THE WHISPERING GLADE

THE
WHISPERING GLADE

Sara Hylton

St. Martin's Press
New York

First published in Great Britain by Century Hutchinson Ltd.

Library of Congress Cataloging in Publication Data

Hylton, Sara.
    The whispering glade.

    I. Title.
PR6058.Y63W5   1985   823'.914   85-11727
ISBN 0-312-86775-1

First U.S. Edition

10 9 8 7 6 5 4 3 2 1

ONE

I HAD NEVER thought that I would ever return to Lexford and it was with some dismay that I found myself miserably aware of the passing scenery as the country train climbed upwards on its single track towards the misted hills. It had been raining on the night I left, almost four years before. Light depressing rain that had chilled me to the marrow, rain that swept down from the fells like drifting smoke across the housetops, obscuring the horizon of bleak rugged hills and endless moorland. Rain hid the hills from me now, heavy driving rain that filled my heart with a remembered pain.

My uncle's letter informing me of my aunt's death had been terse and I doubt very much if he intended it as an invitation to attend her funeral. I have never forgotten however that those two people gave me a home after the death of my parents, and even though the time spent under their roof had not been a happy experience, I could not allow the tragedies of the past to keep me away.

I did not expect to be met. The wind swept along the station platform rippling the puddles under my feet, driving the rain before it so that by the time I reached the station square I felt like some bedraggled waif. The square was empty of any kind of vehicle and although it was only late afternoon the gas lamps flickered eerily through the gloom. It was evident that I would have to walk to the vicarage, so gritting my teeth I took a firmer grip on the valise I was carrying and strode off into the night.

I remembered every cottage and every shop along that straggling High Street. I knew that behind closed curtains fires

1

would glow in shining black-leaded hearths and kettles would already be singing in readiness for the evening meal. Later that night, there would be laughter and friendly warmth behind every cottage door – but I did not expect to find any waiting for me at the end of my journey. Long before I reached the vicarage gate my heart was sick with memories and the dismal echo of the knocker in the hall behind the closed front door seemed like the loneliest sound in the world. I waited, listening for footsteps, but none came and the windows of the house stared back at me, dark and unwelcoming.

I walked over the sodden grass towards the shrubbery. From there, I could see lights inside the church where I assumed my uncle was attending to his devotions. I could hear no sounds, neither organ music nor the chanting of voices, so wearily I wandered back to the house prepared to wait.

The rain dripped mercilessly from the tall elms, finding its way down the collar of my coat but I did not have long to wait. My uncle walked with bent shoulders against the wind, letting himself into the garden from the private path that led from the church to the vicarage. He did not see me until he was quite close and then he started back with surprised uncertainty as I stepped forward to meet him.

He stared at me without speaking, offering no word of greeting, then with aloof resignation he opened the door so that I might precede him into the house. Later, over a meal taken largely in silence, I learned that my aunt's funeral had already taken place and I found myself hating him with the old familiar hatred because he had elected to tell me too late, hoping that I would stay away.

I decided to leave in the morning. I had no wish to stay in this cold unwelcoming house one moment longer than was necessary. In the street outside, the cottage lights had long since been extinguished but I dreaded climbing into that cold bed between sheets that had never been aired – besides, the room was unchanged since I last slept in it and its remembered coldness brought the treacherous tears unbidden into my eyes. In the end I lay on top of the bed fully clothed, shivering and miserable, listening to the wind howling round the house and the bare branches of the elms tapping against the window. I held my hands over my ears just as I had done as a child, reluctant to remember that once I had believed them to be skeleton hands from those ancient graves in the churchyard which gave up their dead every time there was a storm. I did not expect to sleep. Instead, I made myself face the memories which for the past four years I had striven so hard to erase . . .

When I hear people talking about their childhood I keep quiet about mine because I shall always regard it as a singularly unhappy one.

Of the time I spent in Africa until I was four years old I remember little. My father had gone to Southern Rhodesia as a young man intent on making his fortune and to get away from industrial Lancashire and the cotton famine most people believed was inevitable. After long and bitter quarrels with his family who had their roots buried deep in the dark brown soil of North Lancashire, he could see little future in remaining to swell the number of men and women thrown out of an industry that had once been the mainstay of an entire county. He believed he had a choice – life in a new country or a lifetime of regret.

He married my mother, a Rhodesian girl whose family had been settled there for a great many years, and he prospered. He turned to farming and tea-planting and if I search my memory before that last terrible night I can still see our low white house standing in the midst of acres of lush farmland and gardens gay with tropical flowers. I remember the sunlight on long tables piled high with food and carriages arriving pulled by fine spirited horses bringing women dressed in long frilly dresses, with large beribboned hats, and men, immaculate in light-coloured suits, the children laughing and happy as I ran with them across the wide lawns towards the sparkling river. I can still see my father, tall and bronzed, tossing me up in his arms, his eyes gay with laughter, and my mother, lovely in her new ball-gown as she waltzed round my bedroom inviting my admiration.

3

I recall too those dark negro faces with their wide bright smiles, and Anya who had cared for me all my life, rocking me in her arms and crooning softly in her rich contralto. I hear again the songs of the men working in the fields and re-live those long, humid nights when sleepy negro heads nodded over camp fires, and I can still shudder with a delicious thrill at the remembered roars of the great cats as they played out their drama of love and death within the deep inpenetrable darkness of an African night.

Most of all I remember that night when I was roused from my sleep by the shrieking of women and the shouts of men, when the night was lit by flames as our barns and storehouses burned, and rent by the crack of rifle fire and screams of pain. Then Anya came into my room and dragged me from the window, holding me close with my head buried in her shoulder so that I could not see what was happening outside the house.

I could feel the thumping of her heart as she crept down the wide staircase and her screams as I was roughly pulled from her arms. I could see my mother lying just inside the doorway, her long golden hair gleaming against the dark stained wood of the floor and I ran to her, clutching at her hands, beseeching her to open her eyes, terrified by her stillness. My nightgown was dyed crimson with her blood and Anya snatched me away only to stand cowering against the wall while the men with their rifles laughed loudly, enjoying our terror. One of them came towards us with the butt end of his rifle raised on high as though he meant to club us, but then with a sudden cry he seemed to crumple before my eyes and I could see my father standing in the hallway with his gun still smoking in his hands.

'Take the child, Anya,' he called out. 'Get one of the boys and try to reach the Girton place. I'll hold them off as long as I can.'

I screamed after him but he stood alone, firing his rifle as the men advanced towards him, and Anya took to her heels and ran, smothering my screams against her breast.

I was told to lie still in the cart, with my head pressed against a bundle of goatskins. Anya crouched beside me while one of the boys drove furiously along the lumpy country road, rutted by

4

the wheels of farm vehicles during the wet season. We paused just once at the top of the hill so that looking back we could see the flames from our house illuminating the dark sky, then with a crack of the whip the boy urged the horse on until we were met by a group of men on horseback who escorted us to the Girtons' house.

Many of the events which happened after that terrible night have long passed into limbo. Both my parents were dead, murdered by wandering tribesmen, and my home lay in ruins. They had destroyed the young crops and taken our livestock and although the government did their best to salvage what was left it was very little. They had been thorough, those evil men, when they had torn apart the structure of my life.

The Girtons were kindly people. For the next twelve months, they cared for me while Mr Girton sought to establish some sort of order into my father's affairs. All his private papers had been destroyed in the fire and it took a great deal of patient research to discover the identity of his solicitor as well as the names of his and my mother's relatives. My father's solicitors turned out to be in Salisbury, with a branch in London, and once informed, they in turn advised my relatives in England.

It appeared there were only two of them. My father's sister, Aunt Miranda was a spinster lady living in North Lancashire. My mother's elder sister Aunt Edith was married to a vicar, the Reverend James Edisford, and lived in Yorkshire. Between them, they were to decide upon my future.

I felt only lethargy, and I remember how Mrs Girton would kneel with her arms around me saying to her husband, 'If only she could *cry* John. It's unnatural for a little child to be so calm after all that has happened,' and although she tried to interest me in my future I didn't care. For me in those days I had no future. It seemed to me that my life had ended on that terrible night and I could find no more tears.

In England my relatives met to discuss the arrangements and I learned later that although my father's sister offered to take me to live with her, my uncle by marriage persuaded her that since she was unmarried, it was far more suitable that I grow up

5

under the guardianship of a man as well as a woman. Consequently in due course I was informed that I was to make my new home in a country vicarage in a village called Lexford underneath the dark Pennine Hills in distant Yorkshire.

I was placed in the care of an English family travelling home from the Far East and I stood forlornly in their midst just outside the custom-shed waiting to be collected by my relatives who were travelling down from the North to meet me. I was miserably aware of the cold leaden skies and I thought nostalgically of Africa's golden sunlight and bright blue skies.

Leaving the Girtons had meant tearing myself away once more from people I loved but still I could not cry, not even at the sight of the tears rolling down Anya's face as she stood sobbing on the station platform watching the train taking me away from her. None of them were to know that my heart was dying in my breast and that my anguished reserve was more terrible than tears.

Now I listened for several minutes to polite if stilted introductions, then I felt my limp hand taken in gloved fingers and my aunt's swift embrace. I looked up and found myself staring into my uncle's calm, flat face above a stiff clerical collar, the expression in his eyes hidden behind thick spectacles. Although the thin lips smiled and murmured a welcome, I felt no sense of warmth in that erect, darkly clad figure.

My friends of the journey disappeared into the gloom of the winter's day and then we were in the train speeding towards London. I know now that that meeting heralded the end of my childhood and the beginning of a life I have rebelled against ever since. My aunt was totally unlike my mother, but I see now how her personality had been completely subjugated by her husband's narrow prejudices. On that day, as I sat staring miserably out of the window with the grey wintry countryside flashing past, I could find little gratitude in my heart towards these two people who were giving me a home.

We spent one night in a small inexpensive hotel near King's Cross Station and the next morning we were seated in a third-class compartment of a train bound for an obscure village in

Yorkshire. My aunt and uncle conversed hardly at all. He sat in the corner with his head buried in a book, occasionally making notes, but once or twice, when I met my aunt's eyes watching me she smiled, and once she said, 'I'm sorry the weather is so terrible dear, February is a bad month in England.'

'You will soon get used to the weather, Maya,' the Reverend Edisford said crisply. 'The village you will be living in is quite small but the vicarage is very spacious. There is a large room at the top of the house where you can play and take your friends. I don't like the downstairs rooms disturbed as I occasionally hold church meetings there and too much noise is disruptive. You will attend the village school where no doubt you will make suitable friends.'

'Maya is a pretty name,' my aunt said. 'Don't you think so, James?'

'It is not one I am familiar with. Where does it come from, do you know, child?'

I shook my head. I had never thought my name unusual nor had I ever questioned its origin.

'No matter,' my uncle said. 'North country folk are people of few words. They will probably call you May, although I dislike the practice of shortening the name a child was christened with.'

I made up my mind that I would *not* be May to those North country people, I would be Maya, but my uncle was eying me sternly, asking in that cold clipped voice, 'I suppose you were brought up to attend church regularly, Maya?'

'Church was too far away.'

'Indeed. So you know nothing of God's teachings?'

'I say my prayers.'

'I suppose your mother taught you to say those?'

I looked down, my fists clenched tight at my sides. I would not think about my mother. He could not make me think about my mother or else I would see her lying in a pool of blood, her golden hair spread out across the dark stained wood.

In some frustration he turned to my aunt saying, 'If you will look in that chest in the attic you might find some material my

7

mother left behind, enough I am sure for you to run up a few dresses and aprons for the child to wear. My mother was most frugal, she never threw anything away and I notice the child has little luggage.'

'I expect most of her things were destroyed, James. Mrs Girton saw to it that she had enough clothes to see her through the journey and for some time after. We must dress her properly – you know how the villagers gossip.'

'I am not suggesting that we do not dress her properly. My mother did her best with the money available and you should know that a clergyman's pay doesn't run to fancy silks and satins. The child is pretty enough. We don't want to cause resentment amongst the village children who will be her schoolmates.'

I watched my aunt bite her lip, then she looked down at her hands resting in her lap and started to play with her gloves.

'Must you fidget, Edith!' he admonished her. 'I don't like to see you sulking.'

'Oh, but I'm not sulking dear. I was only trying to remember what there was in that old chest in the attic.'

It was raining when the train pulled slowly into the country station bearing the name of Lexford. We were the only passengers to alight onto the platform, a dejected affair with a dimly-lit booking hall at the end of it. Our damp feet splashed through puddles on the way to the wooden gate that led out into a cobbled square. It was almost dark but I could still see the rugged hills that rose starkly above the buildings scattered round the square and that a man carrying a long pole was walking dolefully from gas lamp to gas lamp, leaving pale jets flickering in the gathering gloom. He raised his hat respectfully when he met us and my aunt and I followed the striding figure of my uncle as he marched across the square.

The main street was cobbled except for the pavements. On one side were various small shops and down the centre of the road stood empty market stalls. Obviously it was not market day. A swiftly flowing stream ran down the other side of the street and here and there were narrow bridges leading into

8

country gardens set before neat stone cottages, most of them
with their lamps already lit behind drawn curtains to shut out
the wintry dusk.

At the end of the street I could see the square tower of the
church and I could not help thinking that it seemed a remarkably large church for such a small village. The vicarage stood
nearby, separated from the graveyard by a stone wall and a
shrubbery and on the other side of the road stood the village hall.

The vicarage was large and rambling, with rooms so lofty
they never seemed to get warm, windows through which the
wind whistled and chimneys that smoked, covering the furniture with a fine layer of soot when the wind was a certain way.

I hated it on sight. I hated the sparsely furnished rooms and
threadbare carpets. I hated the paltry cinders in the grate of the
sitting room and the dark tapestry mats on the bedroom floors. I
hated the attic windows that creaked and clattered in the wind
and I was terrified of the branches of the churchyard elms
that tapped against the windows like the fingers of animated
skeletons. Since my window overlooked the graveyard that
sloped upwards towards the grey stone church and the distant
view of the Pennine hills, I was certain I would hear the sound
of those urgent tappings for the rest of my life.

My teeth were chattering with cold as I stood looking
forlornly out of the window and my aunt eyed me dismally from
the doorway.

'I'm sorry it's so cold Maya, but the vicarage takes an awful
amount of heating and there just isn't the money. I'll ask Mrs
Roper to put an ovenplate in the bed as soon as the evening
meal is over, that should warm it up nicely.'

'Who is Mrs Roper?' I asked curiously.

'Just one of the villagers who comes in three days each week
to do housework. Her husband has consumption and hasn't
worked for years so the money we pay her does help out a little
and I am often too busy with church matters to spend much
time cooking and caring for the house. She has a little girl called
Emily, about two years older than you. You'll meet her at the
school.'

9

I said nothing. I was hungry. The last time we had eaten was at breakfast in London and it was now almost dark. I would have liked to ask when the next meal was but my aunt forestalled me by saying, 'I'll go down to the kitchen now and see how Mrs Roper is faring with the evening meal. We eat breakfast promptly at eight o'clock Maya, and your uncle prefers a light breakfast, tea and toast, and he doesn't care for coffee. Lunch is at half-past twelve and we eat our evening meal at six. We don't have anything later unless it's a cup of cocoa before retiring. Are there any questions you would like to ask me?'

'Does my other aunt live near here?'

'Why, no dear. She lives in North Lancashire, on the other side of those hills there. You'll find them just as bleak on that side as they are here.'

'Shall I be able to visit her, then?'

'I'm sure you will when you are older.'

'Will she visit me?'

'Nothing was said about a visit Maya, but then we have only met her once.' My aunt smiled briefly and closing the door quietly behind her left me to stare out at the churchyard with its gravestones and clumps of coarse grass. I wanted to throw myself onto my bed in an agony of weeping but the tears refused to come. Instead, the ache in my throat was an agonising pain that left me trembling. I must not think about the past, I must shut it away behind locked doors never to be stared at and cried over . . . but all the same I was missing Anya desperately and the smiles on dusky faces, their songs and their laughter, and the sound of tom-tom drums in the humid African night.

TWO

GROWING UP IN that draughty vicarage was not a joyful matter. My aunt was immersed in church affairs, holding meetings in the vast room across from my playroom on the top floor. How they survived in that cold cheerless room I couldn't imagine, sitting at long, rough, scrubbed wood tables with a meagre fire burning in the grate and the windows rattling in the wind. My aunt held sewing circles and young wives and mothers came to air their views, as well as young girls preparing to be wives. She also read stories to them from the Bible and I soon discovered that not all of the villagers could read or write.

My uncle would climb the stairs to bid them a polite good evening and deliver a few homilies, whether they needed them or not, then he would retire to his small study at the back of the house which was always warm from the fire blazing in the hearth. There he would prepare his sermon, fortified by rum toddy or a glass of whisky, and there too he would receive his one crony, a retired woollen manufacturer who lived at the large house at the top of the High Street. I always knew when he was there because I would be packed off upstairs, either to bed or to play in the long low attic they described as my playroom. Here Emily and I would read by the light of a flickering gas jet, or we would tell each other exciting stories drawn from our imagination. They had to be, for Emily had never been outside Lexford and my memories of the time before I arrived there were shut away forever.

I loved Emily Roper as I would have loved a sister. She had

bright, red-gold hair that ran riot over her pert little head in shining curls. She was two years older than myself but many years older in her knowledge of life. She was the youngest of Mrs Roper's seven children and the only one left at home. Her mother was a plump cheerful soul, in spite of her troubles, who constantly invited me to their home for meals, and although she did not put anything into words I knew she disliked 'His Reverence' as she called my uncle, and believed I was only half-fed at the vicarage.

Her husband was a frail man who seemed to spend his winters lying in bed in a downstairs room of their cottage, and the summers sitting by their front door racked by coughing. As a young man he had been employed in the woollen industry in one of the large Yorkshire towns, and he now blamed this part of his life for the state of his lungs. As I grew older I wondered how the Ropers survived on the pittance my uncle paid Mrs Roper, until Emily informed me that the rest of their children were very good to them, taking them gifts of food and fuel, while Emily received hand-me-downs from the older sisters which were made to fit her by Mrs Roper's busy fingers.

Although I was younger than Emily we were in the same class together in the grey stone schoolhouse, since I was considered a bright child whilst Emily had no interest in learning. She was good at needlework while I was not, but when it came to subjects that required thought she would toss her pretty head and refuse to concentrate.

'Why should I bother wi' all that,' she would say. 'Like as not I'll marry a chap that works on't land and 'e'll noan want a scholar for a wife. I knows 'ow to milk a cow and feed the chicks, why should I care whether two an' two make four or not?'

I would remonstrate with her, saying, 'But Emily, you don't *have* to marry a farmer. You're so pretty, you could be anything at all if only you'd try a little harder.'

She in turn would throw back her head and laugh. 'Oh Maya, it's a romantic you are, thinkin' the gentry might look at me, or you either for that matter. Mi mother's allus said that money marries money, and since neither of us 'as got any we might just as well be resigned to it. 'Course, you're the vicar's niece so you can look 'igher than a farm'and – besides, one day you'll be prettier ner me, you'll 'ave looks that last, I shan't.'

'Whatever makes you say that! I wish I had your lovely bright hair and blue eyes.'

'I knows I'm pretty now, I can tell by the way the lads look at me. If I'm lucky I might just land me a farmer an' there might be a curate somewhere fer you if you watches yer step.'

'I'd rather marry a farmer than a curate any day,' I retorted, 'particularly if my uncle's an example. At least there'd be good food on the table and a warm fire in the grate.'

'I 'spect I'll finish up like mi sister Rosie. She were the prettiest lass in Lexford, ask anybody, but look at 'er now. She's 'ad three children in three years and she's like a suet dumplin'. 'Er 'air were the colour o' ripe corn an' now there's a lot o' mouse in it although she's nobbut thirty.'

She was right about Rosie but I couldn't believe it would ever happen to Emily. Emily was bright like quicksilver and she made my dull, loveless childhood glow with the warmth of her personality.

The long bleak winters gave way to clear blustery springs, when the moorland grasses waved like a grey tumbling sea under a bright blue sky and the tarn sparkled turquoise in the sunlight. Under the beech trees, the woods were carpeted with bluebells and round the margin of the tarn the buds on the pussy-willows burst out of their silvery fur into fluffy yellow catkins. It was then during the school holidays or at weekends that Emily and I, armed with bread and jam and cakes her mother had packed for us, climbed the long low slopes of the Pennines to sit with our backs against the warm crags looking down on the valleys below.

I was nine years old when I caught my first sight of Greythorn Hall. We had walked in the opposite direction from the one we usually took and I stared down at it with admiration. It was the largest house I had ever seen, with tall chimneys and great mullioned windows staring out across vast acres of parkland at the end of a long curving drive. It was surrounded by a high stone wall and the drive ended in wrought-iron gates bearing a coat of arms which I found suddenly familiar.

When I said as much to Emily she nodded her head saying, 'You've seen it over the pew in the church and like as not in the village High Street. They owns most o' the villages and the land around these parts.'

'If their coat of arms is in the church why do they never come to the services?' I asked her curiously.

'Mostly they goes to the church at Lyndon, it's nearer, but you'll see – one o' these days they'll come to Lexford an' yer uncle won't 'alf make a fuss when they do. 'Is sermon'll go on and on. Last time Sir John were clearly asleep in 'is pew. Works 'isself up into a right old pother 'e do an' makes some folk feel uncomfortable.'

'How does he do that?'

'You know, folk like old Charlie Hardacre who's never bin seen sober, an' Polly Vernon who's friendly wi' Joe Frimsby from Top Meadow Farm, an' 'im wi' a wife an' two chillun.'

There were many times when I wondered where Emily got her information from, and once when I asked my aunt about some of the things she had told me, my aunt was annoyed, saying Emily was too old for her age and no doubt listened to her sisters and her mother talking gossip. I was to take no notice of the things she told me, and perhaps it wouldn't be a bad idea if I saw less of her. After that I kept my own counsel. Seeing less of Emily was something I couldn't bear to think about.

During these summer months, we often sat on the grass looking down upon Greythorn Hall and Emily was always willing to satisfy my curiosity about the family who lived there.

I learned that Sir John Gaynor, the present Baronet, had been married twice although both his wives had died. There were four children, the two elder ones the issue of the first Lady Gaynor, the two younger ones from his second wife.

On probing further Emily responded happily, 'Mr Lyndon'll be the next Baronet. All proud an' 'aughty 'e is, not a bit like 'is father or Master Gavin, but then mi mother says 'ee's more like 'is mother an' she were a Marquis's daughter fro' down south.

'Is sister's Miss Eleanor. She's a rare beauty an' proud as a pea-cock. Mi mother says it'll take a strong arm to tame 'er, 'cause like as not she's bin spoilt. She were only four when 'er mother died.'

'What about the other two children?'

'They be Master Gavin an' Miss Cora. Their mother were a big landowner's daughter fro' the North Ridin'. Poor lady, she were allus delicate an' I reckon Miss Cora takes after her.'

'And Master Gavin.'

She laughed merrily. 'Oh, 'e's a bit of a lad I shouldn't wonder. You'll see 'im durin' 'is school 'olidays. 'E likes to ride down to the village on that white 'orse of 'is, an 'e 'as an eye for a pretty face, young as 'e is.'

'How old *is* he?'

'Sixteen or seventeen. Mr Lyndon looks after the estate since 'is father 'ad a stroke awhile back, and I suppose when 'e leaves school, Master Gavin'll be 'elpin' too.'

Gradually I began to form a picture of the occupants of Greythorn Hall. The squire, bluff and hearty, riding his big chestnut horse behind the hounds on a cold winter's day; his eldest son, tall and aristocratic, proud and haughty as Emily had described him; his sister Eleanor, spoilt and pampered, a proud beauty who needed taming. Then there was Master Gavin who brought a blush to Emily's cheeks each time she spoke of him, and Miss Cora, delicate and pretty as a piece of porcelain.

It was always Master Gavin who became the hero of my childhood dreams, probably because Emily described him more adequately than the others. Once I heard her mother tell my aunt that she had seen him in the village, 'An' a rare 'andsome lad 'e is too, an' no mistake,' she added. 'Like as not 'e'll break a few 'earts afore 'e's much older!'

I first saw them when they attended my uncle's church on Easter Day because the church at Lyndon was undergoing repairs to a leaking roof. I remember that morning particularly well because the house was put into a state from an early hour, and for days on end the villagers had been cleaning the church

15

and decorating it with flowers. I hardly recognised my uncle in his best robes as he walked to the front of the church to greet the carriages when they arrived from Greythorn.

I longed to look up when I heard their footsteps approaching the altar. There seemed so many of them until my aunt whispered that they were servants as well as family and advised me to look straight in front of me and not at the new arrivals.

I did not have to look at my hymn book as I knew the words of the opening hymn by heart and in spite of my aunt's advice I found myself studying the faces of those people occupying the rows of pews underneath the imposing coat of arms. The servants sat at the back, men and women wearing sober black clothing much at variance with that worn by the female members of the Gaynor family.

Sir John was a tall, lean man with a weather-beaten face and dark grizzled grey hair. Standing next to him was a girl of perhaps Emily's age. She was pretty in a pale fragile way, and once I saw her father smile down at her with a special warmth. I moved my gaze, to find a pair of dark bold eyes looking straight into mine, eyes that belonged to a boy of about seventeen. I could feel my face blushing furiously under his regard and I looked down, biting my lip. When I looked their way again he was still watching me as though my embarrassment amused him.

It was not until much later that I dared to take the opportunity to peep at the other members of their party – and this time, my eyes opened wide with admiration. I had always loved red hair, but Miss Eleanor's hair was dark and rich like old mahogany and her blue eyes which occasionally swept over the congregation were fringed by long dark lashes. She was tall and slender and her gown fitted her like a glove. At that moment I hated my raven black hair and grey eyes which sometimes looked like blue slate in my pale face.

Again I felt a pair of eyes trained upon me but this time they were not Master Gavin's. They belonged in a lean tanned face, under dark brows and hair the colour of my own, and again in some confusion I looked away.

There were other people with the Gaynor family, guests, my aunt informed me later. A beautiful blond girl of perhaps Miss Eleanor's age and a stocky red-faced man who could have been her father. At that moment my aunt became aware of my absorption with the Greythorn pew and consequently gave me a little shake, so that for the rest of the service I kept my eyes turned the other way.

Later, as I stood behind my aunt and uncle in the church porch where they both waited to shake hands with the departing Gaynor family, Sir John suddenly noticed me.

'And who have we here,' he said kindly, stooping down to take my hand.

'This is my niece, or rather I should say my wife's niece,' my uncle answered him importantly. 'Her name is Maya Wentworth and her parents were killed tragically in Southern Rhodesia when she was four. We could do nothing else but give the child a home here.'

'Indeed not,' the squire agreed. 'Good of you Edisford, mighty good of you. And have you made friends in the village Miss Maya Wentworth?' he asked, looking down at me with kind twinkling eyes.

'Yes, Sir, I have Emily and other friends,' I answered him stoutly.

'Emily is our cook's child,' my uncle was quick to explain. 'It is difficult for Maya to meet children like herself in such a small community.'

The squire nodded absently, half-turning away, then as though he had had an afterthought he said, 'My daughter Cora has not been well and has been unable to go away to school as her sister did. Would you like to visit us at Greythorn so that you two young ladies can get to know one another?' he asked, looking down at me.

Before I could answer him, my uncle accepted the invitation for me with delighted affability. Although I privately hoped that that would be the last I would hear of the invitation, I had not reckoned on my uncle's determination that I should plant a foot within Greythorn Hall. Two days later I found myself on my way to the Hall, sitting beside my aunt in the trap usually reserved for the Reverend James' visits to outlying parishioners.

I was dressed in my Sunday-best clothes and had been instructed not to get dirty or tear my clothes because money did not grow on trees, and that if I was invited to take tea at the Hall I must eat like a lady which meant refusing second helpings and preferably leaving a morsel of food on my plate – otherwise the Gaynor family might think I received very little at the vicarage. I was not looking forward to the outing, and, once deposited at the door, I watched the trap with my aunt at the reins receding down the drive with acute misgivings.

The house overwhelmed me with its vastness. I followed a manservant across the polished floorboards of the hall, and although I peeped up curiously at the wide curving staircase I hastened my footsteps when he looked behind him disdainfully to see if I was following. I was told to sit outside a door and wait until I was invited to enter. I sat staring out of the window wishing with all my heart that I could take to my heels and run across the parkland towards the gates. I wished I hadn't come, for by this time I felt sure the squire would have forgotten about inviting me, and that he would have other things to do than play host to a young girl he didn't know or really wish to know.

Surely it didn't take so long for the footman to tell them that I was here, or were they merely composing their excuses? I had half a mind to run back towards the door and escape out of this great rambling house, but just then the door opened and the footman motioned me forward. Sir John was sitting behind a huge mahogany desk in a large room lined with books. There seemed to be hundreds of them but now I saw that Sir John was not alone. On the hearthrug, in front of a blazing fire stood a much younger man informally clad in riding breeches and tweed jacket. I recognised him immediately although today he appeared younger than he had seemed in his dark clothes sitting in the family pew. His smile robbed his face of its accustomed severity. It was an amused smile that told me he had not expected his father's visitor to be a mere schoolgirl.

'So here you are, m'dear. I'm glad you came to see us so

promptly,' the squire said, looking at me from across his desk with dark twinkling eyes.

'My uncle said it would only be polite after you had been kind enough to invite me.'

The twinkle became more pronounced. 'Quite right too, quite right. This is my son Lyndon but you must tell me your name again. I have a very bad memory but I do remember that it was a very pretty and unusual name.'

I repeated my name and turning to his son the squire informed him how I came to be living at the vicarage.

'You'll be finding these wild moors a bit different from Africa, child,' he went on, turning towards me.

'I don't remember Africa,' I was quick to answer. 'Only that it was hot and the people were dark.'

'You don't remember anything about the night they killed your parents?' he persisted.

'No, nothing,' I lied. 'It was a long time ago.'

'And such memories are better forgotten, or at least rarely remembered,' Mr Lyndon surprised me by saying.

'Yes, Sir,' I murmured, looking down quickly, wondering at his perception in realising that I did not want to remember or talk about the past, as well as the kindness in his eyes.

Then followed a string of questions posed by the squire to do with my schooling and my ambitions after which the same supercilious footman was summoned and told to escort me upstairs to the old nursery where I would undoubtedly find Miss Cora.

I followed him obediently along a corridor to some backstairs which we climbed towards an upstairs floor. Here, he knocked on a door and after a girl's voice bade us enter held the door open for me to walk into the room. Miss Cora was sitting in front of the fire, curled up in a deep armchair with a book on her knee. Her face broke into a smile when she saw me and immediately she came over and took my hands in hers.

'I'm so glad you've come,' she said, and responding to the warmth in her voice I realised that she was much prettier than she had seemed at first. She was alone in the room and joining

19

her in front of the fire I looked around me with interest. It was a large airy room with chintz drapes at the windows and covering the wide window seats. There was a rich red carpet on the floor and shelves filled with books lining the walls. Across one corner stood a rocking horse and in another corner on a solid oak plinth a sphere representing the world. In the centre of the room was a large table and several comfortable chairs, and I couldn't help comparing it with my sparsely furnished playroom at the vicarage.

I smiled at her shyly and she said, 'This has always been our nursery but I'm the only one who makes use of it now. Lyndon and Eleanor rarely come here although Gavin sometimes comes to play table games with me. Is it very cold outside?'

'No, it is quite warm. My aunt drove me over in the trap.'

'Would you like to walk in the park or do you prefer to stay indoors and read or something?'

'I really don't mind. I would like to do whatever you wish since I'm your guest.'

I had been well primed by my uncle on how I should behave and I felt I was doing his teaching more than justice.

'I would like to walk in the park then,' she answered. 'I get so few opportunities to walk and the park is beautiful at this time of the year.'

'Do you feel well enough to walk?'

'Of course. I am better now, it is in the winter when I am not well.'

I waited while she donned a warm coat and woollen hat, then last of all she took a warm scarf and gloves explaining as she did so that if she was well wrapped up against the elements there would be no complaints.

The spring breeze was warm against our faces as we walked across the park. It brought colour into Miss Cora's pale cheeks and stirred the tendrils of pale golden hair that crept from under her woollen cap. As we walked she asked me questions about my life in the village and the friends I had made, and I began to realise how sheltered she had been from any of the normal joys of childhood.

She had never climbed the slopes of the Pennines or fished for minnows in the stream, never sat with a girl like Emily on a swing in a cottage garden or gathered holly in the woods on a winter's day white with frost. No doubt there had been compensations, and I found myself wondering what they were, as we took the path towards the tarn.

We were walking through a long avenue of beech trees that met over our heads, their pale tender green buds only just beginning to emerge, and I was surprised when Miss Cora caught my arm, pulling me to a standstill.

'Don't say anything Maya,' she said softly. 'Just listen.'

I could hear nothing, only the sighing of the wind through the branches of the trees, sounding much as they did in the churchyard.

'Don't you hear them?' she asked, her small face sharp with anxiety.

'I can hear the wind in the trees, that is all.'

Her hand grasped my wrist so tightly I cried out with pain. It seemed incredible that those slender, delicate hands could grip with such steely strength. Impatient with my lack of comprehension, she cried, 'No, no, Maya, not the trees. Don't you hear the *voices?*'

I listened intently but I could hear no voices, only the low moaning of the wind. Removing her grip on my wrist she said, 'You don't hear them. Perhaps it is only members of my family who are meant to hear them, but they have been here such a long time. They call this avenue of trees the whispering glade.'

'Where do the voices come from? There are no people here.'

'Sometimes I think they are calling to me but I can never be sure. Once, a long time ago, Caroline Gaynor drowned in the lake on the eve of her wedding day. She had been running away from a man she met in the woods . . . some people say he was her lover and that she never wanted to marry the man her family had chosen for her. I don't suppose anybody will ever know the real story, but sometimes, mostly when the leaves are on the trees one can hear voices calling *"Caroline, Caroline"*.'

I shivered. There was something unnerving about this girl

21

with the pale elfin face and haunted blue eyes.

'Who else has heard the voices?' I asked curiously.

'Some of the servants. Some of them won't even walk along the glade, and once Eleanor was frightened by them, so much so that her horse refused to cross the path.'

'There aren't any voices today,' I said stoutly, 'but if you think you can hear them perhaps we ought to go back.'

She laughed, linking her arm in mine. 'Oh Maya, I'm so glad to have found such a practical friend. If we walk towards the stables perhaps we shall see Gavin and the others.'

'The others?'

'Yes, Lyndon and Eleanor and Melinda.'

'Who is Melinda?'

'She's a guest. I think her parents are old friends of my father, and they are hoping that one day she'll marry Lyndon.'

'Do you want them to marry?'

'She's very pretty and very nice too. I don't really mind who Lyndon marries, as long as it's not Jane Sandon.'

'What's wrong with her?'

'She wants him very badly. She's always over here looking for Lyndon to go riding with her, wanting him to dance with her at every ball. I don't think people should get what they want without fighting for it, do you?'

I had no opinion on the matter. I didn't know Jane Sandon or Melinda although it was apparent I was soon to meet the latter.

As we neared the stables we were hailed by Master Gavin riding his horse at great speed down the hillside. He brought it to a halt beside us so abruptly that it reared on its haunches, squealing its protest.

'Hallo,' he said, smiling down at me. 'You're the vicar's niece, aren't you? It didn't take you long to find us.'

I glared at him balefully. 'That was my uncle's idea, not mine,' I snapped.

He grinned, quite unabashed and Cora said laughing, 'Don't mind him, Maya, he's a terrible boy.'

'I don't suppose you ride?' he asked impudently.

'No,' I answered briefly. My pony Kim was locked away with

22

all the other memories I had of Africa and I had no intention of allowing him to escape just to gratify the curiosity of Master Gavin Gaynor.

'You should try it some time. It isn't really very difficult – I would help you.'

'My uncle doesn't have enough money to spend on a horse for me so there wouldn't be much point in my learning how to ride.'

'No, I suppose not. What do you normally do for amusement?'

'We walk in the fields and the woods, and if the weather is good we climb up into the hills.'

'Who is we?'

'Emily and me.'

'That's the girl with red hair I've seen in the village.'

'Yes, Emily Roper. She's fun. She's good about birds and animals and I can wear clothes I don't have to be careful about instead of these Sunday best clothes I hardly dare sit down in.'

Brother and sister laughed, then Gavin said quite seriously, 'Your friend is very pretty.'

'Yes she is, very pretty.'

'She's older than you are?'

'Yes – she's almost twelve.'

'Why don't you bring her with you one day?'

'She hasn't been invited.'

'I'm inviting her.'

'Perhaps I won't be coming again.'

'Oh, but you will Maya,' Cora cried. 'Take no notice of Gavin, you're my friend, not his.' She pointed across the park. 'Look over there, the others are on their way back.'

Gavin spun his horse round and cantered across the park to meet them, and then they all raced their horses back towards us with Gavin urging his mount on to arrive triumphantly in first place.

I stood there self-consciously while Cora performed the introductions, and then to my surprise Lyndon Gaynor leaned down and scooping me up in his arms set me on the horse in front of him while Gavin allowed Cora to sit on his horse while

23

he led him toward the stables.

Melinda rode beside us and for the first time I looked at her face. She was lovely. With her pale golden hair and hazel eyes and in her black riding habit sitting side-saddle on her horse, she was a charming foil for Lyndon Gaynor's dark good looks. I could hear the other three laughing behind me but I was so embarrassed I failed to hear their words.

The rest of that afternoon followed uneventfully. Back at the Hall I ate afternoon tea with Cora in the nursery while the others retired to the drawing room after they had changed out of their riding clothes.

I was careful not to ask for second helpings but I did not leave anything on my plate as I found the tiny sugary cakes and ham sandwiches far too delicious to waste.

Just after five o'clock a parlourmaid came to tell me my aunt had arrived for me so I reached for my coat and bade Cora goodbye.

'Promise me you'll come again soon,' she pleaded. 'I never see Eleanor these days, she hunts and has a large circle of friends. Lyndon never comes to the nursery and Gavin only comes when he's nothing else to do.'

I felt strangely drawn to this wistful fragile girl living in luxury yet unable to enjoy it to the full and I willingly gave my promise to return.

'Bring your friend with you,' she urged. 'Gavin has obviously noticed that she is pretty, and he will enjoy showing off.'

Back at the vicarage I gave a full report of my visit but I refrained from telling them about my ride on Mr Lyndon's horse – or Cora's story of the whispering glade . . .

THREE

IT WAS DURING our walk home from school the following week that I told Emily about Cora and her 'voices' and immediately she was forthcoming with all that she knew about the tragedy of Caroline. It followed faithfully the pattern told to me by Cora but Emily embroidered upon it by saying some of the servants had heard the voices and none of them would venture down the glade after dusk.

I got the impression that Emily felt resentful about my visit to Greythorn Hall when she remarked that I would soon get tired of her company now that I had made friends with the gentry.

Somewhat exasperated I retorted, 'Oh Emily, I'd rather be with you than anybody – surely you know that! Besides, the next time I go I am to take you with me.'

''Ow do they know about me, an' who told yer to take me?'

'Master Gavin, and Miss Cora.'

'Why would 'e ask you to take me? 'E doesn't even know me.'

'He said you were pretty and why didn't I take you.'

Her face was rosy with blushes but she brushed my explanations aside airily saying, 'You'll not catch *me* goin' to Greythorn. I shan't 'ave a word to say for meself, particularly to that Miss Eleanor.'

'Wouldn't you like to see that beautiful house and those fine horses? And what shall I say to Master Gavin if I turn up without you?'

'Mi sister were nobbut a servant there, so why should I want to go an' get mixed up wi' the family, 'specially that Master

25

Gavin who's too sure of 'isself by 'alf?'

'Oh Emily, it's only for one afternoon. I shan't go unless you come with me.'

'Then what would yer uncle say?'

'He'd be furious.'

We both dissolved into laughter and grudgingly Emily said, 'All right I'll come, but the least sign that they're snidin' at me an' I'll come straight 'ome, I swear it.'

The next invitation came shortly after Whitsuntide, delivered personally from Master Gavin himself at the vicarage door on behalf, or so he said, of his sister Cora.

'Bring your friend if you don't want to come alone,' was his parting shot.

My uncle was not at all sure that I should take Emily.

'It will undoubtedly cause jealousy among the other village children and give Emily ideas above her station,' he said, and my aunt, more or less agreeing with him, looked doubtful.

'But Master Gavin wants me to take Emily,' I insisted.

'I daresay,' my uncle said drily. 'Miss Emily is too old for her years and has the makings of a minx. She hears too much gossip from that family of hers.'

'Perhaps there can't be any harm in it if she went just once as company for Maya,' my aunt said. 'The other children need know nothing about it.'

Emily's mother was not entirely in agreement with the arrangements, either. 'Why our Emily?' she asked. 'Why should she go up to the 'All where 'er sister were a parlourmaid an' 'er old grandfather a coachman? It's givin' 'er ideas above 'er station an' she's allus been a one for 'avin' 'er 'ead in the clouds.'

My aunt reassured her that it was only for the space of one afternoon and that she would be taken and brought back, so that in the end, Mrs Roper gave her reluctant permission.

It was a warm sunny day at the end of May when my aunt put us down at the end of the long drive in front of the house, and almost immediately Cora came hurrying across the gravel fore-court to greet us. She looked well and happy in the warm May sunshine. There was a bloom in her cheeks and much of her earlier fragility seemed to have gone. I introduced her to Emily but although she greeted her in the most friendly fashion Emily made little effort to join in our conversation. She walked beside me with compressed lips and a sulky expression but as we approached the house, Master Gavin appeared riding his spirited horse.

Emily's expression became more sulky if anything but he appeared not to notice as he suggested we accompany him towards the stables.

'Oh, Maya's fed up with your silly old horses,' Cora said. 'Take Emily.'

'You come too, Maya, I knows nowt about 'orses,' Emily protested, but brother and sister laughed as Cora drew me towards the house and Gavin got down from his horse and taking Emily's arm, drew her reluctantly across the grass towards the stables.

It was all so normal and innocent on that golden afternoon. A laughing boy with his dark hair falling over his eyes introducing a young girl he admired to the horses he loved, and Cora and I strolling arm in arm towards the house. Did it start then I wonder, or did it come later – that sad, passionate involvement that was to unite and divide us? How could I have known then that it would have been better if I had never set foot inside Greythorn Hall or met those who lived beneath its roof, with their power to hurt and destroy and fill my soul with a hopeless love . . .

I was surprised that Cora did not wish to walk in the park on such a beautiful day but instead we climbed the stairs to the old nursery. I was even more surprised to find Miss Eleanor sitting at the table writing letters, and I was struck anew by her beauty.

She eyed me coolly with the vaguest of smiles, and in some exasperation Cora snapped, 'You knew I was having a friend here, you don't come in here for whole months!'

Eleanor smiled, quite unruffled. 'The house is a mess. Lyndon is interviewing tenants in the library and Father is fast

27

asleep in the drawing room. Besides – there is spring cleaning going on.'

'That was done ages ago.'

'Then they've decided to start again.'

'You could have used your own bedroom to write letters.'

'Good gracious, what's so important between you and this little girl from the vicarage that you have to have the place to yourselves! I can't think that either of your lives is so exciting that you need to chatter in privacy.'

She began to stack her letters together, recorking the ink bottle and in a sudden rush I said, 'Please don't go. Oh, please don't go, we can quite easily walk in the park.'

She smiled. 'Well, at least your friend is more welcoming than you are, Cora. I've almost finished, anyway. What do they call you, little girl?'

'My name's Maya, and I'm not a little girl. I'm almost eleven.'

'And you live at the vicarage?'

'Yes. I'm a niece.'

'That can't be much fun, particularly with the Reverend Edisford. Such a silly, pompous little man.'

'He's not very little,' I objected.

'No, perhaps not, but he is undeniably pompous.'

When I did not correct that remark she laughed merrily and somewhat reluctantly, Cora and I joined in her laughter.

I was completely captivated by her beauty and she knew it. All her gestures were studied. The turn of her head on her long slender neck, the graceful movements of her hands and the honeyed lilt of her voice. She had an audience and she was acting her part while Cora sat quietly and listless beside me, having seen it all before.

She left us at last, sweeping her letters together in one extravagant gesture, favouring us with a swift smile of farewell and saying as an afterthought at the door, 'I suppose you've asked somebody to serve tea here?'

'Of course,' Cora replied briefly.

Then with another smile in our direction she had gone, and

with her going went some of the glow from the sunlit room. Cora's silence made me feel uncomfortable and I began to wish that Emily and Gavin would return. I heard the sound of their laughter in the corridor outside with something like relief. They came in, breathless with hurrying. Emily's hair was a wild russet mass around her rosy freckled face, her blue eyes were sparkling, and the boy too seemed more confidently sure of himself. He made us laugh with his talk of Emily's first attempt to ride on horseback and soon he had Cora too responding to his banter.

He was like Eleanor. Too aware of his charm and ability to amuse and I thought this rather strange as they were only half-brother and sister, while Cora was Gavin's real sister.

Eleanor brought tea to the nursery and served it to us from a table in the corner, gracious and very much the daughter of the house.

'You will soon be having a fine society wedding at your church in the village, Maya,' she informed me. 'Will you be there to watch it?'

Emily and I stared at her in surprise and I asked quickly, 'Who is getting married?'

'My brother Lyndon to Melinda Graves. The church in Melinda's village and the one here in Lyndon are not nearly large enough for all the guests who will be invited, so it has to be your uncle's church in Lexford. Can't you imagine how he is going to enjoy all the limelight?'

There was general laughter and I found myself blushing with annoyance. They were laughing at my uncle and I knew that they saw him as I saw him, a strutting, pretentious figure filled with snobbery and puffed-up pride.

I hated them for laughing at him because somehow, it seemed to reflect upon me. As if she understood something of my feelings, Cora sobered up instantly saying, 'Oh, Maya – it isn't anything to do with *you* You must know how terribly pompous he is.'

'Of course she knows,' Emily said stoutly. "E's more pompous wi' Maya than anybody. Will there be a big ball an' will all the village 'ave to be decorated?' she wanted to know.

'There will certainly be a ball here but I don't know anything about the village. I'm sure the vicar won't let the opportunity pass to organise something,' Eleanor added maliciously.

Her eyes held mine, amused blue eyes looking into grey eyes filled with a strange despair. I was miserably aware of her poise and sophistication and at that moment I resolved that one day I, too, would show the world the same poise – and that as soon as I could, I would leave Lexford and get a decent education. How I was going to do it, I didn't then know, but the resolve that was born in that moment never left me.

I was quiet at first as we walked towards the gates and Emily said, 'You shouldn't let anybody tease you about yer uncle Maya, 'e's naught to do wi' you.'

'He's my uncle.'

'Makes no difference, besides 'e's only yer uncle by marriage.'

Feeling reassured I asked, 'How did you get on with Gavin?'

''E's fond of 'is 'orses, I'll say that fer 'im.'

'And he likes you, Emily.'

She threw back her head, laughing delightedly. ''E'll like any girl 'e thinks is pretty, but come summer when they fills the hall wi' their fancy friends 'e'll 'ave no thought fer me.'

'You don't think enough of yourself,' I rejoined sadly, whereupon she put her arm around my shoulders saying, 'No, Maya, it's you who needs to 'ave yer feet firmly planted on't ground. Now 'urry, I can see yer aunt waitin' fer us.'

We said little on the way home except to reassure my aunt that we had enjoyed our visit. I asked if I could invite Emily in for cocoa and after receiving her permission we made the cocoa and retired to the playroom to drink it.

'You're not sorry you came,' I insisted on asking again.

''Course not, as long as it doesn't make me discontented. I'll be leavin' school come summer. Work be more important than Master Gavin or Greythorn 'All.'

I stared at her in dismay, stunned by her words.

'But you're only twelve and a half. You can't possibly leave school yet.'

'But I am, Maya. Twelve isn't too young to leave school – why, there be children workin' in't mills younger ner me in the big towns. Don't you be worryin' now, it'll be different fer you.'

'Why? Why will it be different?'

'Well, you be the vicar's niece, and besides you're clever. I've never bin much good at school.'

'Then what are you going to do when you leave it?'

She shrugged her shoulders. 'I don't know yet. I could help on't land and I suppose I could allus go into service. One o' the big houses might take me on but I wouldn't go to Greythorn, not to look after Master Gavin. I knows too many stories about the gentry an' their servants.'

'But you won't leave the village, Emily. If you go what shall I do?'

She looked at me solemnly over the rim of her cup and it seemed to me at that moment that Emily was a generation older than me instead of two brief years.

'I 'onestly don't know what I'll do. Mi mother could do wi' the extra money but she'll miss mi 'elp at 'ome an' mi father won't ever work again. Somethin'll turn up, it'll 'ave to.'

I walked with her to the gate and stood for a few minutes listening to her footsteps running along the cobbled street towards her home.

I felt strangely miserable as I walked back to the house. Ever since I had arrived in Lexford Emily had been the one person who had brought some semblance of warmth into my life, and I couldn't bear to think what it would be like if she went away.

FOUR

TRUE TO HER words Emily left school in the summer, but almost immediately the summer holidays were upon us and her mother seemed in no hurry for her to find work. Her father's health continued to deteriorate so she helped out at home and the rest of the family contributed with gifts of food and clothing. There were still whole days when we could roam over the fields and moors and it seemed I had been worrying needlessly.

Another event came along to take my thoughts, indeed everybody's thoughts from the more mundane things of life, and this was Mr Lyndon's wedding to Melinda Graves. My uncle was like a dog with two tails. Never since his arrival as vicar of Lexford had there been an occasion to compare with this one. He was in his element organising an army of villagers to clean the church from top to bottom, weed the churchyard and scrub the gravestones, and my aunt and her sewing circle were completely worn out by the end of every day.

Mrs Roper was scathing to Emily and me in her criticism. 'If King Teddy 'isself was comin' to the weddin' there wouldn't be more fuss,' she snapped. 'You'll see, it'll be His Reverence who'll want to be the centre o' attraction. You'd think the weddin' was for 'is benefit alone.'

Much to my uncle's disgust, Emily and I watched the guests arriving from halfway up a rotted elm tree in the churchyard and I was conspicuous by a torn dress, a scratched knee and dirt on my face. I didn't care, for nothing could spoil the excitement of seeing the carriages arriving filled with elegant men and beautifully dressed women. Gavin was very aware of his hand-some appearance as he shepherded the guests from the church door to their pews, and catching sight of us in our perch halfway up the tree he grinned, while Emily remarked that he seemed well pleased with himself.

We watched the bridesmaids arrive. There were six of them, including Eleanor and Cora, dressed in sweetpea shades of pink, blue and mauve and they hopped and danced about in the churchyard until the carriage arrived bringing Miss Melinda and her father.

A sudden hush fell over the spectators. Melinda's golden fairness and pink and white porcelain skin were enhanced by the frothy veil, making her seem like a fairy creature and not a woman of flesh and blood at all. She glided along the path that led up to the church followed by what I suppose were the prettiest girls in the county and after they had passed I was conscious of a dull ache in my heart, feeling that there would never be such a day for me. Something in the same vein must have troubled Emily because for once her face looked pensive and unusually sad.

We stayed in our tree listening to the organ music and singing from inside the church while below us, the villagers were becoming restive as they jostled for positions in the front row. Suddenly, we heard the triumphant music of the Wedding March and I almost toppled out of the tree in my eagerness to see them emerge from the church.

How handsome they were together, the girl in her frothy veil and white lace gown, the man in his faultless morning dress, darkly austere yet looking down at the girl with obvious adoration.

The bridesmaids were now on the arms of young men marching gaily along the path. Gavin with a laughing dark-haired girl looking up at him with admiring eyes and Cora with a tall young gallant, her eyes shining with excitement. Emily nudged me and whispered in my ear but I couldn't hear her for the noise of the organ and the laughter below as the guests clambered over the gravestones in their attempts to throw their

33

confetti; and then my uncle was there, standing underneath the tree and demanding in a stern voice that I should get down.

In spite of his day of glory and the local dance in the village hall that night, which incidentally was being given for the villagers by the Gaynor family, I was packed off to bed without supper and forbidden to see Emily again that day. I lay with the window open listening to the sound of music floating across the churchyard and the resentment grew in my heart until it became a living thing, and not for the first time I wished I was old enough to leave the vicarage and never set foot in Lexford again.

I was suddenly aware of pebbles being thrown against my window and scrambling out of bed, I ran to open it wide. Standing underneath were Emily and Ned Rakesby. I didn't know Ned well, except that he was a farmer's son and that he lived at Ash Meadow Farm high up in the hills above the village. He had left school several years before and was probably about seventeen by this time. The other children teased Emily about him because he was always hanging around the school gates when it was time for us to go home. Now I expect they had met at the dance but it soon became clear why they were standing beneath my window.

'Come down Maya,' Emily hissed. 'Ned's got the farm buggy so we can go up to Greythorn 'All and see the nobs celebratin'.'

'I can't come out, I've been told to stay in my room.'

'Nobody's goin' to know, yer uncle's dancin' 'is feet off in there an' it'll be 'ours afore they leave. We'll be back by then.'

'How shall I get back into my room without them seeing me?'

'Ned'll 'elp you, that elm tree's right below yer window.'

It was reckless and wild but I needed little encouragement. In no time at all I was letting myself out of the front door and then we were sitting in the farm buggy with Ned urging the horse down the village street. The moon rode high in the summer sky and soon the lights from the Hall windows flowed out into the night. We could hear the music from the road and Ned left the horse and buggy on a grass verge outside the gates.

'Can't yer take it further?' Emily asked indignantly.

"Ow can I leave it up there among all them carriages?' Ned protested. 'We can take a short cut across the park.'

So we took to our heels and ran, finally coming to a halt at a spot where we could crouch underneath the trees with the lighted windows in front of us. Inside the room, couples were whirling round to the strains of a band set high up in the minstrel gallery. I saw Eleanor dancing decorously in the arms of a tall portly man and I wondered why she wasn't laughing and gay like the other young girls, like Cora for instance, who danced by in the arms of the young man who had escorted her out of church, her face wildly happy.

Taking my arm Emily whispered, 'Let's go round to the other windows. Now we're 'ere we might as well see it all.'

Keeping well within the shadows we circled the house, looking in on tables piled high with food, older men and women sitting at card tables, and young couples standing in each other's arms inside the conservatory. Even as we watched them I saw Ned slip his arm round Emily's shoulders and she offered no objection.

Slowly we made our way back to the ballroom through the trees heavy with summer leaves and still the couples danced. I saw Lyndon dancing with Eleanor and Melinda with Gavin, but still Cora waltzed with the same young man and her face was beautiful as she looked up at him so that a lump came into my throat.

It was Ned who brought us to our senses by saying suddenly, 'We should be gettin' back – suppose the vicar finds Maya's gone.'

'Oh, 'e won't. 'E won't 'ave a sudden fit o' feelin' sorry fer 'er, besides it's lovely out 'ere.'

'I should go back, Emily. My aunt might go into my room to see if I'm asleep.'

Emily was reluctant in spite of my anxiety and we lingered on, but then in sheer desperation I said, 'Emily, I *must* go even if I have to go without you.'

'Oh, all right then. Let's go through the glade – I don't believe in ghosts.'

She took to her heels and ran and Ned and I chased after her, and in front of us beyond the mere stretched the glade silent and mysterious, the leaves rustling like a hundred voices in the beech trees.

'We must keep in the shadows,' I whispered.

We passed from tree to tree and in the bright moonlight we could see down the entire length of the glade towards the mere shining silver beyond. We were almost out of it now and ready to run across the grass towards the gates when the sound of a girl's laughter made us pause with swiftly beating hearts under the trees. Emily gripped my arm so fiercely I cried out with pain and then the laughter came again and with it, the deeper sound of a man's voice.

We stood as if rooted to the spot, and then from under the trees a girl seemed to glide in her silver dress, followed by a man who pulled her round to stand within his arms. They were caught up in an embrace that seemed to last forever then she was running along the glade in our direction and as she passed I caught my breath sharply. It was Eleanor, and chasing her until he could take her hand in his was the same young man who had brought the sparkle into Cora's pale cheeks.

We were about to step out from our hiding place when Ned quickly pulled us back. The figure of a man had moved out from under the trees and he stood dark and menacing, watching until Eleanor and her lover had disappeared along the path. I felt myself shivering in spite of the warmth of the summer night, and then the man turned and sauntered slowly along the glade in the direction of the mere, while we ran as fast as we could towards the gates.

'Who was that man?' I asked hoarsely as soon as I had got my breath back.

'Roger Ackroyd,' Ned answered shortly. 'He's a big land-owner from o'er Bleesdale. Mi father's brother 'as a farm on 'is land, that's 'ow I knows 'im.'

'Mi grandfather used to tell us stories about 'is father, right old gambler 'e was, an' so was Sir John Gaynor. They used to 'ave cock fights up at Bleesdale an' mi grandfather did say as 'ow the squire 'ad lost heavily to old Ackroyd an' promised Miss Eleanor to 'is son when she were nobbut a child.'

'But he's far too old for Eleanor,' I protested. 'Surely it can't be true.'

'Well, mi grandfather allus 'ad a lot o' stories to tell about the gentry but mi father said 'e never stayed sober long enough to tell 'em right.'

With the help of Ned and Emily I finally clambered up the ancient elm tree outside my window and with a sigh of relief dropped into my bedroom from the windowsill. The house was quiet but I lay shivering beneath the bedclothes until I heard my uncle and aunt's voices bidding people goodnight along the road. Soon afterwards I heard the click of my bedroom door and the light from a candle shone across the wall. I guessed it was my aunt but I lay unmoving with my eyes closed and eventually she went away.

Back in the village school after the summer holidays there was no Emily to disrupt my progress by her chatter and I knew I had it in me to do well. I read avidly, any book I could get my hands on and I borrowed freely from my uncle's bookcase, with or without his knowledge.

I only saw Emily during the weekends now. We would sit in the attic where we would talk about the future as though it had something to offer us, and it was only when she had gone that I saw the futility of such hopes. Lexford was a backwater and as the weeks and months went by I became more and more determined to get away.

Once I spoke to my uncle about it, asking him if I must leave school at twelve like the other children, and what I would do with my time. He looked at me over his spectacles and after a few moments when he seemed to be pondering the question, he said, 'There is more than enough work to occupy you here at the vicarage, Maya. When you leave school we shall be able to do without Mrs Roper and you will also be able to help your aunt with her work connected with the church.'

'But Mrs Roper needs the money she gets here, it's all they have going into the house.'

'Then Emily must go out to work,' he retorted. 'It's quite ridiculous to keep the girl at home when she could be earning good money doing something useful.'

'But she helps to nurse her father and runs all the errands.'

'I doubt if her father will outlast the winter and there might not be any work about when she is looking for it.'

'Why is it so wrong for Emily to remain at home and so right for me?' I demanded indignantly.

My aunt gave me a warning glance and my uncle put down his paper with some asperity on the table top. 'Your positions are entirely different. You should think of showing us some gratitude for the good home we have given you, after all it is little enough we shall be asking from you. Besides,' he added as an afterthought, 'it will be good training for when you become an adult.'

I couldn't bear it. My whole life stretched before me empty and aimless and my studies suffered because my mind was on other things. When I told the headmaster of my fears for my future he promised he would speak to my uncle.

'You are a bright intelligent girl, Maya. I am sure when I have explained matters to him he will see that you should go on with your studies. I know of several colleges for young ladies that are good but not too expensive and largely for the daughters of professional men.'

'Unfortunately I am not a daughter, I am only a niece,' I said woefully.

'That should make no difference. He is your legal guardian.'

True to his word, the headmaster came to the vicarage and was closeted with my uncle in his study for quite some time, while I hovered about the hall and stairs hoping to hear something that might give me hope for the future. At times, their voices were raised in argument and my heart sank. When my aunt saw me hanging around outside the study she said sternly, 'You should not be listening, Maya. Your uncle is not pleased that the headmaster has filled your head with ideas of further education and possibly going out in the world to work. He believes, and I agree with him, that the world can be an evil place for a girl who is unprotected and alone.'

I had no hopes now that he would agree with my wishes, and one look at the headmaster's face, angry and resigned as he left the house, confirmed my fears.

The following day he sent for me to come to his office, where he informed me that my uncle had been unyielding in his decision to keep me at home. He had also informed the headmaster that there was no money for my education – and that he should allow him to know best how I should spend my future.

I complained bitterly to Emily as we strode off into the hills the following weekend and she listened to me without speaking until my tirade was spent. I didn't really expect her to understand. She had hated school and her one idea had been to get away from it as quickly as possible. I was surprised therefore when she said, 'Didn't you get any money at all fro' yer father?'

I stopped in my tracks, staring at her curiously.

'Well, surely there must 'ave bin somethin', an' if so why shouldn't you spend it on gettin' a better education. Who can you ask?'

'Not my uncle, or my aunt either.'

Suddenly I had an idea that filled me full of hope. Aunt Miranda! We had never met, but every Christmas and birthday I received a card and letter from her enclosed in a paper parcel bringing a present. They were not expensive presents, usually warm woollen gloves and tammies, hand-knitted scarves or slippers, and her letters always bade me be good, heed my elders and go to church regularly.

To say I thought she was in league with my uncle was an understatement. I had no choice but to go to church regularly and I heeded him even when I felt rebellious, but Aunt Miranda was my father's sister and she deserved the benefit of the doubt.

'Emily, I've *got* to see her but I don't know how.'

'Couldn't you write 'er a letter?'

'I could, but how can I possibly say all I want in a leter?'

'O' course yer can. I couldn't to be sure but *you* can.'

When I still looked doubtful she shook my arm impatiently. 'Write to 'er Maya, it's yer only chance an' she'll know if yer father left some money.'

So night after night in the quiet of my room while my aunt and uncle slept on unsuspecting, I composed my long letter by the aid of a candle sputtering low in its holder. I told her I was not unhappy, but I couldn't visualise a future living as my aunt lived. I told her about the headmaster's visit to my uncle and the outcome and I asked her to help me.

I could have written a more coherent letter. On reading it through, it seemed disjointed and wandering but it was a plea from the heart, more convincing perhaps than a studied composition and I posted it at the village post office before I could have second thoughts.

Then began the wait, as day after day I met the postman in the lane only to be greeted by a shake of his head until in the end I felt sure she had decided to ignore my letter.

It was almost three weeks later when I was informed on letting myself into the kitchen after school that we had a visitor, and that my uncle wanted to see me immediately I arrived home.

Mrs Roper's eyes were bright with curiosity as she helped me off with my coat and I was aware of my burning cheeks as I asked anxiously who the visitor was.

'It's yer aunt, all the way fro' Lancashire, an' I don't know what's bin said but the Reverend looks none too pleased.'

'Have you seen her, Mrs Roper? What is she like?'

'I took 'er a cup o' tea, as she said she'd 'ad somethin' to eat afore catchin' the train. She's not a young woman, one would a' thought she'd a' bin glad o' somethin' a bit more satisfyin' than a cup o' tea.'

'Is she very old?'

'No, but a wee bit older than them is my guess. She's small an' wiry an' if yer don't be gettin' in there sharpish 'e'll be out 'ere lookin' fer you again.'

They sat in straight-backed chairs in the drawing room

where a meagre fire burned in the grate. The room was only used for special occasions and I guessed the fire had only been lit since my aunt's arrival. The room smelt musty and I was unusually conscious of the air of dejection about it. My uncle sat nearest the fire, fiddling with several sheets of paper: I immediately recognised them as the letter I had written to my aunt. Aunt Edith sat next to him staring down at the carpet and only Aunt Miranda looked up as I opened the door.

She was dressed in black from her neat buttoned boots to her little feathered hat and I could see that she was small since the big chair dwarfed her. Her face, however, was dimpled and round and her eyes were like my own, slate blue in her bright inquisitive face.

I stood just inside the door until my uncle turned and said in a stern voice, 'Come here, Maya. This is your Aunt Miranda who has travelled all the way from Lancashire in answer to that letter you sent her.'

I didn't speak. All their eyes were on me now, and at last Aunt Miranda said, 'Come here child, let me look at you.'

I stood before her looking calmly into her eyes while she studied me slowly. At last she snapped, 'Well, you've got the Wentworth eyes, I'll say that for you, but you're far too thin girl, too pale and too thin. Your mother was a beauty and it's true you haven't her colouring, still I reckon a few more years, a bit of flesh and colour in your cheeks'll make all the difference.'

'We've encouraged Maya to be good and dutiful,' my uncle said sharply, 'surely more enduring qualities than beauty.'

'Perhaps, but there's no reason why she shouldn't combine the two. Now Maya, can you tell me something more about this letter you sent me?'

'I shouldn't have sent it, Aunt, it was wrong of me.'

'Did you think it was wrong when you wrote it?'

'No.'

'Well, then. I take it you don't want to leave school at twelve to work here in the vicarage. You'd rather get some more education and perhaps find work elsewhere when the time comes?'

41

'Yes. There are so many things I don't know, so many things I shall never know in that village school. Besides, the headmaster says I should go on, and Aunt, Mrs Roper needs the money – I would be doing her out of a job if I stayed to work here, her husband has consumption and there's no work in the village and little enough on the land.'

'Did you think I might finance your education, child?'

'Oh no, Aunt, I never thought that for a moment. I thought you might know if my father had left provision for me.'

'Couldn't you have asked your uncle that?'

'How could I when he never mentioned it, and when I knew he wanted me to stay here to help Aunt Edith?'

I did not dare look at my uncle at that moment, but I sensed his discomfiture from across the room. I knew that I was fighting for my future and even if my aunt couldn't help me or if that wretched letter came to nothing, at least I had tried.

Aunt Miranda now directed her steely-eyed gaze on my uncle sitting haughty and disapproving in his chair.

'I'd like to talk to my niece alone, Sir,' she snapped primly.

'Is that necessary, Miss Wentworth? I am her legal guardian and as such have only her wellbeing at heart.'

'Nevertheless, as this is the first time we have met I should be glad of a chance to get to know her and see what sort of a child she is.'

Stiffly, he rose to his feet and without looking at me motioned to his wife to follow him out of the room.

As soon as the door closed behind them my aunt beamed at me with her twinkling dark eyes. 'So they'd turn you into a skivvy Maya, and have you looking like that poor downtrodden woman in half the time, would they? Well, not if Miranda Wentworth has anything to do with it!'

I looked at her with a new hope in my heart and she laughed, patting the chair so that I could squeeze in beside her.

'I didn't agree with my brother going off to Africa, and him dying at the hands of those black heathens only proves that I was right, but he left enough money for your education Maya, that I do know. I'm not disputing the home they've given you but not all the money that was left has gone in providing it. I'll fight him tooth and nail to see that you get that education, Maya.'

I threw my arms round her small, lavender-scented form and I couldn't help seeing that her eyes were bright with unshed tears.

Strangely enough, no fight was necessary. My uncle capitulated far more easily than I had expected and in less than a month it was arranged that I should go to the ladies' college mentioned by the headmaster for the daughters of clergymen and such. When I say that he capitulated I do not mean that he ever forgave me for that letter, or for my aunt's involvement. Between us now was an ever-widening gulf which he made no effort to close. I had committed the cardinal sin of thwarting his wishes and never again would he look upon me as other than a rebellious nuisance. Aunt Edith tried to bring us closer but he would have none of it, and because I was so soon to leave the vicarage, it did not worry me as much as it once would have done.

'You'll write to me, won't you Maya?' Emily insisted. 'Don't expect me to write back though, yer knows 'ow I 'ates writin' letters, 'sides I niver know what to say.'

Cora too asked me to write to her but promised to answer my letters. There was a new air of well-being about her these days, borne out by a bloom in her cheeks and a sparkle in her eyes that had always been missing. When I mentioned it to Emily she replied knowingly, 'That's 'cause she's in luv wi' that young Mr Carnwood fro' Buckley, the one she were wi' at Mr Lyndon's weddin'.'

We were in her kitchen at the time, sitting at the white wood table eating newly-baked scones straight from the oven and her mother cut in sharply, 'You shouldn't be sayin' such things, our Emily, it be all hearsay.'

When her mother had returned to the stove I whispered urgently, 'But Emily – *that* was the man we saw kissing Eleanor so how can he be in love with Cora?'

'Why don't you tell Maya about mi grandfather takin' old Sir

43

John to those cock-fights up at the Ackroyd 'ouse, Mother,' Emily said quickly. 'Mi grandfather allus 'ad a lot o' stories about the gentry an' their 'abits.'

Mrs Roper returned to the table with two glasses of milk and snapped, 'Yer grandfather couldn't allus be relied on to tell the truth, he were a great one for exaggerating.'

'Please Mrs Roper, do tell me,' I urged her, and sitting down with a steaming cup of tea she seemed nothing loth to repeat some of the tales told her by her father.

'Many were the times 'e was out all night. I remember mi mother lockin' the door an' makin' 'im sleep the rest o' the night in't privy. Next day when 'e were sober 'e'd say 'e'd bin wi' old Sir John over at the Ackroyd 'ouse, gamblin'. Ay, sometimes there were cock-fights an' the old man'd lose a lot o' money. It were on one such night that 'e lost too much and couldn't settle 'is debt. That were the night 'e gave old Ackroyd 'is promise that Miss Eleanor would marry 'is son Roger when they were old enough. Mi mother said it were all rubbish but mi father swore it were the 'onest truth.'

'But how old was Miss Eleanor then?' I cried.

'She were nobbut a little un, three or four, not a year more an' Ackroyd's lad would a' bin about thirteen or perhaps more. Mi father stuck to 'is story till 'is dyin' day.'

'What other things did mi grandfather tell ye?' Emily asked, her eyes wide with curiosity.

'Old Mr Ackroyd died soon after that so there were no more cock-fights over at Seaten, then Lady Gaynor died an' soon after Sir John ups and marries the second Lady Gaynor. I've seen Miss Eleanor drivin' in the carriage wi' Mr Ackroyd. It makes ye wonder if mi father mightn't a' bin right, doesn't it?'

'But Eleanor's so lovely and he's so old,' I objected.

'Ay well, the gentry's not like us Maya. Money marries money, an' if they don't marry fer it, they luv wheer it is.'

Such vagaries did not worry me for long. I was leaving Lexford behind me and since no man was every likely to marry me for my money I hoped to fill my mind and my heart with so much knowledge I wouldn't care whether I was married or not.

FIVE

WITHOUT WISHING TO dwell too long on the next few years, I can only say they were an enchantment that remained with me long after they had ended. The college was a lofty Victorian house standing in the midst of a large garden tended lovingly by an army of gardeners. The large rooms were bright with chintz and flowers and I rejoiced that the next four or five years of my life were to be spent beneath its roof.

The other girls were mainly the daughters of the clergy or other professional men and amongst them I made friends but not of a lasting quality. They took their studies light-heartedly whilst I did not so it was not surprising that they regarded me as something of a bluestocking. I played croquet and tennis as a matter of course and without excelling in either, but it was in the classroom that I came into my own. I absorbed learning like a sponge absorbs water and most of the girls stood in awe of my thirst for knowledge.

I was introduced to parents as the girl who was always at the top of her class, the girl who set an example to all for diligence and hard work. Not surprisingly, those same parents invited me to visit them in the company of their daughters for long summer holidays, in the hope that some of my prowess might be passed on!

True to my word I wrote to Emily without receiving letters in return. Cora wrote often but letters from my aunt and uncle were sparse, although the usual packages arrived from Aunt Miranda on birthdays and before Christmas. My uncle was nothing loth that I should visit the homes of my friends, since the invitations came from bishops, doctors and solicitors. Thus my trips home to Lexford were infrequent and in the end practically nonexistent.

In the next few years I grew tall and slender and my black hair gleamed with a new lustre. I would always have a fine pale skin but my slate blue eyes were unusual and my mouth had begun to curve with a passionate warmth.

I became aware of my newfound beauty in several ways. By the trembling hand of Mr Jacobson our piano tutor, as he turned the leaves of the music I was playing, and the attention of my friends' brothers whenever I stayed with them. I would not have been female if I hadn't rejoiced in my power to attract men, but it was a small thing compared with the harvesting of knowledge that would make certain I never returned to Lexford.

It was with this aim in view therefore that I asked to see Miss Lawford the headmistress several months before I knew I must leave the college after acquiring my diploma. She received me in her study overlooking the garden bright with flowers and beech trees in full leaf. She sat behind her large walnut desk, a slender silver-haired woman with a calm lovely face, and looking into her blue eyes I felt a surge of love and affection for this woman who had made my life blossom, a life starved of affection as well as knowledge.

I told her that I must work, that I could not go back to Lexford *ever* and I asked her to help me, then I stood trembling before her waiting with bated breath for her advice.

'Sit down Maya,' she said kindly. 'I have been meaning to send for you and I realise time is now getting short. Your stay with us is almost finished.'

I nodded, hardly trusting my voice to agree with her.

'Have you any thoughts about your future? I am expecting you to do well in your examinations but this is still a man's world, Maya, and unfair as it may seem work for a woman is precarious and often hard to find.'

'But there must be something, Miss Lawford. I have worked

so hard, surely now I could be a governess, a companion or even a secretary?'

'Would you be happy teaching young children, caring for an invalid or even doing secretarial work when you have learned so much more?'

'I am not thinking of happiness. I know I shall have to find work or return to my uncle's house and I couldn't bear that. I should die in that cold draughty vicarage reading Bible stories to the young wives or stitching worn sheets together with fingers numb with cold.'

She smiled gently. 'Is that what I would be condemning you to, Maya? It hardly seems appropriate that my star pupil should lay her beauty and her learning on the altar of mediocrity.' She paused, smiling a little, then in a voice that might have been offering me a choice between tea and coffee she said, 'How would you like to remain on here Maya, always providing your exam results are good enough, as a junior teacher?'

I stared at her, hardly daring to believe what I had just heard. It was as though the sun had just shone over a world buried under the snow, as though roses had bloomed riotously in the wilderness, and in a voice trembling with joy I breathed, 'Oh Miss Lawford, could that be possible?'

'There is only one post, Maya. You are my best pupil and if you do not want the post then I must offer it to Mary Reardon. Would you like to think about it and let me know later?'

'Oh no, Miss Lawford, I don't need to think about it, I can tell you now. More than anything in the world I would like to remain here to teach.'

'I shall of course need to write to your guardian. Is there any chance that he might object?' she asked.

Momentarily my heart sank but then I reassured myself. How could my uncle object to such a chance for me? Teaching in a good school, I would be off their hands earning my own living, instructing the daughters of men in a similar profession to his own . . . Surely he would not object to such a plan – and yet I would have been happier if I could simply have accepted

47

and informed my uncle later of my decision.

Miss Lawford sensed my doubts. 'You are under age, Maya. I must consult him but I cannot see why he should object. The salary is not large, and you would not at first be able to contribute anything to your aunt and uncle, but in time this would come about. He might be glad of that. I will write to him today and by the end of term I should have his reply and matters can go ahead.'

I thanked her warmly, then with joy in my heart I went racing along the corridors outside so that I could impart my news quickly to the girls I believed were my special friends. They found it hard to believe that I wanted this to be my future life. In the main, they could not wait to leave the schoolroom and take up their adult life in a world peopled by loving families and a string of suitable beaux. Only Mary Reardon appeared sulky at my news. She was a plain, insipid girl whom I always suspected of having hidden depths. She was naturally clever, and as the only daughter of a Derbyshire clergyman, I guessed her life had been as uneventful as mine.

I had tried to make friends with her, but my efforts had met with a frigid reserve. What had lingered however, was a strange rivalry and the fact that she would be offered the teaching post if my uncle refused to allow me to take it, built up a further barrier between us as I waited impatiently for the headmistress to send for me again.

The days and weeks crept on towards the end of term. I worried myself into a shadow as I wondered why I had heard nothing. It was the morning of the prize-giving ceremony and one of my duties was to help in arranging the flowers on the long tables where pupils, parents and teachers would take their lunch. Impatient with the flowers, I snipped carelessly at stalks and leaves, and then was suddenly aware of Mary Reardon standing beside me, watching me with a half-smile on her face.

'I'll finish the flowers if you like. The headmistress is asking for you,' she said quietly.

I looked at her sharply but her plain, prim little face gave nothing away. Hastily I wiped my hands on my handkerchief then handing her the scissors I said, 'Somehow they are not going right this morning. Perhaps I am trying too hard.'

She smiled, 'Perhaps. Miss Lawford is in her study, I have just come from there.'

I stared at her again, but unperturbed she devoted all her attention to the flowers. My heart was racing oddly as I made my way to the headmistress' study. She was standing at the window looking out across the gardens, but on my entry she turned round and walked back to her desk.

'Sit down, Maya, this will not take long.'

Feverishly I searched her face but she was looking down at the letters on her desk and our eyes did not meet. She took a letter from among the others and as her eyes at last met mine I could feel my heart hammering in my breast. I knew at that moment that I would hate what she was about to tell me.

'I have heard from your uncle, Maya, and I am sorry that I do not have good news for you. He has rejected my offer to find you a position here in the school. He tells me your aunt is unwell and quite unable to cope with all the work she does in connection with the church so your presence is required at home. They have not informed you before because they wished you to finish your education, but see, here is the letter, you can read it for yourself.'

I knew my uncle's writing, that large round scholarly hand, using phrases I was familiar with, but the page in my hand trembled so much I was unable to read it. Miss Lawford rose from her chair and came to take it from me. I wanted to cry but the tears would not come, instead the bitter ache in my throat was a searing pain. I felt that my life was over.

'I am sorry Maya,' she said sympathetically. 'I wanted you here, you have worked so hard but you will see that my hands are tied. I must respect his wishes.'

I rose to my feet and stood trembling before her.

'I have asked Mary Reardon if she would like to accept the post and she has accepted. Obviously I shall have to consult her father but she assures me he will not put obstacles in her way. If it is any consolation Maya, your examination results are the

49

best in the school. We are all very proud of you.'

As I stood on the platform that afternoon holding my diploma and an armful of prizes listening to the applause I could only respond with weary resignation. What did it matter? How could anything matter, ever again? I would go back to Lexford, to the dreary round of a life of stagnation, and this time, there would be no hope of escape.

Thanks to my uncle's reluctant permission, I spent several weeks with Aunt Miranda in North Lancashire before returning home to Lexford. How I loved her warm cosy cottage in the pretty stone village overlooking the Pennine hills. Here in Lancashire the countryside was softer . . . and when spring came, it smiled in the leafy lanes and shimmering tarns. I delighted in the pots of geraniums on the windowsill and the fat ginger cat that purred on the hearth, but now I was far from all that loving comfort, sitting in the train that climbed upwards on its single track towards Lexford.

Here, on the other side of those sweeping hills the spring was cold and bleak, and I was relieved to see the one cab the village could lay claim to standing in the cobbled station yard. My case was heavy with books and the cabdriver came forward to assist me, raising his cap and saying, 'So yer 'ome at last Miss. We've not bin seein' much of yer these last few years.'

'No. I spent most of my school holidays with friends I met there and I have just been away at my other aunt's house.'

'Ay well, there's bin one or two changes. Ye knew that old Mr Roper'd died, ye were allus freiendly wi' that lass of 'is.'

'Yes. Emily didn't like writing letters but she did write to say her father had died.'

'It were a blessin' in disguise. 'E'd bin a creakin' gate a long time an' heaven knows they've 'ad more than their fair share o' troubles.'

He shook his head lugubriously and urging the horse on we set off at a brisk trot along the village street.

If there had been changes they were not at first evident. Nothing seemed different in that rambling village street, not even the cakes and bread in the baker's window. A few of the villagers standing gossiping in the street looked up expectantly to see who was in the cab but I leaned back in my seat, disinclined to respond to any smiles of welcome. A smart trap was pulled up outside the post office and an equally smart pony pawed the ground impatiently. As we passed I saw Miss Eleanor coming out, holding a small boy by the hand. She lifted him onto the front seat then took her place beside him. I spun round in my seat to watch them driving quickly in the opposite direction and as the cabby helped me down with my luggage I said, 'Wasn't that Miss Eleanor coming out of the post office?'

'Ay. She lives over at Seaten now. She be Mrs Roger Ackroyd, and that's 'er little boy she 'ad with 'er.'

I stared at him in surprise. Cora had written often in the early days of my absence but she had not mentioned that her sister was married. Curiously I asked, 'Are there any other changes at Greythorn then?'

'Well, Old Sir John died about eighteen months ago so Sir Lyndon's the new Baronet. It's sad they have no little 'uns but they do say 'is wife 'ad a bad fall, fell down the stairs from top to bottom they say, so p'raps it's unlikely the poor lady'll 'ave children.'

'Is Miss Cora still at the Hall?'

'Ay, an' pretty as a picture she is these days. Engaged to a nice young feller, an' Mr Gavin's still 'ere, 'andsome as the devil and twice as mischievous. Well, 'e knows it too, setting all their 'earts aflutter every time 'e rides down the street.'

'And does he ride down the street often, Mr Jarvis?'

'Not as often as 'e used to – which makes me think 'e 'as other fish to fry in some other direction.'

He smiled down at me with twinkling eye. 'P'raps if 'e knows you're back 'e'll be over 'ere again, Miss Maya – I shouldn't put it past 'im.'

I smiled as I paid him the appropriate fare.

'I'll 'elp you up to the 'ouse wi' yer case, Miss. Is it a ton o' coal you've got i' theer?'

'No, just books.'

'Books is it? Well I've never bin a reader misself but you'll need somethin' to occupy yer time. It can't be much fun fer a young girl 'elpin' wi' church matters.'

I watched him walk back along the path shaking his head sadly. It was true, nobody was going to envy me my life at the vicarage and squaring my shoulders I lifted the heavy knocker on the door.

My aunt came to open it, greeting me effusively without her eyes once meeting mine. She seemed much the same. She had always been thin and her pale face above the stiff grey dress she was wearing looked tired. She had pretty hair, but now she wore it pulled back sharply from her face into a tight knot in the nape of her neck and I longed to put my fingers through it and release it around her face. She helped me pull my case into the hall, exclaiming on its weight so that I said, 'I can manage it on my own, Aunt. I'll unpack it later.'

'It's so nice to see you home at last, Maya. Your uncle is out on one of his calls. Poor Mrs Anvers isn't well so I thought we would have tea in the kitchen instead of carrying the crockery into another room. I hope you don't mind.'

'No, of course not. Is Mrs Roper still here?'

'Why no. She doesn't come here now, she left us a few weeks ago.'

'Have you been running the house yourself then, as well as helping with church matters?'

'I've had help from some of the other women, but we thought with you home we wouldn't need Mrs Roper and she had the offer of other employment from a gentleman who has just recently lost his wife over at Buckley.'

'It seems a long way for her to go without transport of any kind.'

'She enjoys walking and she's accustomed to rising early.'

I followed my Aunt Edith into the kitchen where cups and saucers were laid out on the kitchen table. The kitchen was untidy as it never was in the days of Mrs Roper and the cake she brought to the table was stodgy and had sunk in the middle.

She kept up a string of chatter about church matters of which

I was largely ignorant. The daily round of meetings in that cold bleak room upstairs was explained to me in detail so that by the time I heard my uncle's key in the lock my head was spinning with all the things she had asked me to remember. My uncle was more affable than I ever remembered. He told me I would be doing a useful and rewarding task, far more rewarding than teaching rich children who only accepted learning as a means of securing a suitable marriage.

'These young village girls need to learn how to knit and sew, how to tell the difference between right and wrong so that they will not be ignorant when they stand before the Lord in His church where, I hope, my good example will assure that they do not fall from Grace.'

I looked at him sharply, sensing that his words conveyed something more potent if obscure, but immediately he began to talk to my aunt about the failing health of his parishioner and the moment was lost. My old bedroom was exactly as I had left it except for the rug before the fireplace, which I recognised as having once occupied a similar position in the dining room. I shivered. The room felt cold and unwelcoming, and seeing my bleak expression my aunt said, 'Perhaps we can put up new curtains. You shall help me choose the material, Maya.'

'Thank you, Aunt Edith, that would be nice,' I replied, then busy unlocking my trunk I said, 'I haven't heard from Emily for a long time. Perhaps I should walk down to the Ropers' house tonight to see if she is in.'

'I doubt if she will be,' my aunt answered, fidgeting with the door knob on her way out. 'She spends most of her time with Ned Rakesby and I don't think your uncle would be too pleased if you renewed your friendship with Emily.'

'But Emily and I have never stopped being friends, Aunt. I know I've been away for the last few years but my friendship for Emily is still the same.'

'Then perhaps it should not be, Maya. The Ropers have always been respectable people if they never had much money and none of her sisters brought their mother trouble or disgrace. Emily has caused her mother untold anguish, and it's just as well that her father isn't here to see it.'

'What has Emily done that is so terrible?'

She had spun round to face me, two bright spots of colour burning in either cheek, and her lips compressed in disapproval. 'I'll tell you what she has done Maya, she has got herself pregnant, but what is worse she says she has absolutely no intention of marrying the boy. How on earth she thinks she will be able to look after the baby when it is born I can't imagine. There will only be her mother's money going into the house and she says she wants nothing from the baby's father.'

'But why won't she marry him?'

'I don't know. Your uncle has spoken to her, and shown her where her Christian duty lies but Miss Emily sits in church tight-lipped and unrepentant that she has brought shame onto her family. It's brought trouble to the Rakesbys' household, too. They are upright, God-fearing people, and seeing Emily's child grow up in the village is going to be a constant reproach to their son.'

'Why does everybody think they are so perfect that they can afford to sit in judgment on Emily! How can they be so cruel?'

'She should be made to see how wicked she has been Maya, how wicked she is still being to deny her child its father.'

'Poor Emily. You mustn't ask me to ignore her, Aunt. I loved Emily when I was growing up in this village and I can't forget that she was my friend.'

'You must do as you think fit Maya, but remember that you are still underage and it is our duty to protect you from wickedness as we see it and to make sure that you grow up decent and law-abiding.'

'I won't forget Aunt, but Emily's sin isn't contagious.'

She shrugged her shoulders and without another word left me, closing my bedroom door firmly behind her. I went to stand at the window overlooking the churchyard. Nothing had changed. The tall elms still tapped their fingers against the panes but I was unprepared for the wave of loneliness that flooded me so that I knelt on the floor trembling with the pain of it. How would I be able to endure the months and years that followed without Emily's laughter and the strange truths of her sayings?

The following weeks crawled on, weeks when I only saw Emily at a distance, either sitting next to her mother in church while my uncle lectured on about the sins of the flesh, or in the village street. Whenever she saw me she avoided me, either by running in the opposite direction or hurrying out of the churchyard after the service. In spite of my aunt's advice I called twice at the Ropers' cottage but nobody came to the door and I was forced to turn away.

My hands grew red and dry from the soda used for scrubbing the kitchen floor and table and I developed a husky cough from sitting upstairs in the cold attic while I tried to interest the women and girls who came to the meetings. At first I read them stories from the Bible, then I brought out some books of my own, mostly Jane Austen and the Brontës, and read to them from these. I came to accept their stolid expressions which did not tell me whether they enjoyed the readings or not, and grew accustomed to their red hands swollen with chilblains and their feet shuffling on the bare floorboards in an endeavour to stir the circulation.

I took them through the woods on nature walks and we brought in holly to decorate the room and twigs to add to the fire. Now instead of sitting at the long tables we gathered round the fireplace, and with the lamps lit early and the curtains drawn, the room took on a cheerfulness it did not aspire to in the cold light of day. Younger girls were coming to the meetings now although some of the older ones stayed away, and once I was stopped in the village street by the mother of one of them. She was a thin, pinched woman, holding a child with a runny nose by the hand, and in a whining querulous voice she said, 'Our Janie won't be coming to the vicarage agin Miss Maya, she needs to learn 'ow to 'em a sheet and mend a sock. I don't old wi' ye readin' 'em stories about folk who live i' big 'ouses and don't 'ave to work fer their livin'.'

'But that's all they are, Mrs Holden, just stories. Didn't Janie enjoy them?'

'P'raps she did, but the Reverend's wife'd never a' read such stories to 'em, she taught 'em 'ow to fear God, do a bit o' sewing an' knittin' an' 'ow to make good wives when the time comes.'

Shaking the child who had begun to cry petulantly she set off down the road dragging him behind her. As for me, I could have cried with frustration. I had hoped to open up new horizons for them, to make them see that there was another world outside the village, waiting to embrace those who dared look for it. What chance had they, had any of them when there was nothing around them but bigotry and closed minds?

My aunt too had received complaints. 'They don't want to know about foreign lands or Miss Austen's romances, Maya. If you must read to them let it be from the Bible, there are enough stories in there to satisfy anyone, and teach them how to sew neatly. The more ambitious ones could learn to do embroidery to brighten up their homes.'

My sewing prowess was abysmal compared to my aunt's neat stitching and my knitting nonexistent. The girls soon realised I was inadequate in this direction and I learned more from them than they learned from me. Janie Holden came to apologise for her mother's harsh words saying, 'Don't mind mi mother, Miss Maya. She wants mi to get wed and make room fer the others but I'm not gettin' wed till I'm good and ready. I loved the stories yer used to read us.'

Saturday was the only day the girls did not come to the vicarage in the evening and as the days lengthened and grew warmer I took to walking in the hills. It was the Saturday before Easter when I climbed the long low hill above Greythorn and as I looked up after I had climbed the stile I saw Emily sitting above me with her back resting against the crag. She saw me at the same time, and getting clumsily to her feet made as if to move away.

'Emily stop, please don't go,' I called out to her, and taking to my heels I ran after her. Her figure was ungainly now with the weight of the child she carried and she could not run carefree and swift as she had once, across the fells. In minutes I had caught up with her and she faced me, her face flaming, her red hair a fiery halo about her face.

'You shouldn't be doin' this Maya, it's better that yer don't speak to me.'

'Oh Emily, what nonsense! I'll always be your friend, nothing has changed, just as I hope you'll always be mine.'

'Yer aunt an' uncle wouldn't want yer talkin' to me an' I don't want to get ye into bother wi' them.'

'Emily – I don't care. I've been miserable when you avoided me. I want to know what you're going to do.'

I sat down on the hillside and pulled her down beside me.

She didn't speak for several minutes and I watched her face, still beautiful even though her eyes were shadowed and sad. At last she looked straight into my eyes and said, 'I suppose you've bin told I'm marryin' nobody?'

'Yes, but Emily why not? Ned loves you, I think he's loved you for years and one day he'll have his father's farm and you could have a good life together. He's asked you to marry him I know.'

'Oh ay, 'e wants to marry me all right but it's not what I want. I don't want to wed 'im an' spend the rest o' mi life in this village. We'd never live it down Maya, even if 'e married me. Mi child'd allus be the one whose mother 'ad to get wed afore it were born. I know these folk, they're narrow an' bigoted an' right now I'm all they've got to talk about. You knows 'em too Maya, tryin' to bring a bit o' colour into their lives an' all they can do is criticise.'

I could feel my eyes pricking with unshed tears and that old bitter ache in my throat, more hurtful than tears. As though she sensed my distress Emily put her arms around me and held me against her.

'Don't upset yourself about me, Maya. I allus bounces back an' don't walk back to the village wi me, I'm quite capable o' makin' mi own way back an' it wouldn't do fer us to be seen together.'

'But of course I'm coming back with you. I'm certainly not letting you walk back alone.'

'See there's no need, Ned's come fer me.'

I looked down the hill and sure enough Ned Rakesby was climbing it. He stopped when he saw us together and waited for Emily to reach him. I stood on the crag watching them walk slowly down the hill. Ned held her hand tightly in his, and once when she stumbled he put his arms round her and held her close. Once again the treacherous ache filled my heart and I wondered why I had been denied the solace of tears at the most hurtful times of my life.

I continued my climb until I could sit on the summit of the hill looking down on Greythorn. There was smoke from several of the chimneys and the formal gardens surrounding the house were bright with clumps of daffodils and azalea bushes. There were swans on the mere and I thought about the lives of those people inside the Hall in comparison with the lives of the villagers around them. Sir Lyndon had the reputation of being a good man to work for. He was generous with his tenants and kept their property in good repair, always ready to give to the church and to charitable affairs, but was money enough on its own, I asked myself?

As I pondered on the rights and wrongs of life a solitary horseman climbed the hill and rode along the bridle path towards Buckley. He rode slowly, on a large powerful chestnut which picked its way gracefully across the shallow stream, avoiding the brambles which grew riotously beside the path. I had no wish to encounter anyone, so jumping to my feet I hurried down the hill towards the stile. I was not fast enough, however. As I reached the stile the rider had already dismounted and was bent on opening the gate to allow himself and his horse to pass through.

He smiled briefly, holding the gate open so that I could pass by instead of climbing the stile and I thanked him shyly. I had thought at first that I did not know him, but then I recognised his face. Many years had passed since I first saw Sir Lyndon Gaynor standing in his father's study when I was merely a child of ten. Although he was still austerely handsome, there were wings of silver now at the sides of his face and as I walked away down the lower slopes of the hill I found myself remembering him on his wedding day with his lovely bride laughing up into his face and his eyes filled with joy.

Time! That elusive thing which gives and takes away, joy and sorrow, pain and even love. What would Time do for me, in the years ahead? My thoughts were turned inwards as I walked back to the village. All around me the countryside was bursting with new life but all I could think of was the remote sad smile on Sir Lyndon Gaynor's face and Emily who was stubbornly refusing to marry the man who so desperately loved her.

I had reached the road when I became aware of the sound of hooves behind me. I turned round sharply, expecting to see Sir Lyndon on his big chestnut but it was a white horse which leapt down onto the road, ridden by a young man with a dark laughing face and impudent blue eyes which looked amusedly into mine.

He took off his cap and gave me a mocking little bow.

'Good morning,' he called. 'I thought I knew all the pretty girls in Lexford, so how is it we've never met?'

Gavin Gaynor had changed little in the years since I had last seen him, but I evidently had changed a great deal. He didn't recognise me but as I walked towards the vicarage he allowed his horse to fall into step beside me.

'Now who are you,' he mused. 'Whose daughter – tinker, tailor, candlestick maker, baker, barber – the list is endless. Why not enlighten me so that we can get on to something more interesting.'

I stopped at the vicarage gate then deliberately I opened it and placed one foot on the step. 'Good day Mr Gaynor. This is where we part company.'

He stared at the house and the church, and then light dawned in his face. 'Of course, you're the niece. I remember you now, that pale little girl with the enormous eyes and that long black hair like a miniature witch.'

'Thank you Mr Gaynor, I'm sure your description is very apt.'

He leapt down from his horse and put a restraining hand on top of the gate. 'But not now though,' he said, laughing down at me. 'Now you're as beautiful as a summer dawn. How can anybody so colourless grow up to be so beautiful?'

'Please let me by, Mr Gaynor, I am late.'

'You used to call me Gavin I remember.'

'A child can do many things an adult would not dream of doing.'

'I would like you to call me Gavin now.'

'It is doubtful if we shall meet often enough for me to call you anything, Mr Gaynor. I am very involved with church matters and since you are a non-attender we shall have nothing in common.'

'But you walk on the hills.'

'Very seldom. Now please let me by or I shall be late for lunch.'

He withdrew his hand from the gate and stepped back so that I could pass in front of him.

Again he gave me his mocking bow but his eyes were filled with laughter as he called out to me, 'We shall meet again – I'll see to it. By the way, I've forgotten your name.'

I turned round and smiled at him briefly, but I did not enlighten him about my name.

I felt strangely excited as I took my place at the luncheon table and my aunt remarked, 'Have you been hurrying Maya? Your cheeks have more colour than they normally do.'

'Yes, I was afraid I might be late.'

The fact that I was busy with my own thoughts didn't bother them. Luncheon was invariably a time when my uncle aired his views either about the state of the country or the misdemeanours of his congregation. All that was required of my aunt and me was that we agree with him and he took my silence as a sign that I did. I had decided months ago that if I wanted my future to be reasonably peaceful in this household I should either agree with him or remain silent. Consequently, I allowed my thoughts now

60

to dwell on Emily's predicament. Even so the family at Greythorn Hall intruded into my thoughts as they had always done.

I could not help wondering if Gavin would make good his threat to see me again, if threat it was, and I did not have long to wait.

There were days when I drove my uncle out of the village to visit his parishioners who lived on farms well clear of the village and it was on one of these occasions that I saw Gavin again. I always sat in the trap while my uncle went inside, and quite often his visits were lengthy.

Gavin arrived beside the trap, smiling his impudent smile, as he raised his cap.

'I've made sure that we shall meet again Maya, for that is your name! My sister is inviting you to tea at the Hall.'

'I doubt if I shall be able to come, Mr Gaynor. My uncle keeps me very busy and my aunt isn't well.'

'Your uncle will be delighted for you to come I'm sure, either that or he's changed a lot.'

My eyes snapped at him angrily. 'It doesn't rest with my uncle, Mr Gaynor. I may have neither the time nor the inclination.'

His eyes immediately became contrite. 'But I'm asking you to find time Maya. Asking your uncle is a formality – it is you we shall want to see.'

I was about to say something else when to my utmost consternation I saw my uncle leaving the farmhouse. Gavin greeted him politely saying, 'I thought I recognised the trap, Sir, but I thought your wife was driving it. It is many years since I last saw Miss Maya, and I wouldn't have recognised her.'

'No indeed,' said my uncle, all affability as Gavin knew he would be. 'How are Sir Lyndon and Her Ladyship?'

'My brother is very well but Melinda doesn't improve I'm sad to say. She spends most of the time sitting out in the garden with her embroidery. It is a sad state of affairs for one so young.'

'Terrible, terrible. Are there no signs of improvement then?'

'None. She has had the best physicians in London so the prospects are not good.'

61

'Regrettable, most regrettable. But Miss Cora now, she'll be getting married soon. I hope the wedding is to be in Lexford. I well remember your brother's wedding, it kept the villagers' tongues wagging for months.'

'Yes, I'm sure it did. You will have to ask my sister herself, for I have no doubt she will be calling on Miss Maya now that she knows she is home.'

He bowed to us both, entirely correct, and as he turned his horse to gallop away I devoted my attention to turning the pony and trap in the narrow lane.

Two days later a smart carriage deposited Cora Gaynor at the vicarage gate watched by groups of villagers along the road. She greeted me with great warmth and I marvelled at the change in her. Gone was the listless, pallid girl whose every step had seemed an effort in the windy months of spring, whose pale blue eyes had seemed haunted by the sad spectre of ill-health. Now her eyes shone with a new light, her pale hair gleamed in the sunlight and she ran rather than walked along the path to meet me.

She found me in the garden taking the faded flower heads off the rosetrees, and immediately I felt shabby beside her elegant silk dress and pretty flowered hat.

'How well you look,' I exclaimed. 'I would hardly have recognised you.'

She held me at arm's length and looked searchingly into my face. 'Gavin was right, Maya, you are a beauty. He talks about you all the time. He had me come down here quickly, it's years since I've seen him so interested in a girl.'

'I should have thought he was always interested in some girl or other.'

She laughed, showing pretty even teeth, then taking my arm in a conspiratoral manner she whispered, 'Oh I know there have been girls, lots of them. He's handsome and gay but he's really taken with you Maya, so I've got to make sure you come to see us soon.'

'My aunt and uncle are in the house, shall we go in now?'

'No, can't we sit in the garden for a while, it's far too warm to go indoors. Perhaps I ought to greet them first and then can we sit outside?'

My uncle expressed his delight at her visit and my aunt said if we wished to sit outdoors she would serve us tea. Immediately we were comfortable, Cora began to talk about her engagement. It was obvious that she was very much in love. Her eyes sparkled when she spoke of her fiancé and she held out her hand so that I could see the ring on her finger, a large opal surrounded with diamonds.

'Eleanor said opals were unlucky but I have always loved them. I love the fire underneath and diamonds haven't been too lucky for her.'

'You mean she isn't happy?'

'How could she be with Roger! He drinks too much, he gambles heavily just like his father did and I wouldn't be surprised if he didn't beat her.'

The thought of that beautiful, high-spirited girl being at the mercy of such a man appalled me.

'Oh surely not,' I cried. 'She would leave him. I can't see Eleanor putting up with that.'

'What else can she do, she's his wife and then there's Jamie. She had Jamie in the first year of their marriage and he's rather delicate. He's such a shy, withdrawn child and so fanciful, I can't see him ever going away to school and mixing with other children.'

'Why did she marry Roger Ackroyd?'

'When I was a little girl I used to hear the servants talking. They said my father had promised Eleanor to Roger in payment of a gambling debt but I never believed it. Once I asked my father and it was the first time I've ever seen him angry with me! All the same, since then I've often wondered if the stories were true. No smoke without fire they say.'

'If it is true it was a terrible thing to do.'

'Yes, I'm glad I wasn't the answer to another gambling debt.'

'Eleanor lives out at Seaten doesn't she?'

'Yes, in a great dark house which she hates but Roger won't change it in any way.'

I was trying to visualise Eleanor with her vibrant beauty and her zest for living in that great dark house with a strange fanciful child and a husband who drank. But now Cora was asking me about my life at the vicarage and why the teaching position about which I had written to her had not materialised.

She was sympathetic with my plight and I reflected that with all her happiness before her she could afford to be.

'What are they going to do when you want to get married?' she asked.

'Where am I ever likely to meet a man who wants to marry me?' I replied somewhat acidly. 'My only chance is a curate my uncle might take on some day, but I don't want to marry a curate and in any case the size of the parish doesn't warrant it.'

'Well, something will have to be done. Leave it to me . . .'

SIX

ONE WEEK AFTER Cora's visit I received in the post an official invitation to take tea at Greythorn Hall. I laid it dutifully beside my uncle's breakfast plate. He read it through twice, then passed it across the table to my aunt. She looked at him uncertainly but when he nodded agreeably she smiled.

'This will be nice for you, Maya. Miss Cora is a delightful girl! I shall lend you my cameo brooch, it will go well on that green dress.'

'Thank you, Aunt.' The cameo brooch was her most prized possession so I had every reason to feel grateful, and not to be outdone my uncle said, 'I shall not be needing the trap that day, so you may use it, Maya. I don't expect you to be late but your aunt will take the meeting in your absence.'

I thanked them politely while inside I was bursting with delight. To visit that beautiful house and take tea off paper-thin china, to see bowls of roses on highly-polished furniture and long velvet drapes at small-paned windows overlooking beautiful gardens. It was another world, and as the day drew nearer my excitement increased.

I spent all morning cleaning the trap and grooming the pony, then in my Sunday best I drove happily along the village street watched by groups of gossiping villagers who put their heads together immediately I had passed by. It was a day of high summer with the drone of bees in the air and birdsong from the tall trees. As I entered the park I revelled in the speed as the pony scampered along the winding drive towards the house. I had only gone quarter of the way however when I saw Gavin on his white horse galloping swiftly towards me, reigning in his horse so abruptly that it reared above me, whinnying shrilly.

'I've been waiting for you,' he said, smiling down at me. 'I thought you would appreciate an escort.'

'That was kind of you.'

'Oh, when you know me better you'll find out that I am often kind. Green suits you Maya, but red would suit you better. Something bright and vibrant to make you look like a gypsy.'

Oh, but he was impudent, this handsome dark-eyed young man who felt confident enough to give me advice on the clothes I should wear. I hoped that he would think the colour in my cheeks was caused by the exhilaration of the drive and not because of his words, and I concentrated fully on handling the spirited pony so that I did not need to talk to him.

Not in the least perturbed he said, 'We'll drive to the stables.' He pointed to where they lay in the hollow near the path leading down to the mere.

'The grooms will see to the pony, he'll be well looked after,' he said, with his horse prancing and cavorting to show off his horsemanship.

It was a fair walk from the stables to the house and he took my elbow leading me towards the glade. It was dark where the trees met overhead and in a voice designed to tease me he said, 'I suppose you've heard the legend of the glade?'

'Yes, but isn't a legend merely a fable, a myth to scare or frighten?'

'Perhaps it is, but there have been people who have heard voices in the glade. Some of the servants returning to the village. One or two of the tenants. They do say it isn't good for a member of the family to hear them, for that person would be certain to encounter tragedy of some kind.'

'You are surely not telling me you believe in such nonsense?'

'Oh but I do, and aren't you the least bit afraid, Maya?'

'Not the least bit. Like I told Cora years ago, it is only the wind whispering through the trees.'

'What must it be like, to be so beautiful and so sure?'

I didn't reply but I was very aware of his arm against mine. The beech trees were in full leaf over our heads and the light summer wind rustled through them plaintively so that I began to believe that anyone imaginative could well believe they heard the sound of voices whispering urgently, their words lost on the wind.

'This is the place where the voices are loudest,' he said, drawing me towards the side of the drive. Before I was aware of it his arms had crept around me, then he was kissing me, long ardent kisses and I was fighting him madly with all my strength.

'How dare you,' I said angrily, twisting my head away from him at last. Uncontrite he threw back his head and laughed.

'Come on now, I'm a man and you're a beautiful girl, isn't it the most natural thing in the world?'

'Don't think I enjoyed the experience,' I snapped. 'You're conceited enough to think every girl should fall willingly into your arms.'

'You think I'm conceited?' he said. He sounded surprised.

'Yes I do, I've always thought so. You think you can strut through the village and every girl's going to swoon at the sight of you. Well, I'm not every girl and quite honestly I don't think you'd ever be the sort of man I'd swoon over.'

'Well, well, that's certainly telling me where I stand.'

'Yes it is, and perhaps you will now allow me to walk on unmolested. If not I shall return for the pony and trap and drive home.'

He stepped out beside me whistling cheerfully, but I knew my words had stung him. I felt cheapened by his embrace instead of flattered, and after a while the whistling stopped and he took my reluctant arm, turning me to face him.

'I'm sorry Maya, I didn't mean to offend you. A chap gets lonely for the company of a pretty girl. I thought you might be a bit lonely, too. After all, it can't be much fun for you living at the vicarage and talking to those villagers when you have nothing in common with them.'

'I'm not in the least lonely, and what makes you think we should have more in common? You assume too much, Gavin.'

'I'll apologise again then,' he said. We stared at each other for several minutes and then the corners of his mouth twitched into a smile and in spite of myself I found myself smiling with him, then suddenly we were laughing and taking my hand in his he said, 'Come on, I'll race you to the house.'

We arrived minutes later breathless on the terrace but still laughing and Gavin said, 'In the drawing room I think. Melinda usually officiates at tea-time so I expect we shall find them all there.'

'I thought there would just be Cora and me.'

'Cora should have told you. Afternoon tea is a ceremony and Melinda will expect us to be duly appreciative. Give me your hat and gloves and take a look in the mirror at your hair, you look as rosy as that cherub up on the ceiling.'

It was true. My face was shining and rosy and the soft summer breeze had disturbed my hair so that it fell in shining curls about my shoulders. Hurriedly I smoothed it with my hands into some sort of order then I sped on, urged by Gavin's voice saying, 'Come on, we mustn't keep them waiting.'

I had never been into the drawing room before but I was immediately struck by its beauty. It was a large room with three great windows overlooking the formal gardens, and Melinda sat on a couch in front of the fireplace, now filled with summer flowers, pouring tea from an ornate silver teapot. A maid-servant stood beside her, handing out plates and passing cups and saucers, and Melinda smiled at our arrival, indicating that we should sit on the settee facing Cora and her fiancé.

I felt strangely shy, too diffident to do other then concentrate on the cup and saucer in my hand. Gallantly Gavin placed a small table beside me and I was glad they did not expect me to balance it on my knees as well as the plate that was being handed to me. It was several minutes before I found myself able to look up but Cora's smile reassured me and I was glad of Gavin sitting next to me on the settee.

A soft rug covered Melinda's knees in spite of the warm summer day and a wave of compassion swept over me as I took in her pale delicacy. She seemed like a figure made out of porcelain, her pale golden hair falling softly over one shoulder, like a beautiful doll, a child, acting the part of a grown-up, playing at being the mistress of Greythorn Hall.

Lyndon had been standing with his back to the room staring out across the parkland when we arrived, but now he came forward courteously to take my hand.

He smiled down at me, a singularly sweet smile in his grave face and I knew that my hand trembled in his.

Gavin's face was obviously handsome, made more so by its vitality and daredevil assurance, but his brother's face had more character, more charm, enhanced by the wings of silver hair that grew on either side of it.

'You must forgive me, Miss Wentworth. I did not recognise you when we met on the fell the other day.'

'I was only a little girl when last we met, Sir Lyndon.'

'Yes, a pale little girl with large blue-grey eyes and hair as black as my own. They tell me I have inherited mine from an Italian great-grandmother. I wonder where you got yours?'

'I have no idea, but I agree it is unusual. My mother was fair but my father was very dark.'

I felt suddenly stunned. I did not normally refer to my parents. Why had this man's charm made me resurrect them from that hidden place where I had locked them up so long ago?

'Have you met my sister's fiancé?' he enquired.

'No, but I have seen him before, on your wedding day.'

He smiled. 'Of course, from halfway up that tree I seem to remember.'

I found myself blushing and the rest of them laughed so that suddenly I felt at ease.

Cora's fiancé stood beside him and bent to take my hand. He was introduced as Roland Carnwood and I was informed that he lived in Buckley which was a neighbouring village where his father was a gentleman farmer. Cora told me all this and I smiled up into his good-looking fair face.

As we settled down once more to finish our tea I remarked, 'This is a beautiful room, indeed it is a beautiful house.'

'We like to think so,' Sir Lyndon said smiling. 'Have you seen the rest of the house?'

'Why no, Sir Lyndon. Only the old nursery upstairs and I was once taken into the study.'

'I remember. To be interrogated by my father. I thought you stood up to his questions rather well.'

'I'll show you the house, Maya,' Gavin said quickly, but Cora just as quickly snapped, 'Maya is my guest Gavin. Must you always monopolise my friends?'

'I don't monopolise Roland,' Gavin said mischievously.

'That's because I'm not a pretty girl,' Roland laughingly replied.

'Well, to save any arguments I shall take Maya round the house,' Sir Lyndon said, and unreasonably I felt I could have danced with joy at his offer. I did not want to be shown around by Gavin. He wished to be alone with me and I knew what form our inspection of the house would take! All the same, I looked quickly at Melinda, expecting her to demur a little.

The dispensation of afternoon tea seemed to have exhausted her. She lay back against her cushions staring into the fireplace. It was almost as though she had not heard the conversation going on around her, but as I rose to my feet to accompany Sir Lyndon from the room, she looked at me and smiled.

'Ask Lyndon to show you the orchids Maya, they are particularly beautiful this year.'

I smiled with all the warmth that was in me. She was so vulnerable, this beautiful sad girl sitting on her couch like a china doll while all around her was youth and vitality.

Walking through that great house with Sir Lyndon beside me was a joy and I was grateful for the five years I had spent at Miss Lawford's school which had taught me to appreciate the beauty of fine pictures and delicate china, the sheen on priceless furniture, so that I was not unknowledgeable in the eyes of this man who valued his home and all it contained.

Time seemed to have no meaning as we stood at last in the conservatory where he pointed out the many varieties of orchids that grew there. I exclaimed with delight over their unusual

70

beauty and he reached out and plucked an exquisite bloom in shades of blue and mauve which he handed to me with a smile.

'No doubt other men will give you orchids Maya, but allow me to present you with your first.'

I took it with a blushing face. It had no perfume but I knew that I would keep it always. I would press it in the pages of my Bible with other flowers that had been precious to me. The hibiscus which I had gathered as a child under the warm sun of Africa and the rose I had received on my confirmation day. In time the colour would fade and the petals lose their bloom, but in my heart it would always remind me of the joy of this moment and the first faint agonies of love. This was a day when I had received my first kiss, but as I looked up into Lyndon's dark eyes, and although I responded automatically to the impersonal smile on his lips, I was wishing with all my heart that the kiss had come from him.

In some confusion I tore my eyes away from his face and moved towards the door. I wanted to get back to the others. I was unused to the strange hammering of my heart and the brush of his fingers against mine as he opened the door for me to pass through made me feel gauche and incredibly stupid.

As though he sensed my desire to return to the drawing room he said, 'Well, perhaps you have seen enough for one day. You are too young not to be bored by talk of pictures and furniture and the history of my sometimes doubtful ancestors!'

I was quick to say, 'Oh no, Sir Lyndon. I have loved it all – I just don't want Cora to think I have deserted her.'

'Of course not, and as she was quick to point out, you are her guest.'

'It is nice to see her looking so well these days. I remember that she was always ill in the winter time.'

'Yes, but now she has what she has always wanted. Perhaps it is true that love can work miracles.'

I did not know how to answer him. His voice had been noncommittal, stilted almost, and I was glad when we reached the drawing room. Almost immediately he was making an excuse to leave us, saying that his presence was required in the

71

study. He kissed Melinda's cheek dutifully, but her sad eyes followed him as he left the room.

'It's far too nice to stay indoors,' Cora said gaily. 'Shall we walk in the park or would you like to play croquet?'

'I really don't mind what we do,' I answered her. 'I mustn't be too late in case my uncle needs the trap.'

'Make the most of your day of freedom Maya,' Gavin advised, 'for who knows when you'll get another.'

I looked at Melinda uncertainly. It was obvious she would not be able to join our activities and as though she sensed my hesitancy she said quickly, 'Of course you must go out. I always rest before dinner and the day is too beautiful to waste.'

I thanked her for inviting me and graciously she replied, 'I hope you will be able to come again, Maya.'

It was the conventional reply and I couldn't help wondering if she really meant it. I was not of their world. They must have many young people they could invite but as I strolled across the lawns with Gavin beside me he urged, 'You will come again, won't you Maya? I promise to be good but I get very bored here at Greythorn.'

'Don't you have work to do? I thought you helped your brother to administer the estate.'

'I suppose I do my share, but it's never going to be mine, so why should I break my back caring for it?'

'But of course it will be yours, as Melinda may never have children.'

'She won't have children, but if she dies young Lyndon'll get married again and then there could be children.'

'That's a particularly callous way of looking at things.'

'It's a practical way of looking at things. You've seen Melinda, and heaven knows she isn't getting any better, worse in fact.'

'I'm sure he loves her, and if she does die he may not wish to marry again.'

'He will. He loves this house and the title should be passed on. He thinks I'm too wild, too uncaring. I can't see old Lyndon handing all this on to me without a struggle.'

72

Inwardly I agreed with Lyndon, but I was careful not to say so. Instead I asked, 'How did Melinda come to have her accident?'

'Oh, it was a Christmas party several years ago. The house was full of people, it had been a good party and we decided to play forfeits. During the revelry somehow or other Melinda managed to fall down the stairs. Completely knocked out she was. Lyndon carried her into the drawing room and a doctor was sent for immediately. She quite put paid to the party.'

'Were any limbs broken?'

'She broke her thigh and a couple of ribs. The doctor said she'd be fine when they healed, but unfortunately arthritis set in and now she's become a chronic invalid. I don't suppose we'll ever have another party in this house, not while Melinda's alive at any rate.'

'The party seems more important to you than Melinda's health. I'm not surprised your brother thinks you are uncaring.'

He grinned, quite unabashed. 'I'm quite fond of Melinda actually. She's well looked after and Lyndon is very patient.'

Cora and Roland had walked on ahead and were now out of sight somewhere in the garden. Gavin seemed in no hurry to catch them up and as we stood on the lower terrace looking out across the park he touched the orchid I had pinned through my aunt's cameo brooch.

'I see Lyndon presented you with one of his precious orchids.'

'Yes, isn't it beautiful? It's the first orchid I've ever had, I never saw them before today.'

'You're not really an orchid girl, Maya. You should wear poppies, great scarlet poppies. Orchids are for cool blondes, not wild passionate gypsy creatures.'

'I am neither wild, passionate nor a gypsy.'

'How do you know whether you're passionate or not? Passion has to be inflamed and where is the man who is going to do it?'

'Not you Gavin, for all your fascination.'

'Don't be too sure, my girl. You have admitted I fascinate you, that is always the first step.'

Later that day in the soft scented dusk I drove slowly back to the village. I felt strangely bemused. I had discovered in myself a new person, a woman who could love and a woman who could flirt and I felt disquieted and shaken. It was as though I no longer knew myself.

I could dismiss Gavin with all his charm, but I could not dismiss Lyndon. For a long time that night I lay sleepless listening to the leaves rustling outside in the churchyard but I was seeing his face, dark and grave, the sudden sweet smile, and the low timbre of his voice found an echo in the soft night wind.

Seven

I LIVED WITH that day long after it had passed into limbo, and meanwhile the summer was passing and once more the leaves turned golden on the elms outside my window.

Occasionally I saw Gavin riding his horse across the lower fells but he did not come into the village and I saw nothing of Cora. It was said she was visiting an aunt of Roland's living in the Midlands and I guessed she would also be busy preparing for her wedding the following Easter.

Most of it was gossip heard in the village shops and deliberately I entered into none of it. The villagers looked at me expectantly knowing I had been invited to visit Greythorn, but I merely smiled politely and said I knew nothing of Cora's plans.

Every day I looked for Emily in the village but again she seemed to be avoiding me and for two consecutive Sundays she had not appeared in church. I asked her mother if she was well.

'Well enough Miss Maya, but she resents the looks some folk are givin' 'er, an' His Reverence don't 'elp matters wi' 'is strictures.'

'I would like to call to see her but she doesn't seem to want me.'

'No, an' yer aunt and uncle wouldn't like it. 'Ere's yer uncle condemnin' 'er and you visitin' 'er, it wouldn't be right now would it?'

'I'm not condemning her, I'm her friend.'

'Yer might prove to be a better friend by stayin' away. I'll tell 'er you've bin askin' about 'er, that'll cheer 'er up I'm sure.'

I nodded and moved away. I thought Mrs Roper looked ill. She was much thinner and more careworn than I remembered her.

When I said as much to my aunt and uncle later that day my uncle was quick to retort, 'Of course the poor woman looks thin and careworn. She is worried about her daughter. It's a pity the daughter isn't more concerned about her mother.'

I bit my lip wishing I had not brought up the subject, but since I had I was prepared to flounder on.

'I can't help thinking how uncharitable everybody is being towards Emily.'

'Uncharitable!' he snapped, his eyes blazing in his pale face.

'Yes. Who are any of us to sit in judgment on Emily? The poor girl is being driven to desperation.'

'The remedy is in her own hands. She should marry that boy and they should bring up their child together in the ways of Christianity.'

'There doesn't seem much Christian charity in the way Emily is being treated. I'm not surprised she isn't coming to church.'

'You will apologise for those remarks immediately, Maya. I am trying to do my duty as I see it. If her mother and I cannot shake some sense into her silly head then she is forever damned.'

Trembling, I rose to my feet, hating him and longing with all my heart to tear that self-righteous pompous mask from his face to reveal the mean petty soul beneath. With an unsteady voice I said, 'I cannot apologise for something I said when I earnestly believe it. Who are any of these people to criticise Emily? You are a vicar of God, Uncle, did not Christ say, "Let he who is without sin cast the first stone"?'

He stared at me open-mouthed and I turned on my heel and left the room.

I wished I could leave the house and never return to it. My uncle would never like me, nor I him, my aunt was a clinging shadow, her individuality forever swamped beneath his, and who knows, if I remained long enough under their roof I might lose mine also!

I saw Emily only once after my outburst at the vicarage. It was dusk and a chill wind moaned along the village street carrying a scurry of leaves before it. I had been to post letters and I was hurrying back to the vicarage with my head lowered against the wind when I felt someone touch my arm gently. I looked up in surprise to see Emily beside me. She was pale and there was none of her bright red hair showing underneath the shawl she wore on her head.

'I thowt it was you Maya, I waited til ye came out o' the post office.'

'You shouldn't be standing here in the cold Emily, come into the shop doorway.'

She allowed me to pull her into the doorway of the baker's shop.

The window was empty and evidently having sold all they had to sell they had decided to close for the day. It was cold in the doorway, the leaves scurried round our feet and Emily pulled the shawl closer round her face while I, who had come out without gloves, buried my hands deep inside the pockets of my coat.

'I wish we could talk inside,' Emily said plaintively.

'I could come to your cottage – it's only just down the street.'

'No, Maya. If ye were seen enterin', they'd know at the vicarage afore we'd even closed the door. I won't keep ye longer than a minute.'

'But I want to talk to you, Emily. I want to know what you are going to do and I want to help in any way I can.'

She smiled, and I could have wept at the sad bitterness of her smile.

'Nobody can 'elp me now Maya, it's too late fer that. I just wanted ye to know that I was 'appy bein' friends wi' you when we were children. We did 'ave some good times, didn't we?'

'Oh Emily, you know we did. You were the one bright beautiful thing that saved my childhood from disaster. You brought joy and laughter into it and I'll never forget you for it, never.'

Her small pinched face lit up into some semblance of the old Emily and I could feel the old familiar ache in my heart that would not allow me to cry.

'You'll 'ave other friends, lots of 'em, more proper friends – more suitable-like.'

'I'll never forget that you were my best friend Emily, whoever else comes into my life. I don't want to be the silly superficial sort of woman who puts friendship on one side because something better turns up. There's never going to be anybody better than you, Emily. Is there any way at all I can help you? I haven't any money but there must be some other way.'

'Don't worry about me, Maya, I'll be fine. I've 'eard there's all sorts of 'ospitals an' 'omes that looks after the likes o' me.'

I stared at her in amazement. 'You shouldn't be talking about homes and hospitals Emily, you should be thinking of marrying Ned soon, before the baby is born. Your time is getting near.'

'Somehow I don't seem to be able to think straight at all.'

'Promise you won't do anything foolish like running away?'

'I shan't run far Maya, that's fer sure. Time was when I could run down this street an' mi feet never touched the ground. Mi 'ead was filled wi' nowt but jolly robins an' when I saw yer uncle leavin' the church I'd slow down to a walk an 'e used to watch me till I were out o' sight. Do ye remember?'

'Oh yes, I can hear him now saying, "Walk don't run child, or your shoeleather will last no time." '

We looked at each other in the fading light and to my surprise I saw that her eyes were bright with tears, then she reached out and put her arms around me, holding me close for several minutes.

'Better go now Maya, I don't want them to come lookin' fer ye.'

'Are you going home?' I asked her.

'O' course, where else is there for me to go?'

'I'll see you soon, Emily, and please think about what I said.'

She smiled, and although she started to walk in the opposite direction, when I turned round at the vicarage gate she was standing in the lane looking after me.

I thought about Emily often in the evening that followed. I could not concentrate on the teaching of embroidery to girls with fingers swollen from too much scrubbing or toil on the land and I was sharp with one or two of them when they could not follow the simple intricacy of feather-stitching and herringbone.

I was particularly abrupt with Phoebe Henshaw who lived in the next cottage to Emily when she remarked, 'I saw ye talkin' to Emily Roper Miss Maya earlier on. 'Ow long's it goin' to be afore she marries Ned Rakesby?'

There was a sudden hush in the room and I knew that for the moment they all listened for my reply. There was a sly look on Phoebe's round vapid face, and a smugness which I longed to wipe off with a curt rejoinder. Casually, to show that I was in no way ruffled by her question I said coolly, 'Emily and I are old friends, but I wouldn't dream of asking her anything so personal.'

One or two of the girls tittered, and I was glad to see the red ugly colour suffuse Phoebe's cheeks. She was the first to look away.

I was relieved when they finally put away their sewing and I heard them chattering in small groups as they left the house. How could I blame them? Their lives had been set in strict narrow paths since the day they were born and in due course they would bring up their children in a similar pattern. I had tried. I had tried to open the windows of their world, to let in the sunshine and the fresh air, but in the main they were uncaring, being satisfied and complacent with their lot.

I felt strangely troubled as I tossed and turned in my bed that night. There had been something fatalistic in Emily's attitude that I couldn't entirely define, but it kept me awake until the early hours and when I finally slept my dreams were tinged with sadness. I awoke with the tears still fresh on my cheeks and vague, intangible fears in my heart.

I could not rid myself of a deep feeling of misery as I went about my household tasks. My aunt had one of her sick head-aches and my uncle was short-tempered and impatient. I was glad to escape into the fresh air after lunch, and armed with my shopping basket I set off at a brisk walk down the village street. There was an autumnal nip in the air and the dry leaves crunched beneath my feet. The stream too gushed and gurgled along its way which told me that there had been heavy rain on the moors during the night but it was not the scenery that occupied my thoughts, it was the behaviour of those I passed.

They stood in little groups deep in conversation, only pausing to acknowledge me before they put their heads together again. What scandal were they discussing now, I wondered? Their faces wore long woeful expressions and hastily I scanned the cottage windows looking for drawn curtains which always signalled a death in the house. It was the same in the shops, where conversation instantly stopped whenever I entered.

Phoebe Henshaw's mother finally enlightened me, and with a certain degree of relish.

'Ye might like to know Emily Roper's gone missin'. She didn't sleep in 'er bed last night.'

'But I was with her last night,' I exclaimed. 'She can't be far away.'

' 'Er mother's out o' 'er mind wi' worry. The trouble that girl's caused!'

I had no intention of carrying on a conversation about Emily with Mrs Henshaw. Instead I paid for my purchases and hurried out of the shop. A small crowd had gathered outside the Ropers' cottage and I recognised Emily's sister Mary trying to elbow her way through the crowd. I didn't care what my aunt and uncle would say, I walked quickly towards them and following Mary's example, pushed my way through them fully aware of the curious stares they levelled on me and their whispers.

I knocked sharply on the door which was opened only a few inches by Mary. When she saw it was me she opened it wider and said, 'Come in, Maya,' closing the door sharply behind me.

There were others of Emily's family gathered there but it was her mother who caused me the most concern. Her face was red and swollen from too much crying and she rocked herself to and fro in the old wooden rocking chair, dazed, as though she could not fully comprehend what had happened. Quickly I turned to Mary asking, 'Is it true Mary that Emily has gone?'

Mary nodded. 'She were 'ere all last night wi' mi mother. They never went out and mi mother says she were much as usual, p'raps even a little 'appier than she's bin of late. When mi mother went to rouse 'er this mornin' 'er bed 'adn't bin slept in an' she left this note.'

I took the note she handed me with shaking fingers, recognising Emily's large round handwriting immediately.

I have to go away for a time, perhaps for ever, but please don't have them look for me. I love you Ma, I loves you all, Emily.

'Have you asked at the Rakesby farm?' was my first thought.

'She's not bin there. Ned's bin out sin' breakfast time lookin' for 'er,' Mary said.

'I spoke to her last night. She talked about hospitals and homes for girls in her condition. Did she have any money?'

'She 'ad a bit put by, but we've found that. Maybe she 'ad some we didn't know about.'

'What will you do now?' I asked fearfully. What was there to do when a girl left her home without money in the middle of the night?

'Mi brother's told the police. They say they'll drag the lake an' the stream. They're 'igh this mornin', there were a lot o' rain durin' the night.'

How could I believe that they were dragging the stream for Emily, Emily who had been a joy with her lovely bright face and her impish humour, Emily who could make my world sing just by being there.

I let myself out of the cottage and pushed my way through the gathering crowd. As I walked quickly towards the vicarage I saw my uncle coming towards me and I felt an unreasonable surge of anger against him. He would visit the Ropers and he would pontificate about the sins of the flesh and the ingratitude of an erring daughter as if the Ropers hadn't enough to worry about.

'Have you heard about Miss Emily?' he asked quickly.

81

'Yes,' I answered tersely. He had always called her Miss Emily, as though even as a child he had wanted to turn her into a baggage.

'I must go down there,' he said importantly. 'They will need the comfort of God at this time. Your aunt is very upset Maya, you had better go up to the house and see what you can do for her.'

I wished I had Emily's courage to run away, but I was so very frightened. I hoped that was all she had done.

They searched the fells and dragged the stream, they tracked through the forest and searched the lake but they didn't find Emily. Then after a few weeks they stopped talking about her and concentrated instead on the Harvest Festival.

That was the first Sunday my uncle didn't offer up special prayers for the saving of Emily's soul, living or dead and I was glad he had decided to let her alone. They came from Greythorn to the service, Sir Lyndon and Gavin, Miss Cora and Roland and after the service my uncle offered them hospitality at the vicarage because one of the horses that pulled the chaise had cast a shoe and the blacksmith was forced to open up the forge to attend to it.

'Hurry on home, Maya, and add some wood to the drawing room fire,' my aunt cautioned me and I was glad I had done so when I felt the chill of the room and the old mustiness invading my nostrils. By the time they arrived the fire was blazing up the chimney and a huge vase of late roses adorned the top of the sideboard.

I helped my aunt to serve sherry and shortbread and my uncle tried to inveigle Cora and Roland into holding their wedding ceremony at his church.

I met Lyndon's eyes across the room and I knew that the colour had flooded my cheeks, treacherous betraying colour that I wanted no part of.

Addressing me Lyndon said, 'I have been hearing how diligent you have become in educating some of our village girls Miss Wentworth, but it seems a great pity that this should be the reward for all your superior education.'

I did not speak. My aunt looked uncomfortable and I could almost feel my uncle bristling across the hearth.

'My niece is young and unworldly, Sir Lyndon,' he said primly. 'Her aunt and I wish her to remain with us where at least she is protected from the more doubtful things in life.'

'Protected – or stunted, Edisford? I doubt very much if this young girl should be asked to hide her prowess from the world. It should be allowed to grow and flourish where it is most appreciated.'

'I think Maya is happy and contented with her lot, Sir Lyndon. She has a good home with us and does a worthwhile thing in teaching these village girls how to cook and sew and make a comfortable home when the time comes.'

'Which could all be done by the mothers of any one of them, Edisford. I heard from my sister that you had been offered a teaching post at Miss Lawford's college, Maya. Didn't you wish to take advantage of it?'

'Yes, but my aunt was ill and I was needed here. The position was offered to another girl.'

The atmosphere was heavy in the room. I could feel it and I was wishing fervently that Sir Lyndon would change the subject quickly or I would bear the brunt of it at a later time.

He had no intention of doing anything of the kind, however. Unperturbed, his smooth even voice went on, 'I have an idea which might appeal to you, Maya. My sister Eleanor's little boy is a shy withdrawn child in need of a governess. He is only just four years old but he would benefit from some lessons if only for part of the day. I know that she is anxious to find someone. Would you be interested?'

'I don't know, Sir Lyndon. It would depend on how much I am needed here,' I answered.

Of course I was interested, I was desperate for it, but I had been desperate before and my uncle had denied me, he could do so again and I couldn't take that chance.

'What do you say, Edisford? You could surely spare Miss Wentworth for part of the day at least, perhaps even the entire day as Jamie becomes older.'

He was watching my uncle with a small amused smile on his lips, enjoying his discomfort. My aunt sat fidgeting with the ties on her blouse while the rest of them looked on, waiting with barely disguised anticipation for his reply.

I could see that he was confused by the question. He did not want to offend Sir Lyndon, indeed he was already revelling in the honour of having me teach Eleanor's son, but he was also counting the cost. Could he afford to take in a woman to cook and clean and would my aunt take kindly to sitting in that cold bare attic again instead of working at her tapestry in the comfort of the drawing room?

Sir Lyndon nonchalantly pressed home his point. 'Can you see any disadvantages, Edisford? Here is your niece, adequately able to help my sister out of a crisis and here are you with all the village to assist you. Transport will be no problem. I know you need your pony and trap for visiting outlying parishioners but I have one I could lend your niece and Mr Ackroyd has several he would not be averse to lending out, I am sure.'

'It is some way to Seaten,' my uncle objected weakly.

'Oh come now, it is no further than you drive most days and if the weather is bad I am sure my sister will allow Miss Wentworth to stay. How about the young lady herself – I think we should ask her if she has any thoughts on the matter. Maya?'

'Oh yes, please. It would be so wonderful, to teach a young boy, to have his mind grow and blossom and know I have made it so. I feel lost and stagnated with these village girls. They only want to get married quickly and have lots of children. They've grown up with the idea that this is all there is to life.'

'It's what the good Lord intended them to do, Maya,' my uncle put in briskly.

'But there are other things, Uncle. There's a whole world out there and I know I shall never make them see that.'

'Well, Edisford,' Sir Lyndon said again. 'How can we ignore such a plea, how can you deny this girl the right to express herself?'

'You will need to ask Miss Eleanor. She will want to see Maya before she makes up her mind.'

'But of course. Eleanor and I have always been very close, and I feel sure she will take notice of me in this. I knew you would see it my way, Edisford. I felt sure I could rely on your good sense and fair play.'

I doubt very much if my uncle knew what had happened to him. I knew. For the first time since I entered the vicarage I didn't mind the chill of my room or the skeleton fingers of the sturdy elms in the churchyard. I didn't mind the endless search for perfection in the execution of feather-stitching and the like and I willingly helped Phoebe Henshaw turn up the cuffs of her father's frayed trousers, which he required for church on Sunday.

Tomorrow afternoon I would drive with Sir Lyndon to be interviewed by his sister Eleanor and soon my life would take a dramatic new course.

EIGHT

MY AUNT EYED me critically for several minutes before she gave
her approval. I had braided my hair into two plaits which
I wore neatly round my head and the white lace collar on
my plain navy-blue dress gave me an unusually businesslike
air.

Navy-blue was not really my colour, I was too dark and too
pale but the white collar relieved its plainness and the dress had
always given my figure a mature grace.

'You will wear a hat of course,' she remarked, eyeing me
doubtfully.

'I hadn't thought of doing so, Aunt. It is a beautiful day,
perhaps one of the last really warm days we shall have before
the winter comes.'

'Well perhaps not then. You have managed your hair very
well. Are you quite sure you want this position, Maya? I rather
thought it was thrust upon you and I'm not sure if you will fit
into Miss Eleanor's household at Seaten.'

'Yes, Aunt I do want it. Why should you think I won't fit in?'

'Well, one can't help hearing talk. You won't find it anything
like Greythorn.'

'I'm not expecting to. I shan't be part of the household Aunt,
I shall only be there to teach the little boy and I haven't got the
post yet, they might not consider me suitable.'

'Well, we shall see. Mr Ackroyd is known as a hard business-
man and I always considered Miss Eleanor to be a bit wild. No
doubt she has settled down to married life and I hardly think Sir

86

Lyndon would have mentioned the post if he hadn't thought you would be happy there.'

Sir Lyndon arrived promptly at two o'clock and I was glad to see that he was alone. As we drove down the village street I was aware of curtains being pulled back and inquisitive eyes staring after us. The few villagers we did meet did not try to hide their curiosity but I merely smiled at them then looked straight ahead.

I enjoyed that drive in the warm autumn sunshine with Sir Lyndon's hands expert on the reins and the two horses trotting happily ahead. My hands were warm as toast under the rug he had spread over my knees and I was very aware of him sitting beside me. Most of the time we drove without speaking but it was a companionable silence and I gave myself up to thinking what it must like to be married to a man like this. I was young enough and foolish enough to daydream, to cry for the moon and believe it was not impossible. He was my knight in shining armour, the one person who had seen my frustration and unhappiness, the man who right from our first meeting had shown me a sensitivity as rare as it was beautiful, and although he was as far removed from me as the stars above I would never be able to settle for less.

As we drove slowly through the village of Seaten with Ackroyd House standing large and forbidding on the hillside above I could not help comparing it with Greythorn Hall. It was a square house, unremarkable for its architecture and there was an air of neglect about it. As though he read my thoughts Sir Lyndon said, 'It is nothing like Greythorn, Maya. The Ackroyds did not build it, they only acquired it from old Sir George Pilsworth who was some sort of kinsman, very remotely connected I think. He was a bachelor and died at his sister's house in the West Riding. At his death Roger's father bought the property but they have never had much interest in it as a home.'

'Does Miss Eleanor enjoy living here? I asked curiously.

'I see my sister very seldom these days. She only visits Greythorn occasionally.'

'But she knows that I am to see her regarding the little boy?'

'Of course.'

He turned and smiled at me, a warm smile that gave me courage and somewhat hesitantly I asked, 'I would like to know something about your sister's house Sir Lyndon. It seems a trifle overwhelming, it is so dark and stolid.'

'I agree. It has not mellowed with the years as Greythorn has done. When I was a small boy I came here with my father and I remember driving with him towards it just as we are doing today. I hated it on sight and I was not looking forward to the night ahead of us.'

'Why was that?' I asked sharply.

'Old Mr Ackroyd had a reputation for coarseness and cruelty. He seldom came to Greythorn but when he did the dogs wouldn't go near him and the Persian cat that belonged to my mother, Caliph, would arch his back and spit at him – much to Ackroyd's amusement – and once, he tore open his hand with his claws. I think Ackroyd would have killed him if it hadn't been for my mother.'

'Why didn't the animals like him?'

'I don't know. They can sense things about people that humans can't and it was said he used to whip his horses. On the night I came here we found the old man in a downstairs room lying in his bed surrounded by other men he had invited from some of the large towns in the area. Several months before he had suffered a slight stroke but he was now almost recovered. I remember the room was filled with cigar smoke and the wine and whisky were flowing pretty freely. I was the only child there but I was made to sit with my father while we witnessed the entertainment of the evening.'

'And what was that?'

'Cock-fighting. Birds as beautiful and proud as peacocks with the courage of lions. They wore spurs on their legs and they fought until one of them lay like a mangled bunch of feathers on the floor and the other was so badly injured it had to be destroyed. I hated every moment of it, the looks on the men's faces, the money they were wagering, the pitiless bestiality –

and I hated my own father for taking part in it.'

'How could he have taken a young boy to witness such a spectacle?'

'Such things were meant to make a man of me. A man was only a man when he could see creatures tearing each other to shreds, and not just cocks, dogs too, fine noble animals with the instinct to kill. For a long time I could not bear to look at a dog lying on the hearthrug with his nose and ears twitching without thinking of them snarling and growling as they tore into one another.'

'How many times did you go with your father to watch these things happening?'

'Only twice. Then I started to have nightmares and my mother forbade it. I doubt if my father ever quite forgave me. My brother Gavin would have been a better pupil.'

'You think Gavin would have enjoyed it?'

He smiled, his warm sweet smile which had the power to make my heart lurch in my breast. 'I don't know, Maya. Such activities are now forbidden by law thank goodness, so Gavin will never be put to the test. Don't look so worried child, nothing of that nature happens at Ackroyd House now.'

We had reached the front of the house but instead of stopping there we drove through an archway into a cobbled courtyard behind. He jumped out of the carriage and came to the other side to help me to descend, then we walked to a brass studded door. It was opened by an elderly woman wearing a severe long black dress, her hair piled high above the stiff black collar. She bobbed a small curtsey and held the door open wider for us to pass into the house.

'Will you tell my sister that I am here with Miss Wentworth, Mrs Markham,' Sir Lyndon said briefly.

'Mrs Ackroyd is in the library, Sir, if you would like to follow me.'

'I know where it is, Mrs Markham, there's no need for you to take us there.'

I felt her eyes upon me, hard dark eyes and I knew she stared after us as I followed Sir Lyndon. The hall we passed through was dark but I was aware of the sound of our feet on the flag floors and the dark wooden staircase and panelled walls.

The room we entered wore a more cheerful air. There was a fire burning in the grate and a warm red Turkey carpet made it look more lived in. Eleanor was sitting in front of the fire with a magazine in her hands and on our entry she rose and came forward to receive her brother's brief embrace, then she turned her attention on me.

She looked older than I remembered. There were tiny lines around her eyes and that beautiful face which had always seemed so animated and vital now wore a faint expression of boredom.

'Perhaps you remember Miss Wentworth,' Sir Lyndon said, bringing me forward. 'She visited us at Greythorn as a child – do you recall our father inviting her to be with Cora?'

She stared at me without recognition and after a few moments Lyndon said, 'Well, it doesn't matter, but I suggest you two have a long talk together while I drive over to Exton. I have some tenants to see there.'

I had hoped he would be with me while Eleanor and I spoke but she accepted his suggestion, indicating that I should take the chair across the hearth from where she had been sitting. I heard the door close behind Sir Lyndon with some trepidation. With his going went much of my courage and all the time she was looking at me with a vague detachment.

'I do remember you now, Miss Wentworth. I remember you came to the Hall with a very pretty girl with bright red hair, and that you have an unusual name.'

'Yes, Maya. I am the vicar of Lexford's niece.'

'Ah yes, the vicar of Lexford, and now you are a qualified teacher.'

'I have no experience of teaching,' I began, and then went on to tell her about my education, my disappointments and my need to find work away from the vicarage. She listened without interrupting, then she made enquiries about transport and whether I would be prepared to live in if the occasion demanded it.

To all of her questions I agreed. It was my one chance and I wasn't going to miss it. I told her that there were days when I could have the pony and trap and that her brother had intimated that he or Mr Ackroyd could find the missing transport when my uncle's vehicle was not available.

'Something should be done on a permanent basis,' she said. 'It would not do for transport to interfere with your regular attendance here. Do you have adequate stabling at the vicarage for another horse?'

'Oh yes, I'm sure we do, and I would look after him.'

'He could be fed here. I see no reason why we shouldn't give it a trial, and if we do find that transport becomes a problem then you might be required to live in here. Are you sure that would not be an insurmountable problem, Miss Wentworth?'

'No, I'm sure it wouldn't. My aunt and uncle are very anxious that I should be offered the position.'

For the first time a mischievous twinkle came into her eyes and a half-smile on her lips. 'Yes, I can quite understand that your uncle would wish to help us! Jamie is a shy fanciful child, would you like to meet him?'

'Oh, yes please.'

She rose to her feet and walked over to the bellrope, then as though she thought better of it she said, 'We will go up to the nursery, that is where you will be working most of the time.'

I followed her across the hall and up the dark staircase to the even darker realms above. There were portraits on the wall but I did not have time to look at them, and as though she read my thoughts Eleanor said, 'You will have time to familiarise yourself with the house later, Miss Wentworth. The nursery is at the end of the corridor on the first floor and the stairs at that end of the house go down to the side entrance, so you need not enter through the main hall. It is nothing like my family home, but I suppose you are already thinking that.'

'It is a very large house, Mrs Ackroyd.'

'Yes,' she said tersely, but that word was enough to tell me that she hated it.

A warm fire burned in the nursery grate but I was surprised

91

to find that it was a small room. A little boy sat at the table drawing with coloured pencils and dozing near the fire sat an elderly woman in a white apron and with a white cap on her grey hair. She started up suddenly when we opened the door and the little boy looked up expectantly with a smile on his face. Hurriedly he put down the crayon and getting down from his chair rushed round the table into his mother's arms.

He was a beautiful enchanting little boy with dark hair and large brown eyes. He stared at me without smiling but his mother said, 'This is Miss Wentworth, Jamie. She is going to come here to teach you.'

'Does that mean that I shall not be going away to school then?' he asked, his face brightening.

'Not just yet at any rate,' his mother answered him. 'Are you pleased that Miss Wentworth is coming here?'

'Yes, Mother. I'm pleased not to be going away to school.'

'Isn't he very young to think of sending him away?' I ventured.

'He would go when he is five like his father and my brothers did, but this is a better arrangement for Jamie. He is very sensitive and seems at times to live in a world of his own making. You must tell Miss Wentworth about your friends, Jamie.'

'He has friends then, I'm so glad about that,' I said, speaking feelingly.

'They are friends of his imagination but he talks to them as though they are real people. It is very disconcerting and just a little unhealthy. I hope your coming here will remove them from his mind.'

'I think that perhaps all young children imagine other children they can play with. I imagined a dog called Toby. He used to share my bed and my games until Aunt Edith found out and consigned him to the infinite. I was careful never to mention him or think of him again, except when I was alone.'

'I think that you too had a very lonely childhood, Miss Wentworth. I had a wonderful youth, but one cannot expect such happiness to last forever.'

I felt troubled by her words and the inflection of her voice, but as though she had shown me too much she said quickly, 'Jamie and I walk in the garden during the afternoon. Perhaps you would like to walk with him today, Miss Wentworth. My brother will not be back until five and I am expecting a friend.'

'Yes, of course. It will give Jamie and me a chance to get to know each other.'

With that she left us and I watched as the servant wrapped Jamie up warmly in spite of the sunny afternoon.

''E soon catches cold Miss an' there's monny a chill wind at this time o' the year.'

'How long does he normally remain outdoors and should I take him outside the grounds?'

'I shouldn't if I were ye, Miss. Like I said, the boy's delicate an' 'is father's allus complainin' that 'e catches cold easily.'

I felt she would have liked to elaborate on other things that Jamie's father complained about but with a swift smile I thanked her and holding out my hand said, 'We're ready now Jamie, where would you like to walk?'

I had not had a great deal to do with young children but I knew that they liked to scamper ahead of their adult companions. Jamie, however, showed no signs of wanting to let go of my hand. I showed him where the conkers were hiding amongst the branches of the chestnut trees and how the leaves crunched and danced in the russet carpet underneath our feet. His face glowed with colour and he laughed with excitement as I took to my heels and ran with him across the grass. When we reached the stone wall overlooking the meadow I said, 'This is the first time I have been here, Jamie. Perhaps you should tell me where we go now.'

'There's a little wood at the back of the house. Peter likes to go there but Nancy says it is dark and there are monsters living there.'

'Have you seen the monsters?'

'No, of course not. Nancy's always saying things like that.'

'Then we should leave her at home, but Peter can come if you like.'

'I only take them when there is nobody else, today you're here.'

I gave him a little squeeze. I could learn to love this child with his delicate charming face and his grown-up way of speaking. Quite suddenly I was delighted to be coming to Ackroyd House to care for him and I resolved that I would keep the laughter in his face and chase away those earlier shadows with my tales of adventure. I remembered all the stories I had ever loved, the Knights of the Round Table and the tales from the Arabian Nights, and the true adventure stories with their feats of endurance and patriotism that had gained our tiny island dominion over a vast, far-flung empire. These were tales to stir the heart and blood of a young boy, and please God this time let there be nothing to tell me I was wasting my time or his.

It was a charming little wood hidden behind the square stone house. We walked along the path that followed the shallow stream gushing and gurgling among the stones and we sat on a dead tree stump to watch a family of blue tits darting in and out of their nest in an old beech tree.

'It is beautiful here, Jamie. Is this your favourite walk?' I asked him.

'Yes, and it is nicer still in the springtime when the bluebells are out.'

'Do you gather them?'

'No. Boys don't gather flowers, only girls do that. Nancy gathers them.'

'Then what does she do with them? I used to put them in jamjars on my bedroom windowsill.'

I was curious about Nancy but he seemed not to know what she did with the bluebells. I had never been able to keep a pet and now I found myself remembering the mythical Toby and how together we had scampered over the fells. 'Do you have a dog or a kitten Jamie?' I asked him curiously.

'No. My father has dogs but they are not friendly. He uses them when he goes out shooting. There are dogs at Greythorn, and I play with them when I go there.'

'Perhaps one day you will have one of your own.'

'Perhaps. Shall we go back now the sun has gone in?'

I hadn't noticed, but it was true, the sun had gone in and the shadows were lengthening along the path. I consulted the watch pinned onto my dress and was surprised to see that it was already four o'clock.

'We should walk quickly, Jamie. It will keep us warm,' I said, stepping out smartly along the path, and dutifully he fell into step by my side.

A grey horse stood at the side entrance to the house and I asked, 'Is that your father's horse, Jamie?'

'No, my father is out with the trap. It belongs to a friend of my mother's.'

'Then perhaps we should go in by another entrance,' I said, not wishing to encounter Eleanor and her friend who I felt confident would be some man or other, judging by the size of the horse.

'We can get into the house over there,' the child said, pointing to the opposite corner of the courtyard.

'Where does it lead to?'

'Across the barn and up the stairs to the kitchens. Come on, I'll show you.'

Obediently I followed but just as we were about to enter the barn I heard the sound of Eleanor's laughter and the deep tones of a man's voice. The voice was familiar and instinctively I turned my head. Eleanor stood at the other door with her back to it, laughing up into the face of the young man about to mount his horse. She looked beautiful and animated as she had looked in the old days and there was a warm smile on the man's face also. I felt a shiver of anxiety wash over me. It was Roland Carnwood, Cora's fiancé, who looked down at Eleanor now with an expression on his face I had never seen when he looked at Cora. I was remembering that long mad embrace in the whispering glade on the night of Sir Lyndon's wedding and I knew their fascination for each other was there still. In spite of her marriage and his engagement, nothing had changed.

'Come on,' Jamie called. 'You won't find your way if I leave you.'

I hurried to keep up with him, surprised by the many stairs and corridors which bypassed the kitchens before we reached the nursery.

'Are you going to have tea with me?' the boy asked, as I helped him off with his coat.

'I don't know, Jamie. Perhaps your mother will want to see me now.'

'Not while Uncle Roland's here.'

'Does he often come here, Jamie?'

'Oh yes. Sometimes he comes with Aunt Cora but mostly he comes alone.'

'Would you like me to read to you, Jamie or would you prefer to show me how well you read yourself?'

'I would rather wait for my mother to say if you are really coming here. Besides, tea will be brought in soon.'

I smiled down at him. He seemed such a strangely adult child and I wondered if he had any real, flesh and blood friends of his own age and what sort of a father Roger Ackroyd was. I went to sit next to him at the table where he had taken up a crayon and was busily colouring a clown's face in the drawing book filled with pictures. We had not been there more than a few minutes when the door opened and the servant came in carrying a tray containing cups and saucers, a silver teapot and a large iced cake. I smiled at her and she said quickly, 'Mrs Ackroyd is on 'er way 'ere Miss. I'm to leave the tray.'

Almost on her heels Eleanor appeared. 'Plates Mary, and forks,' she admonished the servant. 'How can we possibly eat cake without plates and forks?' As the servant skipped quickly out of the room she said, 'Really, these country servants are quite impossible. One has to constantly tell them the rights and wrongs of things.'

She had changed into a green, watered-silk teagown which complemented her colouring beautifully. She wore her dark red hair caught back from her face by a green silk bow and she seemed happy and relaxed as she poured the tea.

'Well, where did you go for your walk?' she asked smiling.

'Through the wood Mother, and we watched the blue tits.'

'And did you get along well with Miss Wentworth?'

'Oh yes, Mother, she *is* coming to teach me, isn't she?'

'What do you think, Miss Wentworth – would you like to teach my son?'

'I would like that very much, Mrs Ackroyd, if you think I shall be suitable.

'My brother seemed to think so. I wonder why he took up the cudgels on your behalf?'

I looked down quickly, hating the treacherous colour that flamed into my face and the amused expression at the corners of her mouth.

I accepted the teacup she handed me with a whispered thank you and she immediately began to speak of the hours I should spend with Jamie, the transport arrangements and the remuneration. She was very generous and seemed delighted to have secured my services and I found myself responding to her charm.

I thought how different she was from Cora, Cora who was at times withdrawn and reserved. Eleanor and Gavin were alike and yet it was Lyndon who was her full brother.

'I think we should go downstairs now, Miss Wentworth, my brother will be here presently. Do you want to see Uncle Lyndon, Jamie?'

The little boy's eyes lit up with expectation and jumping down from his chair he ran to take his mother's hand.

'He adores Lyndon,' Eleanor said laughing. 'It is a great pity my brother has no children and poor Melinda is not very likely to give him any. He is very fond of Jamie.'

'It is sad for Lady Gaynor. Is there no hope that she will get well again?'

'No. Her illness is progressive but it is not a killing disease. My brother does not have a lot of personal happiness to look forward to.'

The sadness of it troubled me later when I saw Lyndon toss Jamie high into the air, catching him chortling with glee into his arms.

As we drove home later in the early evening he seemed pleased that his sister had appointed me and that Jamie and I had got along well together.

'He's a strangely withdrawn child at times,' he said. 'The fact that he was not withdrawn with you augurs well I think for your future together. Did Mr Ackroyd appear while you were there?'

'No. I hope he will approve of my appointment.'

'He is all for sending Jamie away to school but my sister doesn't think he is ready for it. I agree with her, and in any case Roger has never seemed close to the child – he would have wished for a son more outgoing and fearless.'

'He is an enchanting little boy,' I objected staunchly.

'Yes,' Lyndon responded drily, 'but my brother-in-law is not one to be swayed by enchantment or affection. He was raised in a hard school by a father who was a drinker, a gambler and something of a bully. His mother died when he was born.'

'Then he is much to be pitied,' I said feelingly. I knew what it was to be loved but all I had of it were memories that at times seemed elusive and remote.

I wondered if Lyndon knew about his sister's friendship with Roland and saw the danger in it. I could not think that he knew or surely he would counsel her against it, and as though our thoughts ran on the same lines he said, 'Cora will be pleased that you are to teach Jamie, although she is busy with plans for her wedding and thinks of little else.'

'When is the wedding to be, Sir Lyndon?'

'Probably in the spring. Cora's health in the winter months still leaves much to be desired, and I think she will want to look her best on her wedding day.'

'Of course, and they are very much in love.'

'Cora has always been a person with set desires – a favourite book, a favourite doll, even a favourite boy. She has been besotted with Roland since she was little more than a child, and affection of that sort is often crying out to be hurt. One cannot possess another person, body and soul.'

I didn't speak, and next moment almost as though he regretted having opened his heart to me he said in a change of tone, 'I hope your aunt and uncle will be pleased with your news.'

'Oh yes,' I breathed, 'surely they must be.'

That night they both listened while I enthused about the new life that was opening up before me, and with some acidity my uncle remarked, 'You seem remarkably uninterested in how your aunt and I are going to manage without you, Maya.'

'Oh, but I'm not Uncle. Naturally I shall help all I can and I can now keep myself and buy the few clothes I shall need.'

Somewhat mollified, as he always was when finances became a little lighter he said, 'Well, no doubt we shall manage. Your aunt has approached Mrs Roper who will be glad to come back I'm sure. Travelling to her present employment isn't any good for a woman of her age.'

Oh, the insufferable assumption that Mrs Roper would automatically return to the vicarage to suit him! I had no doubt that she would return, but I couldn't help wishing that she would tell His Reverence what he could do with his position, it would serve him right.

'Has Mrs Roper said if she has heard from Emily?' I asked him cautiously.

'Mrs Roper is careful not to mention her daughter to me – she knows what I think about her,' he replied pompously and stalked from the room.

I worried incessantly about Emily, wondering if she had found some home or hospital where they would care for her until the baby was born and if she would be able to get the child adopted. I couldn't see how she was going to take care of it herself *and* find work.

NINE

I SETTLED DOWN happily at Ackroyd House. I enjoyed the preparation of our lessons and Jamie was an intelligent child who worked well with me and appeared to relish our time together. Sir Lyndon provided me with a brisk pony and trap and I loved the creature instantly, taking great pride and pleasure in grooming him and making him comfortable in the stable with my uncle's pony. His name was Rory and it suited his bright chestnut coat and intelligent brown eyes.

I had been at Ackroyd House for almost a month before I saw Jamie's father, even though I had heard his voice outside in the courtyard or in the library where he saw his tenants. We had only just settled down to our history lesson when one of the servants came in to tell me Mr Ackroyd wished to see me in the library.

Quickly, I smoothed my hair and after assuring myself that I looked cool and businesslike I hurried downstairs. His voice bade me enter and I found him standing on the rug in front of the fireplace looking down into the flames. He was more corpulent than I remembered him and apart from the hair that grew above his ears and into the nape of his neck he was completely bald. His face was red and there were heavy lines about his mouth and creases beneath his eyes and in that split second before he looked at me I felt I could understand why his beautiful wife looked forward to the company of her sister's fiancé.

He eyed me narrowly from head to foot and I felt like a prize heifer brought forward for his inspection. Ready to squirm with embarrassment I was glad when he finally said in a dry voice, 'So you're the schoolteacher my wife has brought in to teach my son. How old are you?'

'I'm eighteen,' I gasped, surprised by the question.

'Aren't you a little young to be a governess?'

'I don't think so. Isn't the knowledge I can impart more important than my age?'

A faint gleam of humour came into his eyes.

'Well, at least you're not mealy-mouthed! I like a girl that can answer back. What do you think of my son?'

'He's very bright and intelligent. I think he will do well.'

'Hmm. You might as well know, Miss Wentworth, that you were not my choice. I would have preferred Jamie to have gone away to school. I don't hold with a boy being brought up in a woman's world.'

'But he isn't. You are his father, you have a great deal of influence with him. Naturally he is close to his mother and I am only his teacher until he becomes older.'

'I want him to stand on his own two feet. I don't want you to make a milksop out of the boy.'

'I have no intention of making a milksop out of him. That isn't my rôle here. I think he is an intelligent pupil, and the more boyish activities can surely be taught by you, Mr Ackroyd.'

'How long did my wife say your trial was to last?'

'I was not aware I was on trial. I thought I was employed to teach Jamie until he was old enough to go away to school.'

'Would you be prepared to live in here?'

'If I thought it was necessary, yes.'

I didn't like him. I thought he was lacking in good manners and there was a coarseness about him that I found repellent. Then I remembered Sir Lyndon's version of his upbringing and I softened towards him. I was saved from further conjecture, however, by the entry of Eleanor, looking cool and elegant in her riding clothes.

'Ah, here you are,' she said, addressing me. 'I want to take

Jamie riding, and perhaps you would like to accompany us, Miss Wentworth.'

'I'm afraid I don't ride, Mrs Ackroyd.'

'But you rode as a child – I do remember you telling my sister that you had a pony in Africa.'

I stared at her in surprise. What a strange thing to have remembered, when I had so desperately tried to forget.

'Yes, but that was before I came to England and I have never ridden since.'

'Then you must learn, Miss Wentworth, so that you can accompany Jamie when I have other things to see to. My old riding habit will fit you, we are about the same height and size, and I'm sure there is a horse in the stable suitable for your initiation.'

Ignoring my air of doubtful incredulity she turned to her husband saying, 'You see Roger, Jamie's more manly pursuits are being adequately taken care of. You can't say I am aiming to disappoint you.'

There was a faint mocking smile on her lips and an angry frown on his face as their eyes met across the room. Nonchalantly she walked across the room and stood on the hearthrug beside him, looking into the mirror where she tilted her hat to a more becoming angle.

He watched her with a deepening frustration and in that moment I knew that he loved her with a hopeless passionate yearning which she met with amused tolerance. She did not love him, had never loved him, and her absorption with Roland fed all the wayward wild passions her marriage could not satisfy.

'Come along, Miss Wentworth, Mary is getting Jamie ready. Let us see how you look in my riding clothes. I suppose you will be in for dinner, Roger?'

'I expect so, and you?'

'Of course, where else is there to go in this benighted place?'

Eleanor's 'old riding clothes' as she had called them were by no means old, indeed they looked very little different from her own, and they fitted me perfectly. She held me at arm's length when I was fully dressed and there was speculation in her eyes and a glint of humour.

'You look very beautiful, Miss Wentworth. It will be interesting to see if your prowess equals your appearance.'

'How can it, Mrs Ackroyd, when I have told you I have forgotten how to ride,' I answered her calmly.

'It will come back to you, I'm sure. We will keep to the bridle paths and the horse I have chosen is docile and manageable.'

In spite of all my misgivings I enjoyed riding in the crisp chill of the afternoon and I knew that with greater experience I would come to love it.

She was generous with her praise as we dismounted, leaving our horses in charge of the grooms. Jamie too said, 'You did very well Miss Wentworth, much better than Nancy.'

His mother frowned. 'Really, does the child still talk about these imaginary children as if they were real? I would have thought you might have stopped him doing that, Miss Wentworth.'

'They are very real to him, Mrs Ackroyd. One day he'll forget about them but he has got to dismiss them himself. It is not for me to tell him to forget them.'

'Well, it's all very disturbing and silly. I don't want a child with second sight on my hands!'

'It is because he is an only child and without real companions of his own age.'

'Is that so? Well, since he is likely to remain an only child I suggest you fill his mind with so many other things he forgets about these figments of his imagination. We can't ride tomorrow, by the way. I am expected over at Greythorn for lunch . . . I suppose it will be more of Cora's wedding plans. I'm sure I didn't make half as much fuss.'

I always knew when she had been to Greythorn. She came back restless and vaguely unhappy. All the talk there would be of Cora's marriage, but there were those other days when I knew she had seen Roland. Then she would be wildly affectionate, presenting me with some item out of her wardrobe, a dress or jacket she had tired of, a fashionable hat which I would probably never be able to wear and which my aunt and uncle looked at with extreme disapproval.

I offered to give my aunt some of the gowns, but she said primly that they would need too much altering to fit her, and in any case were hardly the sort of gowns a vicar's wife would wear. Consequently, they hung in my wardrobe waiting for the opportunity that never seemed to come.

I seemed to have been at Ackroyd House for months and the weather grew colder so that now there was ice on the roads leading from Seaten to Lexford and the mornings were misted and chill. I could not help wondering what I would do when the snow came as it invariably did to these villages high up in the Pennines, battered by cold north east winds straight, I felt sure, from Siberia.

If Sir Lyndon came to the house I never saw him although once I thought I heard his voice in the courtyard talking to Mr Ackroyd. I longed to press my face against the window pane, but remained glued to my seat in case he thought I was spying on him. I tried to dispel the companions of Jamie's lonely childhood but they remained – mischievous Nancy and sensible, plodding Peter – and I ceased trying. In time, Jamie would forget about them but I remained surprised by his remarkable perception. There were times when he seemed to know what I was thinking – which was disconcerting, to say the least.

I now came to the house in the middle of the morning and left earlier in the afternoon, but even so it was dark when I arrived back at the vicarage and my aunt objected, saying, 'This is no fit weather for you to be travelling back and forward to Seaten. Any day now the snow will come, and what do you suppose will happen then?'

I was soon to find out. It was about three o'clock that day when I left Seaten and already there was a faint powdering of snow on the lanes and the sky above was grey and heavy with snow. The pony seemed to sense it as he trotted with his ears laid flat against his head and his tail swishing madly. With the sudden dark the snow came, sweeping down from the fells obscuring the horizon, and in no time the pony's feet began to slip on the road and the wheels of the trap skidded ominously. I jumped down from the driving seat and went to guide the pony with my hands. He was frightened that his feet could not now gain a steady grip on the road and he struggled while I talked to him soothingly. The snow was beginning to drift and soon I realised we would not be able to cope with the depth of it. It was quite impossible to see the path now, and I looked round frantically for the sight of a barn or shelter, anywhere to escape from the driving snow and the bitter cold. Suddenly we were in a drift, and it took all my strength to calm the frantic heaving strivings of the pony endeavouring to extricate himself from snow that already reached his shoulders. I dug with my hands, oblivious to his threshing hooves. The trap tilted drunkenly behind him and I knew I would not have the strength to right it.

He writhed until he was exhausted and my voice was hoarse in my ears. I sat beside him, each of us deriving warmth from the other and his head hung dejectedly above the snow. Time seemed to stand still as we waited and I found myself wondering how long it would take for the snow to cover and suffocate us.

It was much later when the blizzard stopped and by the light of a full moon I could look out across the desolation of snow-covered fields and hills. I had no hope that we would be rescued. Nobody would venture out on such a night to look for us, it would be madness, and I resigned myself to waiting for daylight. I felt the pony shivering beside me and I whispered to him gently, stroking the side of his neck, breathing warmth against his frozen face. I prayed for someone to find us even though I had little faith in prayers on such a night. Consequently, I could hardly believe my eyes when I saw a group of people approaching us carrying lamps, and then I heard a voice, Sir Lyndon's voice, and my fears disappeared as though by magic and the snow-covered world became a wonderland of glittering frost.

It didn't take him long to assess our plight and then the men came with shovels and ropes to help us. I was wrapped in a warm rug and placed in the snow sleigh and soon we were on our way to Greythorn with the pony trotting behind. He had taken no harm from his ordeal and had been more frightened than hurt. Now petted by encouraging words from Sir Lyndon's grooms he was quickly forgetting our adventure.

'I have asked them to prepare a room for you at the Hall,' Sir Lyndon told me. 'It is impossible for you to get through to Lexford tonight.'

'But my aunt and uncle will be wondering what has happened to me!'

He smiled drily. 'Your uncle and aunt had already assumed you would be spending the night comfortably at Seaten. Other arrangements will have to be made, Maya. You are not going to make this journey in the winter months, so I think you must reconcile yourself to staying at Ackroyd House. It is large enough to accommodate an army of governesses, and Jamie has taken to you. I felt sure he would, and if you were to leave them now it would be very bad for the child. Obviously you must stay there.'

I looked at his calm severe profile against the arctic night and I wished his voice was not so impersonal. What had happened to me?

Love had been far from my thoughts on that afternoon when he showed me round Greythorn Hall and yet it had touched me with cruel tenacious fingers where it could never hope to be returned.

In the silence of that drive over the snow I asked myself miserably why I should love this man. Was it because I pitied him in his sad passionless marriage? Love born out of pity was a shallow thing, a closing of one's mind to other, more powerful emotions. No, it was not pity I felt for Lyndon Gaynor. I was suddenly aware of a burning need to throw myself into his arms and fiercely I clenched my hands together beneath the rug that covered my knees, pleading with God silently to make me strong.

How could I help comparing my spartan bedroom at the vicarage with the one I was given at Greythorn Hall, with its velvet carpet, and soft subtle chintz curtains and bedcover . . . I was loaned one of Cora's nightdresses and a dressing gown, fine woollen garments that kept out the cold yet caressed my skin with tender warmth.

I saw little of either Lyndon or Gavin during the next few days because they were out on the estate assisting tenants who had been sorely hit by the bad weather. A message was sent to the vicarage informing them that I was safe and staying at the Hall, and for the first time since I had left college I was inordinately happy.

I had access to the library and hundreds of books, and the opportunity to play the piano. I had always loved music and had been doing well with my lessons, but the vicarage did not own a piano so my studies had had to cease. Now I was able to find pieces of music that matched my skill and the hours flew by on winged feet.

Only one thing troubled me and that was Cora's absorption with her wedding plans. She had me looking through numerous pattern books which she had had sent up from London fashion houses. Swatches of silks and satins, brocades and chiffons were all there for her to choose from and the list of guests seemed endless. She was fretful because Roland couldn't get to the Hall on account of the weather and I found myself wondering if he had been able to get to Ackroyd House . . .

Eleanor and Cora were very different, so what was there about Roland that could bring that look of love into both their faces? I acknowledge that he was handsome in a fair English way, that he could dance with grace and ride with panache but compared to Lyndon with his steely reserve he was a nonentity in my eyes. With Lyndon there would always be things to discover, slowly and with wonderment, but then I was in love with Lyndon even though it was a love I must hug to my heart, for it could never find expression.

On the few occasions I met Gavin he flirted with me and once he waylaid me on the stairs, putting an arm on either side of me so that I could not escape. It was Lyndon standing at the foot of the stairs saying in an icy voice, 'When you have finished dallying with Miss Wentworth Gavin perhaps you will remember there is work to be done,' that sent him hurrying away.

I felt cheapened that he had seen us together. I wanted none of Gavin's embraces but that evening over dinner Lyndon was unusually distant, addressing me only when it was absolutely necessary and Gavin too seemed suitably chastened. Surely he couldn't think that I had encouraged Gavin and that I was some sort of fortune hunter with one foot already in Greythorn Hall!

I was left very much to my own devices on the day that Cora returned to her bed with a bad chill. Winter was still the worst possible time for her and although she was now much healthier than she had been as a child, she had to take care and this was an unusually bleak winter. The snow outside had settled down into a hard core of ice. The roads were treacherous for both man and beast and the snow clouds still hung ominously on the Pennine hills. A warm fire burned in the music room grate and I joyfully occupied my time playing the piano, glad of the opportunity which would not come again once I had left Greythorn.

I was surprised when the door opened and Melinda came in, walking painfully on two sticks.

'May I listen to you Maya? It is so seldom the piano is played these days.'

'Do you play yourself, Lady Gaynor?' I asked her.

'I learned as a child but I was never a very apt pupil. I had brothers who considered it a frothy pursuit and because I liked to keep up with them I spent most of my girlhood on horseback or walking over the fells with the dogs.'

I felt sad as I tried to visualise this sick woman so immersed in manly activities.

'What would you like me to play?' I asked her.

'Anything you like. It will be restful sitting here listening to music.'

I played until the maid came in with afternoon tea and Melinda said, 'Thank you, I have enjoyed that. Now come closer to the fire and have tea.'

The firelight shone on her pale flaxen hair and delicate pink and white skin. This was the kind of beauty Lyndon liked, I told myself, this soft gentle beauty so ethereal it seemed almost unreal, not my black gypsy hair and eyes that flashed like blue steel.

As she straightened back in her chair after pouring out the tea I saw her wince with pain and today the shadows seemed more pronounced under her blue eyes.

'Can I make you more comfortable, Lady Gaynor?' I asked gently.

'No, it is the weather. I am always unwell in the winter. It is very wearisome, this slow, creeping illness, but it is worse for Lyndon to see me like this.'

'Would you be better in a warmer climate, do you think?'

'Perhaps, but there is no certainty and this is our home.'

'You don't think it is worth a try?'

She did not speak for several minutes but remained looking pensively into the flames, then she turned to face me. 'If a certain cure was guaranteed then I might be prepared to take that chance, but not unless. I couldn't bear to watch Lyndon hating every day he was away from this house that he loves, wondering if it was being looked after, caring about the land and the men and women who work on it – simply to give me a chance. It could destroy both of us if it failed.'

'But if it *succeeded* Lady Gaynor.'

She shook her head. 'I have no faith in present-day miracles and we have received no definite answers to the questions we have asked. I have accepted my disability and yet it seems on looking back that one day we had everything, Lyndon and I, and the next we had nothing. I remember I was so happy that day preparing for the party. It was New Year's Eve and guests were coming from all over the North Riding. It was one of those beautiful clear winter days and we had decorated the house and there was a giant Christmas tree standing in the hall. Oh how we danced that night . . . I had never felt so alive. We were all enjoying ourselves, even Cora who had been ill over Christmas and Eleanor was still here, captivating all the men as usual. Just after midnight somebody suggested we play games, you know, those silly games where somebody has to hide and the others have to search for him or her. It was my turn to hide and I knew the exact place where they would never find me. Old Sir John told me about it, a secret panel in the master bedroom at the head of the stairs. It had been used in the old days to hide monks during Henry the Eighth's purge on the monasteries. The abbeys suffered terribly at that time and many of the old houses have these sanctuaries where they used to hide the monks. I could hear them searching for me, then suddenly it went very quiet and after a time I wondered if they had given up the search. I thought of all the fun I might be missing so I climbed out of the panel and ran towards the landing. This, it seems, was what they had been waiting for because suddenly they were all around me at the head of the stairs.

'We started to go down the stairs and then suddenly I didn't know what was happening to me. One moment I was standing at the top – and the next I was rolling over, unable to stop myself.' She shuddered.

'Did you trip over your gown, do you think?'

'I don't know. It was very strange. I had walked down those stairs so often, run down them like a child. They were shallow and wide but that night there was something different. I have always had the strangest feeling that someone pushed me. Oh, it can only have been accidental, how could it have been otherwise?'

I stared at her in shocked surprise. She was not looking at me, her mind was back on that long-ago night and her stricken face was strangely puzzled. As though by a great effort, she dragged her thoughts back into the present and then she was Melinda again, smiling and asking gently if I had settled down happily with Jamie at Ackroyd House.

'I do hope so,' I answered her. 'He is a delightful little boy and very intelligent.'

'Yes. Lyndon tells me that he is.'

There was a sadness in her voice and I knew that she was thinking of the son she would never give Lyndon. Wishing to turn her thoughts elsewhere I said, 'I think he was a very lonely child before I went there. He had invented two playmates – a little girl called Nancy and a boy called Peter, but I don't hear him speak about them quite so often now.'

'Then you have done wonders for him already, Maya. Does he see much of his father?'

'I very rarely see Mr Ackroyd myself but I am sure he sees his son in the evenings when I have left the house.'

'But he rides with his mother each day, I believe?'

'Not every day since I started to ride. We only ride in the grounds of the house but quite often Jamie and I ride alone.'

'And what does Eleanor do in your absence, Maya? I cannot think that she spends it poring over a book or working at her needlework. Eleanor has always pursued her own ends regardless of others, and now I have heard that she is recklessly pursuing her sister's fiancé.'

I stared at her with wide eyes, completely taken aback that she had voiced her fears to me.

'Perhaps I shouldn't be saying this to you, Maya, but I am unhappy with the situation. Once Eleanor and Roland were very close but there was no escape from her marriage to Roger Ackroyd and in those days Roland had very little money and few prospects. It would have been better if he had stayed away from Greythorn Hall. It was cruel retribution that made him turn to Cora.'

'You do not think he loves Cora?'

'I would like to think so but how can I when I know that he visits Eleanor as often or more often than he comes here.'

'Do you think Cora knows?'

'No, and she is so much in love she would never believe he could do such a thing. She is a quiet girl but underneath that quietness is a strong will and a determination equal to Eleanor's own.'

I shivered in spite of the warmth of the room. I was remembering Cora's grip on my wrist in the whispering glade, and I was also remembering Eleanor's look of love as she waved farewell to Roland Carnwood on the doorstep of Ackroyd House.

'Does Sir Lyndon know that Roland visits his sister, Lady Gaynor?'

'I cannot think that he knows or he would have tried to do something about it.'

'May I ask how you know?'

'Sometimes in the summer I go out alone in the carriage. It is one of the few pleasures left to me and I like to visit my friends whenever it is possible. Twice I have seen Roland riding across the fells with Eleanor and once I saw him leaving Ackroyd House. I told him I had seen him but he gave an excuse that he was returning a book Mr Ackroyd had lent him. Perhaps he was, but Mr Ackroyd is not often at home in the middle of the afternoon!'

She rose painfully to her feet and stood for a moment leaning on her sticks, steadying herself for the walk to the door. I walked over to open it for her.

She smiled and I wished I was not quite so tall as I looked down at her dainty, childlike figure.

'I have spoken to you in confidence, Maya. I would not like you to repeat what I have told you.'

'You can rest assured that I will not repeat a word of it.'

She patted my hand gently. 'Thank you, Maya. You know, the sick see more because they have nothing better to do and perhaps they brood more. Thank you for playing for me. Is there a piano at Ackroyd House?'

'I don't know. I have only been in the library and the nursery.'

'It would be nice if you could continue with your music.'

'Yes, I would like that, Lady Gaynor.'

I stood at the door and watched her walk slowly into the drawing room. My thoughts were confused. Was Melinda warning me that she would know if I showed too clearly my infatuation with her husband, or were her words merely an indication of her fears for Eleanor and Cora?

I saw little of Sir Lyndon during the next few days but once I received an impudent wave from Gavin as he raced his horse across the park. The days were cold and frosty even though the sun shone and I took to wrapping up warmly so that I could walk in the gardens. Once, I even plucked up enough courage to walk the length of the whispering glade, and stood for a long time looking out across the mere. The bare branches were still. The leaves of summer had gone and I could hear nothing except the lonely cry of a curlew as he flew high above the lake. Much of it was still frozen under a layer of ice and I shivered, thinking of its depth. Emily had always said that nobody really knew how deep it was.

Why, oh why, had Emily left Lexford? By this time, the baby would be born and I wondered if she had managed to find work where she could keep it with her, or if she was destitute in some lonely city. Why couldn't she have married Ned and stayed close to her family and friends? It had been madness to go away, and I refused to face the thought that a more terrible tragedy could have overtaken her.

Like the deaths of my parents I placed Emily's memory in that part of my mind where it was locked away, never to be thought about or cried over, and in four days the roads were sufficiently clear for me to return to Ackroyd House.

TEN

JAMIE GREETED ME happily on my return, and very soon we had taken up our former routine. We worked in the morning before lunch which we ate together in the nursery, then in the afternoon we either walked or rode in the grounds. The weather was still cold after the snow had gone so we did not stay out too long before returning to our studies.

Now that I was living at the house, Jamie and I ate tea together in the nursery and one day, as an afterthought, Eleanor said to me, 'What do you do in the evenings Miss Wentworth, after Jamie has gone to bed?'

'Usually I read. I asked Mr Ackroyd's permission to borrow books from the library.'

'Well of course, Roger doesn't read them. I don't suppose they were ever acquired because anybody wanted to *read* them, no doubt they were bought simply as books to fill the shelves!'

She laughed merrily at the expression on my face.

'Don't look so surprised. The Ackroyds were never noted for their intelligence, only for their dissipation and their vulgarity.'

I wished she had not started this conversation. I was only a governess in the house and it seemed disloyal on her part to speak of the Ackroyds in this manner.

Unrepentant she said, 'Don't you get lonely in the nursery reading your books by the light of that one small lamp?'

'Why no Mrs Ackroyd, and there is plenty going on in the daytime.'

'Well, in future I think you should dine with us. It would

relieve the monotony and there are times when I am alone.'

'But the Master may not agree to that, Mrs Ackroyd. He might feel that I was intruding.'

'You will not be, and from now on I shall call you Maya. This "Miss Wentworth" is all wrong when you have visited my sister at Greythorn and she calls you Maya.'

'Very well, Mrs Ackroyd.'

'How do you see your future, Maya, when Jamie grows too old to have a governess?'

'I haven't thought about it. I am simply grateful for these few years and the chance they are giving me to set Jamie's feet on the right path, educationally I mean, of course.'

For a moment she looked pensive, then with a shrug of her shoulders and a little laugh she said, 'You are still very young. I remember what a solemn little thing you were and so much on the defensive when we poked fun at that uncle of yours. I was brought up to expect all the good things of life to come to me without a struggle, I only found out later that I didn't have a choice – that I must accept blindly and without question, the only thing I should have been free to choose for myself.'

'You have a beautiful little boy, Miss Eleanor, and perhaps if you understood Mr Ackroyd more . . .' I floundered, wishing I hadn't been so presumptuous. It was really none of my business and who was I to give her advice? I thought she would be angry, cut me down to size with well-administered words, but instead she walked over to the window and stood with her back to me looking out across the courtyard. Then, to my utmost surprise she said, 'I am told you play the piano rather well, Maya?'

'I wish I played better but I am out of practice.'

'There is a piano in the drawing room and you have my permission to use it.'

Without another word she turned on her heel and left the room, while my murmured thanks fell on empty air.

Later in the afternoon I heard the sound of her horse's hooves crossing the courtyard and I knew she intended to ride across the fells. I felt sure she would be meeting Roland out there and again I felt that old sensation of foreboding. In a few months he would be married to Cora . . . surely their friendship must end soon.

I changed into my Sunday dress for the first time I dined with Eleanor and her husband in the gloomy dining room at the back of the house. Although a bright log fire burned in the grate its glow never reached the corners of the room, nor did the light of the gas bulbs set in the alcoves on either side of the massive stone fireplace. The table had been set with exquisite cut-glass and silver which reflected Eleanor's taste, but the food was mediocre and barely warm.

Eleanor played with her dinner, pushing it about her plate until her husband snapped angrily, 'If you don't want the food Eleanor send it back to the kitchen.'

'I don't know why we don't get rid of Mrs Markham. She's no good as a housekeeper when she can't get better service from her staff.'

'She suits me well enough,' was his terse reply.

'That is because you haven't been used to anything better! Your father was neither interested in good food nor good service.'

I looked down at my plate unhappily, wishing I was back in the nursery with a book in my hands.

'I don't require my wife to tell me what I've been used to,' he replied shortly, but Eleanor merely laughed flippantly saying, 'We never know what time you are coming in for dinner, consequently the food is often spoilt.'

'I must make a habit of coming in at a set time in future then,' he said meaningfully. 'It would suit you better, wouldn't it Madam?'

'And what exactly do you mean by that remark?'

'For instance the middle of the afternoon,' he went on, ignoring her interruption.

'I'm sure Maya isn't interested in your inferences, and nor am I.'

'A man likes to dine in peace in his own home at the end of the day, not listen to these constant tirades against the servants and the state of the house.'

116

'Well, look at it! This room is miserably dark and the lighting inadequate. There is only one decent room in the house and that is the drawing room – and that wouldn't have been like it is but for the things I brought over from Greythorn.'

'Greythorn, always Greythorn! We never have a meal but what I don't hear of the excellence of life at Greythorn. I'm surprised you don't return to it.'

'Then you will not be very surprised if I do.'

He flung his table napkin on the table and got to his feet. His face was red with anger and in a flustering voice meant to intimidate he shouted, 'Be very sure, my fine lady, that I should bring you back, by the scruff of the neck if necessary. You're my wife and here you'll stay until one of us is dead.'

She was pale but she met his eyes fearlessly and with a half-mocking smile on her lips, while I looked from one to the other wishing I could put a considerable distance between them and myself.

'Perhaps, Miss Wentworth, you will inform them in the kitchens that I will eat dinner in the library tonight, and every other night until my wife learns her manners.'

'Gracious me,' Eleanor taunted. 'There has never been any-thing wrong with my *manners*. I cannot vouch for my other misdemeanours, but my manners have always been above reproach.'

I had got to my feet and was hurrying to the door. Roger Ackroyd went through it before me however, allowing it to swing behind him, almost into my face.

'My husband's manners are non-existent, Maya. Do as he has asked and you and I will finish our meal alone.'

If the servants were surprised by my request they didn't show it, which made me think it was not a new occurrence. When I returned to the dining table, I found Eleanor happily eating her food and for the rest of the meal she chatted amiably on about all sorts of things, travel, clothes and even the latest dance steps.

After that night I dreaded the evening meal. Mr Ackroyd ate alone in the library for several nights until one evening when they had guests, then he was forced to return to the dining room. I made my excuses on that occasion, saying they would wish to dine alone with their guests, and Eleanor agreed with me.

Christmas was now approaching and I wondered whether I would be expected to stay, or if I would be given a holiday. When I broached the question to Eleanor she said, 'Heavens above, I'd forgotten about Christmas! We always go to Greythorn for the festivities – it was a stipulation I made when I came here as a bride and up to now Roger hasn't tried to alter it. Perhaps you should go to your aunt and uncle in Lexford Maya – after all, it is a great celebration in church circles.'

'But not only in church circles, Mrs Ackroyd. Jamie is looking forward to it.'

'Well of course he is, he gets thoroughly spoilt at Greythorn and has far too many presents. I'm not too sure I want to go this year . . . I'm so sick already of hearing about Cora's wedding plans, she's so single-minded about everything.'

'Don't you think that is very natural?'

'Possibly, but so incredibly boring. I'll see what Roger thinks about it.'

I knew that the subject would arise that same evening over dinner, and I found myself dreading it, wishing I could make an excuse to be elsewhere.

We had reached the coffee stage when Eleanor asked nonchalantly, 'I suppose we shall be going to Greythorn as usual this Christmas?'

'I don't see why not, we've gone every Christmas since we were married.'

'Isn't there somewhere else we could go – some nice hotel in the country, say, were there's plenty going on and lots of people.'

'When I've suggested that before you've always disliked the idea. Why don't you want to go to Greythorn this particular year?'

'Oh, there's no special reason . . . however I am so tired of hearing about Cora's wedding. It's not until the spring – we're surely not going to have it every day until then.'

'You don't see her every day. I doubt if she ever sets foot in this house.'

'Oh well, Cora and I were never bosom chums. She was a strange, withdrawn little thing, I'm sure Maya would agree with me.'

'She was never very well,' I murmured unhappily.

'And didn't all the household know it,' Eleanor snapped, 'having to creep about on tiptoe and not raise one's voice in case dear Cora was asleep.'

'Well, next year she might not be there so I think we shall go to Greythorn as usual,' Mr Ackroyd said firmly.

'What do you mean, next year she might not be there? Where else should she be?'

'I take it young Carnwood will be expected to furnish a home for her. He should be able to afford it – he's come into his aunt's money and that's the usual procedure for married couples, to move into their own home.'

Eleanor was staring at him with a strange expression in her eyes. I doubted if the question of Cora's whereabouts after her marriage had ever troubled her, but now that the marriage was coming closer, such mundane matters were being discussed openly.

Mr Ackroyd was watching her through narrowed eyes and I thought I detected a malicious gleam in them. How much did he know of his wife's friendship with Roland Carnwood, I wondered? And how long would he allow it to last . . .

In the end I went home to Lexford for Christmas and the Ackroyd family made their usual visit to Greythorn Hall. The weather was unseasonably mild but it meant that I could drive myself home. As I headed towards the vicarage along the village streets the lamps had already been lit and from the church came the sound of organ music and carols being sung. My uncle had started his Christmas festivities early by making sure that the church choir were properly rehearsed.

I saw to Rory in the stable next to my uncle's pony, then I let myself into the vicarage by the side door. There was a good smell of food cooking and putting my head round the kitchen door I saw Mrs Roper busily basting the joint she had taken from the oven.

'That smells good Mrs Roper, what are we celebrating?'

'Nothin' special Maya, only yer uncle's got a young curate visitin' an' I suppose 'e wants to show willin'.'

'You mean he's coming to work here?'

'I knows nothin' Maya. As Heaven's my witness yer uncle doesn't tell me 'is business, but the young feller turned up this mornin' an' now they're over at church. Didn't yer 'ear 'em?'

'I heard the choir and thought it was a little early. I don't suppose there's a cup of tea?'

'Sit down there an' I'll soon make yer one. You're lookin' well Maya, got a bit o' colour in yer cheeks, I expect that's the fresh air if you've driven over.'

'Yes, it's going to be a frosty night. How is my aunt?'

'She's over at the church 'elpin' the girls to decorate it. She might be glad o' your 'elp too, Maya, after you've 'ad your tea.'

'Have you heard from Emily, Mrs Roper?'

'No, not a word. I worry about 'er somethin' shockin' an' I get angry too. She should a' written, she should niver a' gone off like that wi'out a word.'

'No, I agree with you, but Emily always knew what she wanted to do and she didn't want to marry Ned Rakesby.'

'No, an' there's the poor lad 'avin' trouble wi' 'is parents about it. I'll bet they make 'is life a misery between 'em.'

'It isn't Ned's fault Emily's gone off.'

'Well, they seem to think different. The lad were willin' enough to wed 'er, what more could 'e do?'

'I don't know, Mrs Roper. It's all very sad for both of them. I suppose nothing has changed here?'

'Well, there's new curtains in the study but that's about all. I think they were plannin' to put the curate i' your room Maya – so where will you be sleepin'?'

'I don't know. I couldn't send a message to say I was coming home. The Ackroyds only decided to go to Greythorn last weekend, and by then it was too late to let my uncle know.'

'I'll tell ye what. That Miss Eleanor don't look any too 'appy to me.'

She was watching me with sharp shrewd eyes but I had no wish to enter into a conversation about Miss Eleanor with Mrs Roper.

'I haven't noticed anything, Mrs Roper, she always seems the same to me. I suppose none of the other rooms are aired or the beds made up?'

'Eh, bless ye lass, there's not enough beddin' in the 'ouse for another bed to be made up! The vicar's allus bin frugal, allus just enough an' never anythin' left over. I reckon the curate'll 'ave to find a room at the inn now that you're 'ere.'

My uncle made it quite plain that they were put out by my arrival. In particularly censorious tones he accused me of being guilty of extreme thoughtlessness, even when I explained the circumstances.

The young curate Mr Lowndes hovered uneasily in the background, feeling I am sure that he was the innocent cause of our argument and offering to move out immediately to make room for me.

'No, please Mr Lowndes, that won't be at all necessary. I can easily sleep in one of the downstairs rooms – after all, it is only for a few days.'

I hurried into the kitchen, leaving him to argue matters out with my aunt and uncle. When I told Mrs Roper what was happening she said, 'You can allus come an' stay at the cottage with me Maya, ye can 'ave Emily's room. I can soon get it aired an' I'll be glad of a bit o' company.'

To my relief her offer was accepted by all concerned. It did solve the curate's move to the local inn but although Mrs Roper and I sat up chatting well into the night, I was not looking forward to spending the rest of it in Emily's room.

It was a far nicer room than mine at the vicarage and a great deal of Emily's personality was stamped upon it. The wallpaper had a delicate rose design and the curtains were a pretty shade of green, her favourite colour. I sat up in the single bed feeling the warmth of the oven plates that had been put in to air it while

I hugged the stone hot water bottle on my knees.

I tried to get the room to tell me something. I had always heard that houses absorbed some element of the tragedies enacted within their walls but these stared back at me, stolid and impersonal. What had Emily's thoughts been during those last few days before she walked out, never to return? She must have cried in this room, sobbed and prayed, but whatever scene the room had witnessed it was closed to me.

I left my bed and opened the wardrobe door. One or two of Emily's dresses still hung there and on the shelves were old schoolbooks and pencil-boxes. The drawers in the tiny dressing table were mostly filled with old birthday cards and the usual fripperies a girl collects long after they are any use to her, but one thing disturbed me. Emily's hairbrush. I remembered that once she had said to me, 'I could never go anywhere without mi 'airbrush. My 'air's unruly, not heavy and shinin' like yours Maya.'

I slept badly. The hairbrush nagged at me all through the night but during the day I was kept so busy I didn't get much chance to think of anything except the festivities centred around the village hall and my aunt's insistence that I accompany her. She had acquired a new assistant, a Miss Peabody, who was a retired schoolmistress. Listening to her encouraging the young women around her, I felt sure my aunt would be better served by her than she ever was by me.

Miss Peabody was a small, erect woman whose eyes snapped behind rimless spectacles. Her first words to me after our introduction were, 'Hmm, so you're the young woman who is teaching the Ackroyd child. I don't hold with private education myself, the boy is old enough to attend the village school for a few years to see if he can adapt to other children.'

'I am sure his parents thought they were doing the best thing for Jamie. He is a shy, imaginative child but he's also very bright.'

'One hears talk of course. Mrs Ackroyd came from quite the wrong background for her husband.'

'You know the family well?'

I didn't want to get into a conversation with her about my employers, yet I was surprised that she had been so forthcoming, particularly to someone she had only met that afternoon, and especially a girl who was already employed by the Ackroyds and living in their house.

'I know the Ackroyds all right,' she snapped in acid tones. 'I was brought up in Seaten and only came to Lexford to live with my brother when his wife died. My father was an acquaintance of old Mr Ackroyd.'

Her face was disapproving, with compressed lips and a heightened colour. All the same I couldn't stifle a mischievous twinge of amusement that made me wonder if her father had sat up half the night wagering his money on those wretched birds and animals, to the despair of his wife and children.

She bent her head curtly and with a bleak, 'Good afternoon, Miss Wentworth,' she moved on.

Miss Peabody had made it very clear that she did not approve of me and I sensed she was already more than familiar with my many shortcomings. I smiled grimly to myself. Miss Peabody might see my uncle as the Almighty's representative on earth but in my book it took more than a clerical collar to turn a man into a saint. Besides, I told myself, why should I worry about her opinion anyway when she had obviously judged me without knowing me.

As I mingled with the villagers, moving from stall to stall, I was greeted by little groups of them, and always there would be one of their number asking sly questions about the 'gentry'. Carefully I parried their questions, saying, 'I am only there to teach Jamie. I know nothing of the family's plans.'

After one of these encounters I heard somebody say, 'You'll get nothin' out of 'er, she's never really bin one of us.'

They were right of course, I had never been one of them. Right from the first moment my uncle's profession had set me on a different plane so that in the village they had made the barrier, not I. Only Emily had found a way through it and yet my uncle had wanted me to be a child with a foot in two worlds, the world of the village to suit his pocket, and the world of Greythorn to suit his pride.

Although it was a cold and frosty afternoon and the dusk would come down early across the fells I longed to get out of the village hall and into fresh air. I saw that my aunt was surrounded by people she knew and I didn't think I would be missed. I did, however, tell the woman sitting at a table just within the doorway that I was going out for a breath of air and that I would not be long.

The village street was deserted but frost clung to the hedge-rows and glistened against the window panes and I was glad that I was not spending the night in my room at the vicarage. The curate was very welcome to it! I much preferred Emily's snug little room in the cottage.

I turned up the collar of my coat and slid my hands into the deep pockets then I set off to walk across the hard frozen ground leading out of the village. I knew I would not be able to go far, but I was enjoying the peace and quiet after the clamour in the village hall. Consequently, I felt unreasonably irritated to hear a voice behind me calling, 'Miss Wentworth, may I have a word with you?'

I turned to see the curate heading up the hill towards me, his head bent against the wind. He was flushed with hurrying and I had no smile of greeting on my face which must have disturbed him.

'I can see you wanted to be alone, but I tried to get to you in the hall. It was a bit of a crush, wasn't it?'

I smiled then and moved forward to meet him. 'Yes it was, and very stuffy in there.'

'I really do feel very badly about turning you out of your room. Are you quite sure you are comfortable at Mrs Roper's?'

'Of course I am, Mr Lowndes. I've known the Roper family since I was a little girl.'

'Would you mind if I walked with you a little way? I feel like stretching my legs.'

'No, of course not. We shan't be able to go far – the clouds are racing in and the fells can be treacherous.'

'How long did it take you to get accustomed to living in Yorkshire?'

'I feel I have never lived anywhere else.'

'You mean you never think about Africa or your parents?'

'Never, Mr Lowndes. What would be the point of it? I can never have my parents or the old days back again. I don't like to speak of them.'

'I'm sorry, Miss Wentworth. I seem to be spending most of my time apologising to you.'

There was something very nice about this young man with his anxious air of seeking the right thing to say, like a confused puppy trying to please.

'Your aunt tells me you are teaching a small boy at one of the big houses in these parts?'

'Yes, his name is Jamie Ackroyd, and I am enjoying it. You are not from Yorkshire, Mr Lowndes, so what brings you here at Christmas time?'

'I'm originally from Lincolnshire. My uncle is a Dean at the Cathedral there, expecting me to follow in his footsteps probably, but I doubt if I have his dedication.'

'But why Yorkshire?'

'Well, one has to start somewhere and I love this county. It is big and wide and steeped in history. I love the old abbeys and the cathedral cities, and when I got the chance to come here for a few days I rather jumped at it.'

'I wasn't aware my uncle intended to take on a curate. Surely the size of the parish doesn't warrant it?'

'No, but it's experience for me. I shall be expected to try out a few such places before some poor vicar believes I am what he is looking for.'

I didn't often get the opportunity to talk to a man as a friend. Gavin never wanted to talk, only to make love to me, and Lyndon who had talked to me was a dream in the heart, intangible and unrealistic. The best thing I could do was forget him but immediately I was remembering Emily's laughing face in this same meadow years before when she said, 'There might be a curate somewhere for you if you watches yer step!'

Why, oh why, did I have to think about Emily just then? It was as though she had stepped out of limbo to remind me of that long golden summer in our childhood and I paused on the hillside, momentarily confused, while Mr Lowndes stared down at me perplexed.

'Is anything wrong, Miss Wentworth?'

'No. Just a ghost walking over my grave.'

'An unhappy ghost?'

'Oh I hope not, I do hope not.'

I was surprised how far we had walked and how high we had climbed. There were lights in the houses of the few farms scattered on the hillside and in the distance the village of Buckley nestled under the bulk of Chagmire Hill while Lexford was completely hidden at the other side of the fell.

'We've come rather a long way Mr Lowndes. I think perhaps we should be getting back.'

He had gone to stand on a small jutting crag several feet away, looking down to where the parkland and chimneys of Greythorn formed a perfect setting against the darkening hills.

'That house, Miss Wentworth – whose is it?'

'It belongs to the Gaynor family. It is Greythorn Hall.'

'Oh, this is what I love about Yorkshire, these great country houses that seem such a part of the wild hills and crags, almost as if they had grown there from the beginning of time . . .'

'Yes, they seem that way to me, too.'

He turned reluctantly away and came down the hillside to join me. 'Isn't it a member of the Gaynor family you are with now?'

'Yes, Sir Lyndon's sister Eleanor. She lives over at Seaten in another great house, but it is nothing like this one, although with love and care it could have been perhaps.'

'If I had a house like that I would nurture it and love it above all things.'

'Above all things?'

He laughed a little. 'Well, perhaps that is an overstatement, but then I'm not married.'

'I think that perhaps that is how Sir Lyndon loves his house, above all other things. It is the only thing in his life that will last.'

'But he is married, I believe?'

'Yes. Lady Gaynor is an invalid and not likely to get better. It is very sad.'

'Gracious yes. And who will the property go to eventually; as I take it there are no children?'

'No, so the house will probably go to Gavin Gaynor, Sir Lyndon's younger brother.'

'Oh, that's all right then. At least it will stay in the family and I suppose the younger brother will care for it.'

'I don't know, the two brothers are not in the least alike.'

We were walking quickly now, almost running. I had visions of my aunt's doleful face and my uncle's annoyance if they were kept waiting for dinner. Some of my anxiety must have conveyed itself to my companion who put his arm under my elbow and broke into a gentle trot.

We need not have worried. Only my aunt had arrived home by the time we arrived and I set to immediately, helping to lay the table in the dining room as well as building up the fire. I had never been fed so well. My uncle was obviously trying to impress our visitor with his hospitality and cynically I wondered if it was the young curate or the Dean in Lincoln Cathedral who had prompted this generosity.

ELEVEN

THE ENTIRE VILLAGE was taken by surprise on Christmas Day when the Gaynor family arrived for the morning service. Only Lady Gaynor and Mr Ackroyd stayed away and even Jamie was with them. I stole a surreptitious look halfway through the service at the Gaynor pew but on meeting Gavin's bold dark eyes and impudent smile I looked quickly away. I did not linger afterwards with my aunt and uncle in the porch to exchange greetings with the visitors, but instead walked slowly through the churchyard chatting to other worshippers. It was only when I heard my name called that I spun round to see Jamie running as fast as his legs would carry him towards me.

There was such a wealth of joy on his beautiful boy's face that I instinctively gathered him into my arms, touched by the warmth of his welcome. When I released him I could see that the others were watching us from the porch and then Sir Lyndon came forward with a smile on his face to take the child's hand.

'It is obvious that you have made yourself popular with Jamie,' he said lightly. 'I was sure you would.'

I smiled without agreeing with him, then I joined the others in their walk back to the lane where the carriages were waiting. My uncle introduced Mr Lowndes, who immediately informed Sir Lyndon that only the day before we had stood on the hillside looking down on Greythorn Hall.

'It's a very imposing pile,' the curate said enthusiastically. 'I was telling Miss Wentworth how much I loved Yorkshire for

128

her fine old buildings. It must be wonderful to live in a house like that, sir.'

'Yes, perhaps it is, but it needs a great deal of upkeep. Every year it gets more difficult to maintain and owning land isn't the easygoing, profit-making life people seem to think it is. One of these days some wealthy woollen manufacturer from one of the cities may make me an offer for it.'

I looked at him in surprise, unable to tell whether he was serious or not. There was a faint smile on his lips and Mr Lowndes too didn't know whether to commiserate or agree with him. To change the subject I said, 'I hope Lady Gaynor is quite well, Sir Lyndon?'

'Winter is not good for her complaint Maya, and she finds difficulty in manoeuvring these steps and the long walk up to the church.'

He smiled down at me, that sweet impersonal smile that tugged at my heart and then wishing me good morning and a Merry Christmas, he moved away. I turned disconsolately and it was then I saw Roland walking with Eleanor while Cora strolled behind with Gavin.

I was seized suddenly by such a strong feeling of foreboding that I felt quite shaken. Surely every person in the churchyard that morning must see the ravaged look on Eleanor's face – and the concern on that of the man who walked beside her. She was pale, paler than I had ever seen her and there was a tautness about her . . . like the restless tigress who paces her cage, knowing that only those strong slender bars keep her from the freedom that lies beyond.

She played nervously with her gloves while Gavin and Roland climbed into the first carriage with Cora, then taking Jamie's hand she walked to where Lyndon waited at the door of the second carriage. With one foot on the step she turned towards me as though it was the first time she had seen me that morning.

'How long are you intending to stay in Lexford, Maya?' she surprised me by asking.

'I can return to Seaten at any time Miss Eleanor, whenever I am needed.'

'We intended to go home before the New Year, on Thursday, immediately after lunch, I think. We will call for you then.'

'Very well, I shall be ready.'

'I am sorry if it upsets any of your plans for the New Year festivities.'

'It doesn't. I had made no plans, Miss Eleanor.'

She nodded, almost absentmindedly and Lyndon looked down at her, faintly troubled.

We watched them drive away then we walked back slowly towards the vicarage. My uncle seemed entirely gratified by their visit as I knew he would be. After a few minutes I found myself walking behind with Mr Lowndes.

'It's a strange time for you to be going back to Seaten, Miss Wentworth. One would have thought Mrs Ackroyd and her husband would have wished to stay at Greythorn over the New Year.'

'Perhaps Mr Ackroyd has business matters he wishes to attend to. I don't think he is one for family festivities.'

'It is the younger woman who is marrying Mr Carnwood in the spring you said?'

'Did I Mr Lowndes, I don't remember, but you are quite right.'

I saw the puzzlement on his face and thought to myself that already he was becoming a student of human nature, an attribute that would serve him well in his chosen profession.

The following Thursday came round quickly and I was all ready and packed long before lunch. I had spent my last night in Emily's room and as we left the cottage together in the early morning her mother said, 'I 'ope you've bin comfortable stayin' wi' me, Maya.'

'Very comfortable. I wish a curate could be here every time I come to Lexford!'

''E's a nice young gentleman, not much trouble and friendly-like.'

'Yes, he seems very nice. I hope he gets fixed up somewhere.'

''Ere perhaps – Maya?'

I laughed. 'Oh Mrs Roper, you're matchmaking and I'm not rising to that bait.'

'Well, there's not much round 'ere for a girl like you. This young feller's educated and nice.'

When I didn't answer her she gave me an anxious look and said, 'It's not that Mr Gavin I 'ope?'

'Oh Mrs Roper, of course it isn't Gavin! He doesn't visit Ackroyd House and he's not my type.'

'I used to think 'e were our Emily's type. She talked about nothing but Master Gavin an' 'is 'orses all that summer, long after you'd taken 'er up to the 'All she did.'

'But she was only a child then, Mrs Roper, and young girls get these silly ideas.'

'Ay, but she wouldn't marry Ned, would she?'

I stared at her surprised. 'You are surely not suggesting Gavin Gaynor had anything to do with her not marrying Ned! Gavin was fun, I agree, but Ned was a real friend.'

'She 'ad funny ideas in 'er 'ead, 'ad our Emily. One day after 'er sister Mary'd bin round she said, "That's 'ow I'll be, married to Ned, Mother, there must be somethin' else in life." '

'I wish there were some answers Mrs Roper. I wish we knew where to look for them.'

'Ye know what I think?'

'No.'

'I think she's 'ad that baby adopted an' she's livin' in some big 'ouse somewhere in service, settin' 'er cap at any young feller she thinks is goin' to make 'er into a lady.'

I stared at Mrs Roper but I didn't agree with her. Somehow I didn't see Emily in that rôle: it didn't measure up to her honesty or her levelheadedness.

The Ackroyds arrived promptly at two o'clock at the vicarage and after my luggage had been placed on the rack I climbed into the back seat to sit with Jamie and his mother. Eleanor's maid Janine sat in front with Mr Ackroyd, an arrangement which I thought exceptionally strange since Janine was one of the bones of contention between them. To Mr Ackroyd, brought up in a man's world with neither mother nor sisters, a ladies' maid seemed an unnecessary presence in the household, but to Eleanor who had never been without a maid Janine was as necessary as the horse she rode and the food she ate.

On the whole it was a silent drive. Even Jamie seemed wrapped up in his own imaginings and Miss Eleanor stared straight ahead, her face remote, her thoughts elsewhere. It was only as we drove through the gates and started the long pull up to the house that she turned to me with an absent smile and said, 'Perhaps you would like to have a tray in your room tonight, Maya. I intend to do the same, as there are some letters I want to write.'

'Of course Miss Eleanor, that will suit me very well.'

'Tell me Miss Wentworth,' Mr Ackroyd said drily, 'why you address my wife as Miss Eleanor when she has been my wife for several years.'

Before I could reply Eleanor snapped, 'Really Roger, Maya has known me as Miss Eleanor since she was a child. I see no reason for her to change now, after all it is only a title. I don't care what she calls me.'

'In that case, in future Miss Wentworth, you will address my wife as Mrs Ackroyd. *I* care what you call her.'

'Very well Sir,' I murmured unhappily. 'I am sorry.'

I should have known that day that they had reached an impasse in their life together and that what came after was only a tragic and inevitable ending to a marriage that should never have taken place.

I was entirely bound up in my time with Jamie. I enjoyed our lessons and I loved our walks together in the early spring and the rides we now felt competent to take along the bridle paths beyond the gates. The late days of February were warm and sunny and I felt the sweet familiar pull of summer that always filled my heart with old yearnings and memories, as potent as they had ever been.

It was on one such venture outside the gates that we met Sir Lyndon riding his big chestnut across one of the lower fells from an outlying hamlet. Jamie suddenly urged his pony forward and my heart skipped a beat when I realised it was because he had seen his uncle riding below us. Sir Lyndon caught the pony's bridle and headed back towards me. He was smiling, bending down in the saddle so that he could hear the boy's chatter, and it was only when he drew alongside that he raised his head and greeted me.

'Are you and the boy riding alone?' he asked, surprised.

'Yes Sir, we often ride alone now. Jamie rides well and I have become more proficient.'

'But you stay with the bridle paths I hope and do not risk riding across the moors?'

'Yes, of course.'

I was puzzled by his concern. Surely he must know I would not put either myself or Jamie in any danger by being foolhardy, but still the concern lingered on his face, then he surprised me by saying, 'Are you returning to the house now, Miss Wentworth?'

'It is a little early for us, Sir Lyndon.'

'I will ride with you. It is several days since I saw my sister. Come Jamie, let me see how well you ride.'

There was nothing else for us but to retrace our steps and Jamie was nothing loth to show off his prowess. Sir Lyndon paid no further attention to me and I thought miserably that sometimes he addressed me quite naturally as Maya and at other times appeared so formal. Left to my own thoughts I began to worry. Suppose Roland was with Eleanor. We would be back at the house hours before we were expected, and I wondered how Sir Lyndon would greet him or if he already knew how matters stood and thought it was perhaps time he did something about it.

Eleanor came out of the drawing room when she heard our footsteps. She looked beautiful and elegant, and there was a bright welcoming smile on her face which wavered at the sight of us.

'Perhaps you were expecting somebody else?' her brother said astutely whilst he bent to kiss her cheek.

'No of course not, but I certainly didn't expect to see you. Your visits have been very spasmodic of late.'

'I found these two young people riding alone on the fells and I was surprised you were not with them.'

'Why should I be? Maya is perfectly capable of taking Jamie alone and I had a headache. Oh it's better now, I took something.'

'I don't suppose Cora's been here?'

'Cora never comes here, or at least hardly ever.'

'Then she must have met Roland near the village. She set out early hoping she might meet him.'

He was watching her closely and I saw the rich red colour suffuse her cheeks and the clenching of her hand against the skirt of her gown. Acutely embarrassed, I hurried Jamie upstairs but neither of them looked at us and I was glad when we reached the upper landing so that I did not have to listen to their conversation. Sir Lyndon knew about Eleanor and Roland, that much was sure, and we could still hear their voices. Lyndon's urgently persuasive, Eleanor's passionately vehement.

'Why is Uncle Lyndon quarrelling with Mother?' Jamie asked anxiously.

'I don't think they are quarrelling, Jamie. Lots of grown-up people have arguments.'

'My mother is very unhappy.'

Silently I agreed with him. Eleanor was desperately unhappy. In a few weeks the man she loved would marry her sister and the snatched moments they spent together were foolish and ill-advised. Roger Ackroyd was known for his fiery temper which would be unleashed in its entire fury if he should ever find them together, and what of Cora, blissfully immersed in the plans for her wedding?

I found myself wondering again if there was any truth in the old rumour that Eleanor had been promised to Roger in payment of a gambling debt. If it were true, then it had been utterly contemptible of old Sir John to ever have made such a commitment, but I could not think that Eleanor would ever have married Roger Ackroyd if there hadn't been some dark and hidden reason.

Sir Lyndon had deliberately told her that Roland would not be visiting Ackroyd House today – Instead he would be at Greythorn Hall with Cora. I dreaded the evening ahead when I would have to sit at the dining table in complete silence or listening to the Ackroyds' veiled sarcasm or open resentment.

Jamie sat huddled on the window seat looking across the fields. Recently the child had been more natural and outgoing, more like any other small boy, but now I was afraid that he would retreat once more into his world of imaginary characters, with his friends, who seemed more predictable than the people of flesh and blood around him.

'Would you like to come over to the fire, Jamie, and I will read to you?' I asked him anxiously.

Instead he shook his head. 'I am waiting to see Uncle Lyndon leave the stableyard,' he answered, and disconsolately I set about tidying the table of the schoolbooks we had used that morning.

I was busy putting them away when after a brief tap on the door Sir Lyndon entered, and Jamie, with a little cry of joy flew into his arms.

He sat on the window seat with the child and they talked about horses and fishing, long walks over the fells and long summer evenings filled with the scent of honeysuckle. I sat at the table listening to the low charm of his voice and I could have wept with the normal sweetness of it all. This was how a father should talk to his son, but Jamie's father never talked to him like this and Sir Lyndon had no son.

At last he rose to his feet and ruffling the boy's curls he said gently, 'One of these days, Jamie, you must come to Greythorn and you and I will spend long days together doing whatever you like best – in the summer, when you can stay for several weeks.'

'Oh, yes please, Uncle Lyndon! I should like that,' the boy answered with shining eyes.

Lyndon turned to me. I had risen from my chair and stood near the door knowing that he was about to leave. I did not want him to go. I wanted him to talk to me as he had talked to Jamie for I too knew the enchantment of long summer twilights and days filled with the scent of clover, but instead he took my hand and held it for a few moments. There was a half-smile on his lips and I took my hand away in case he should feel its trembling.

'I want you to promise me something Maya,' he said quietly.

Surprised, I stared at him. 'Yes, Sir Lyndon?'

'That you will confide in me if you are troubled and that you will do whatever you think is best for Jamie and yourself, even if it means bringing him to Greythorn.'

Without putting it into words he was telling me that there was danger for us here at Ackroyd House but if that danger came we had a friend we could turn to.

I nodded, meeting his dark serious gaze with eyes filled with trust and no doubt that other emotion I was trying so desperately hard to hide.

With a brief smile he seemed to accept my confidence, then surprisingly he bent his head and gently brushed the top of my hair with his lips.

TWELVE

I LIKENED THE days that followed Sir Lyndon's visit to living with a volcano and not knowing when it was likely to erupt. Roland did not come to the house and I guessed that perhaps Lyndon had spoken to him, but Eleanor could be seen galloping madly across the fells and I wondered if they were meeting elsewhere.

Taut as a bow, Eleanor barely disguised her restlessness and at the dinner table her husband spoke infrequently and consumed large quantities of port and brandy. She appeared not to notice that he was drinking more than usual, and immediately after dinner I excused myself and retired either to the nursery upstairs or to my own room.

How they spent their evenings I never knew, except that sometimes I could hear their voices, harsh and quarrelsome, the slamming of doors and his beating upon the bedroom door with loud aggressive fists, demanding to be let in.

Twice I found Jamie sitting shivering on the stairs while the tirades went on below him, and more and more he spoke of his old imaginary playmates as though they were real people. One afternoon Eleanor herself heard him and she turned to me petulantly saying, 'Really Maya, I thought you had talked him out of all this nonsense!'

Stung to retaliate I said, 'He is upset by you and Mr Ackroyd quarrelling. It is bad for the child – there seems no permanence or stability in his life.' She merely glared at me balefully and stalked out of the room.

Matters came to a head two weeks before Easter, when Mr Ackroyd informed us he would not be in the following evening for dinner.

'I don't suppose it will inconvenience you,' he remarked gruffly. 'I have business in Leeds.'

Uninterestedly, Eleanor asked, 'Will you dine in Leeds or will you require something here later on?'

'I shall dine in Leeds.'

He left immediately after breakfast the next morning and Eleanor was like a caged bird suddenly released from captivity. She ordered the pony and trap to be brought to the front of the house and I watched her depart in a flurry of rain and blustery wind.

The long day stretched ahead of me and she had omitted to say if she would be back in time for dinner. I would always have preferred to eat off a tray in my room but more and more I realised that my presence in the dining room meant that real feelings had to be restrained. The outcome was that Eleanor remained silent, in a festering silence deadlier than words, and Mr Ackroyd turned to the bottle for solace.

Dusk came – and she had not returned. When night fell, it seemed to me that the house was alive with menace, just waiting for the right moment to erupt into terrifying reality. I saw Jamie safely settled into bed, and waited by his side for a while until I saw his eyelids close. There were dark shadows under his eyes and he seemed pale, as though the atmosphere of the house was already haunting him, and for the first time in months I left a nightlight burning on the mantelpiece.

I dawdled over my toilet, wishing I could simply ring for a tray and spend the rest of the evening curled up with a book, but I had not been excused dinner and reluctantly I left my room to go down to the dining room. The house was quiet . . . even the sounds from the kitchens seemed muffled but as I entered the dining room I could see that two places had been laid for dinner.

I hated the décor of the dining room with its ponderous furniture and rich, gloomy wallpaper. I could imagine Mr

Ackroyd's wicked old father holding court in this room. There was a painting of him hanging above the mantelpiece, a skinny, wispy-haired old man with a narrow skull and sharp piercing eyes over a long, thin, hooked nose. In the dim light it seemed to me that there was a bitter sneer on his thin lips and silently I agreed with Eleanor that the portrait was a monstrosity, a defilement of the wall which could have been put to better and more cheerful use.

Suddenly, I heard the opening of the front door and a blast of cold air crept beneath the dining room door. I had not heard the sound of the trap returning along the drive, but next moment the door was flung open and Mr Ackroyd stood glaring at me. His face was red, whether from hurrying in the wind or drinking I couldn't at first tell, but then I realised his voice was slurred as he came over to the table and leered into my face.

'Where is my lady wife Miss Wentworth?'

I could smell the whisky on his breath and I edged away from him. Jumping to my feet I stepped behind my chair but his hand came out to grip my wrist painfully.

'*I asked you where my wife was.*'

'I don't know, Sir. She went out early this morning.'

'You mean she's not returned?'

'I don't think so.'

I made myself meet his burning eyes bravely, and muttering to himself he dropped my wrist and turned unsteadily towards the door. My wrist was bruised with the marks of his fingers and I could feel my heart fluttering painfully in my breast. He stood beside the door uncertain what to do, and then with relief I heard the sound of hoofbeats on the drive and realised Eleanor was returning, driving the pony to the rear of the house where the stables were situated. Roger Ackroyd's gaze met mine and the sight of his narrowed gleaming eyes made me suddenly very afraid. I wanted to take to my heels and run out of the room, warn Eleanor not to enter the house but to drive away, anywhere out of his reach – but he stood between me and the door and I dared not move.

She came into the hall from the back of the house humming

139

cheerfully to herself and a cynical smile spread over his face. I wondered if she would come straight into the dining room, but instead I heard her running lightly up the stairs, well-pleased with herself.

In the quiet of the house we heard the distant closing of her bedroom door and then without another look in my direction he went out of the room and I heard his footsteps mounting the stairs. I stood still, my hands clenched against my breast. It seemed a lifetime before I heard the opening of a door then the sound of their voices. Almost immediately I heard Eleanor cry out with pain and I remembered that he had been wearing riding clothes and had carried a horsewhip in his hands . . .

Dinner was served to me but I do not know of what it consisted. All hunger had left me and I sat fearful and quiet while the food congealed on my plate and the vegetables grew cold in their silver tureens. A servant came to remove the dishes, sniffing fretfully when she saw that the food had not been touched.

I heard Mr Ackroyd descend the stairs unsteadily, then move across the hall in the direction of his study. He had been muttering to himself, but until I was sure that he was safely shut away in his study with the door closed I dare not leave the room. I paused for a moment outside Eleanor's room but all I could hear were the muffled sounds of her sobbing, then I went into Jamie's room.

The child was sitting up in bed, his eyes wide with fear, and he was trembling so that I gathered him into my arms to comfort him.

'You must go to sleep Jamie,' I said soothingly. 'There's nothing to be afraid of.'

'He was hitting my mother. I heard her screaming,' the boy said, his eyes searching mine for reassurance.

'She's not screaming now, Jamie. Would you like me to read to you?'

'No thank you, Maya. You can take away the nightlight. Peter and Nancy are here so I'm not afraid.'

I stayed with him for several minutes until I was sure that he felt relaxed and less frightened, then I went to my room. I couldn't sleep. I felt the dismal foreboding of something dreadful about to take place. I lay, watching the tracery of branches on the ceiling of my room, listening to the low moaning of the night wind in the trees outside my window and I resolved that the next day or the day after I would ask Sir Lyndon to help us. Even as the thought entered my head I stifled it. Wasn't the danger to my heart as powerfully potent as any danger from another source?

It was only just light when I washed in luke-warm water and dressed by the aid of a candle. It felt cold in my room and I was glad of the warmth of my robe as I hurried along to Jamie's room. I had slept only fitfully, my waking moments filled with the sounds of doors closing, muffled voices and before it was light, the sound of a horse's hooves galloping madly along the drive.

Jamie's bed was empty, the drawers of his dressing table and wardrobe flung wide. With dismay in my heart I ran along the corridor towards Eleanor's room, my first thoughts being that Mr Ackroyd had left the house and taken Jamie with him. To my relief I heard the child's voice inside his mother's room and I tapped tentatively on the door.

Jamie was already fully dressed and there was a pile of his clothing neatly folded inside a valise on her bed. Eleanor was wearing her robe but her face was tragically pale, her eyes wary and filled with a strange excitement.

'I am sending Jamie to Greythorn,' she said instantly. 'One of the grooms will take him.'

'One of the grooms!' I echoed, surprised.

'I have given Jamie a note to give to my brother asking if he can stay there until I can go for him.'

'Don't you think your brother will come here and demand to know what is going on?'

'He already knows what is going on. He will realise that matters have been precipitated, that is all.'

'Shouldn't I take Jamie to Greythorn?'

'No Maya, I need you here. You can leave later with us but I

141

can't stay another night under this roof.'

'Does Mr Ackroyd know that you are leaving him?'

'How could he know? He spent last night in his study, no doubt in a drunken stupor and this morning he left early.'

'Then he could come back at any time! What are you going to tell him?'

'He will be over at Bleasdale – there's trouble with some of the tenants. By the time he gets back, I want to be gone. Please Maya, do stop arguing and help me with these things.'

I stared at Jamie, sitting disconsolately on the edge of Eleanor's bed. He had that remote, faraway look on his face which I had come to dread. Already his mind was far removed from his mother's and father's problems and he was in that other world of his own imaginings. As though Eleanor sensed my worries she snapped, 'Jamie – do come alive darling. Maya will take you down to the stables and Mr Arthern will take you over to Greythorn. You know how much you will love that.'

'I don't want to go with Mr Arthern. Can't I go with you and Maya later?' he asked plaintively.

'No, darling, you are to go now. Maya and I are going to be very busy.'

Reluctantly I took Jamie down to the stables but already the pony was harnessed to the trap and waiting in the yard. I did not like Arthern the head groom. He was a man who usually looked at me with a sly, one-sided smile on his face, a man who missed nothing and kept very close to his employer. As he lifted Jamie into the trap he said pointedly, 'You're not comin' wi' us then, Miss Wentworth?'

'No. I have things to do here.'

'Ay well, t'little un'll be alright wi' me I reckon.'

'Yes. Thank you, Mr Arthern.'

I hugged Jamie, but he sat stiffly in the trap, not even bothering to turn his head as they drove out of the stableyard.

On my way back to Eleanor's room I saw her maid hurrying down the main staircase wearing her outdoor clothing. From the hall I watched her scuttling along the drive, her head bent against the wind and then she broke into a little run and I wondered where Janine could be going without transport. Puzzled, I returned to find Eleanor flinging her gowns onto the bed while a cabin trunk stood open on the floor.

'I should take most of them,' she said, half to herself. 'Heaven knows when I'll be able to buy such things again. If there's anything you want Maya, help yourself.'

'I can't take your gowns, Miss Eleanor.'

'Why ever not? I shan't be needing them, besides they could be out of place where we are going.'

'At Greythorn!' I exclaimed, surprised.

She stared at me helplessly, then sitting on the edge of her bed she said, 'I can see I shall have to tell you. I'm going away with Roland, possibly to Australia, and if you tell my husband or another living soul until we are gone I think I shall kill you.'

For a moment I stared at her in horrified silence, then unable to stop myself I cried, 'But what about Cora? Oh Miss Eleanor, you can't do this terrible thing, it will break her heart, she loves him so.'

'But I love him too, Maya. I loved him long before she did. I loved Roland when she was little more than a child, but what's more important, he loves me. He was desolate when I married Roger Ackroyd. I think he only got engaged to Cora to punish me, or to stay within the family, I don't know which.'

'Then it was cruel of him to use Cora in that way.'

'Yes it was cruel, but Roland hasn't had the monopoly on cruelty. It would be far more cruel if he were to marry Cora when he isn't in love with her – and in time she would come to feel it. Cora's young, she'll meet other men, men who don't love some other woman. You'll see Maya, in time all this will be for the best.'

'But what about Mr Ackroyd? He'll never let you get away with it.'

'I'll never live with him again. I'll never let him touch me again and if I thought he was going to bring me back I'd die before I let him take me. For Heaven's sake Maya – don't look so tragic. See what he did to me. Could you live with a man who did this to you?'

143

She dropped her robe off her shoulders and I gasped with horror at the blood-red weals that lay across her shoulders.

'He's beaten me before,' she said steadily, 'but he's never taken a whip to me until last night. I've sent Janine over to Roland's house asking him to come for me today, as quickly as possible. Neither of us had intended it to be like this, but you must see we have to go secretly before Roger has time to stop us!'

'He is capable of killing Roland when he knows.'

She stared at me mournfully. 'When he finds out, he is capable of killing both of us. I have always known of the savagery under the veneer. It is that same savagery that demanded a cruel and wicked price from my father. It was raw and evident in the father and the veneer that covers it in the son is only superficial.'

I shall never forget that day as Eleanor and I waited for the sound of Roland's carriage on the courtyard below her room. The hours dragged by painfully and every noise made us look up quickly, our eyes full of hope, only to be extinguished.

At times she paced relentlessly backwards and forwards, at others she stood looking down morosely at the long drive in front of the house. We heard the sound of the trap returning from Greythorn and Eleanor said, 'It has taken a long time to deliver one small boy to my brother's house. Who took him?'

'Arthern took him.'

'I don't trust that man. He is too close to my husband but I don't suppose he's had time to get a message over to Bleasdale.'

'You should have allowed me to take him.'

'You Maya, you with your wide-eyed innocence, Lyndon would have known immediately that something was afoot! Besides, you are in love with Lyndon are you not?'

I could feel the colour flaming in my face, feel my heart hammering as I rushed to deny it, but she was smiling gently. 'It doesn't matter, Maya. My brother is a man who always honours his obligations, and if he returned your love you would never know it. Melinda will never need fear his rejection or his betrayal.'

I could not answer her, for what she said was true – and guessing my pain she said, 'If Lyndon was more like me he would see the futility of his life with Melinda and at least he would try to salvage some semblance of happiness while there was yet time. However, if my father put stains upon the family name my brother will *not* do so. You can remain assured, my dear Maya, that your honour and his will remain intact.'

'Your brother does not love me Miss Eleanor, that is fantasy.'

'Of course, but a very sweet and tender fantasy and one you no doubt hug closely to your heart when you are lonely. I want no sweet and dreaming fantasies for myself, Maya. I must have the real thing or nothing.'

Again the restless pacing began, backwards and forwards across the space between the window and her bed, and in exasperation she snapped, 'Where can that girl have got to! Surely there has been time for Roland to get here.'

'It is a fair walk to Mr Carnwood's house from Seaten.'

I thought about Janine walking across the fell, battling with the wind and the clouds ominous and lowering, filled with rain. Eleanor too looked up at the sky knowing as well as I how treacherous the fells could be at this time of year.

She continued her pacing but I was thinking now of Eleanor having to endure Cora's outburst of grief and fury, when they called for Jamie at Greythorn. Suddenly my own plight dawned on me. With Jamie gone I would be without employment and the thought of returning to the vicarage and my old life there seemed like death itself. As if she read my thoughts, Eleanor said, 'Is it going to be very terrible, Maya? Can you bear to return to your uncle's house?'

'I don't know.'

'Oh well, he'll have you back I'm sure. You are just the innocent sufferer in the affairs of that wicked Mrs Ackroyd. He'll be able to sermonise about me for months, then perhaps they'll stop talking about that poor child Emily.'

'You knew about Emily?'

'Only from servants' gossip. Her sister worked at Greythorn for a time, and Emily is the one you brought up to the Hall before you went away to school – I remember her clearly.'

'Yes. She was my friend.'

'She was very pretty, at least my brother Gavin thought so. I remember him talking about her one evening over dinner, but even then my brother Lyndon maintained you would be the beautiful one later on.'

I stared at her, unable to believe that Lyndon would ever say such a thing, and she laughed a little at my confusion.

The rain struck the window like tinkling ice and Eleanor spun round with a frown on her face. 'Oh gracious, that's all we need,' she snapped. 'Get your things, Maya, there won't be much time when Roland arrives.'

'You are taking me with you?'

'Well of course! You don't think I would leave you here to face Roger's wrath alone, do you? See – I have written you a good reference in case you need to seek other employment, and there is one for Janine, too. I shan't need a maid where I am going.'

I ran to my room and hurriedly gathered my few belongings together. It only took a few minutes but by the time I arrived back in her room Roland's carriage was already pelting up the drive. I felt strangely excited by this race against time, watching anxiously as Roland jumped from the carriage followed by Janine who stood fearfully in the doorway.

I helped Roland carry the trunk downstairs while Janine cowered helplessly at the foot of the stairs. It took both of us to lift it onto the luggage place and by the time we returned to the house Janine was creeping fearfully up the stairs. I waited in the hall while Roland leapt up stairs calling urgently to Eleanor to hurry. I felt sick with terror in case something should happen at the last minute to prevent us leaving the house. Standing with the front door wide open, my feet prepared for flight, I heard the chiming of the grandfather clock in the library, unnaturally loud – until I realised with a sickening shock that the library door was open . . . Spinning round, I saw Roger Ackroyd standing in the doorway – looking steadily up the stairs.

Rooted to the spot, my mouth was dry with apprehension.

His face terrified me as no other person's face had terrified me before. There was sheer cruely in his expression . . . the sadistic cruelty of a cat playing with its victim before the kill. He never once looked in my direction and I watched him cross the hall and slowly, deliberately mount the stairs, then – as though unknown fingers suddenly snapped me out of my hypnotic state, I took to my heels and ran. I reached the stables in seconds to find Arthern about to unsaddle Roger Ackroyd's horse Indigo. In desperation I cried out, 'Leave him Arthern, I want him.'

He stared at me in dismay. 'Ye want 'im, miss? Ye'll never ride this black devil, an' that's fer sure!'

'Help me up Arthern, I've got to try.'

The horse had already been ridden hard and was sweating profusely. I had no thought of danger in these circumstances. Fear gave me the spur to ride a horse which normally I would have viewed with more than trepidation. In desperation, I urged him on and Indigo responded, galloping fiercely along the drive so that I wondered if I would ever be able to stop him.

I had to reach Greythorn Hall but as we raced across the fell the rain slanted in a steady downpour, drenching my clothes and saturating my hair, but I didn't care. I rode that horse as though the hounds of hell pursued us and I felt a sudden exhilaration fill my being. Assured that I had no fear of him, the horse was behaving beautifully, and I thanked God for his speed and his unerring instinct for a safe pathway through the deepening gloom.

Indigo was tiring as we entered the great iron gates and his spirit was almost subdued as we began the long gallop up to the house. Lights shone through the darkness but as I rode through the whispering glade towards the stables, grooms came as if from nowhere to lift me down and take the reins.

'Please care for the horse,' I gasped. 'I must see Sir Lyndon immediately!'

'But this is Mr Roger's 'orse miss! 'Ave yer ridden 'im all't way fro' Seaten?'

I didn't wait to answer but took to my heels and ran, gasping for breath, my heart beating painfully until I was able to hammer on the great front door of Greythorn Hall.

It was opened to me by a servant but almost immediately Lyndon was there, staring at me incredulously while I strove to regain my breath, and speak to him.

At last my story was told and thankfully he asked no questions, but issued commands. 'Stay here, Maya. I'll go to Seaten immediately.'

I followed him out into the rain, gasping that I must go back with him. Something of the urgency of my appeal made him take my arm so that we arrived at the stable running as though for our lives. 'Saddle the horses to the chaise!' he commanded, and then for the first time taking stock of my streaming hair and wet clothes he went inside one of the stables and came out with a long black riding cloak.

'Put this round your shoulders, Maya. It won't stop the damp but it will keep out the wind a little.'

We drove fast, and in silence. The horses were fresh and he guided them with expert skill along the narrow winding roads that climbed and dropped suddenly over stone bridges. We passed through the village of Buckley where people on the roadside turned to stare after us in the rain. Seaten stood stolidly beneath the Bleasdale fell, with the lights from Ackroyd House shining eerily through the gloom.

As we neared the house I could feel my heart hammering fearfully against my ribs. The front door stood wide open as I had left it and the rain had swept into the hall, falling like glistening globules on the polished floor.

I followed Sir Lyndon inside, both of us looking upwards into the darkness at the top of the stairs, but there were no sounds in the stillness. It was as though the house was a dead thing, a mausoleum . . .

Lyndon ran up the stairs but I waited below, until I became aware that Janine sat on a step, cowering against the balustrade, her face white, her lips shaking.

I ran to sit beside her but her face was vacant – she was unaware of my presence. I stood near her, looking helplessly into the darkness, paralysed by the dread in my heart.

I shall never know how long I waited there but after what seemed an eternity Lyndon came walking slowly down the stairs. In his arms he carried Eleanor, her head and arms hanging limply, lifelessly, and I knew that she was dead.

I shall never forget his face – stern, shaken with horror. Helplessly, I followed him into the drawing room. Tenderly he laid her on the couch and I saw then that the front of her gown was stained with blood. I met Lyndon's pain-filled eyes and asked with trembling voice, 'But how, how did she die?'

'She's been shot, killed instantly. Roland's dead too, both of them shot.'

Weakly I sat down in the nearest chair, unable to take my eyes off Eleanor's pale beautiful face and the spread of blood across her light green gown.

'I must search the house, Maya. Will you stay here?'

I nodded wordlessly. I heard him go out of the door and his footsteps crossing the hall but still my eyes were riveted on the gentle figure of the girl, who looked as though she could be sleeping if it had not been for that dark, telltale stain.

I heard the sudden closing of the library door and then Lyndon was back with me, his face pale. As our eyes met he said, 'He's dead too. His body is in the library, he kept the last bullet for himself.'

'What must we do now?' I asked wearily.

'I've sent one of the servants for the police. I found them huddled together in the kitchen – they heard the shots and were too terrified to come out.'

'At least Jamie is safe,' I murmured.

'Yes. I suspect he would have killed the child too if he'd still been here. Can you bear to go upstairs Maya, and take off those wet clothes? It will only add to our troubles if you catch pneumonia.'

I thought about my clothes packed away in my valise on the luggage rack of Roland's carriage and realised that the only other clothes I could change into were Eleanor's and I was too afraid to enter her room. When I explained this to Sir Lyndon he immediately said he would ask the housekeeper to get them for me and again I waited, my heart resigned and already familiar with death.

The police came. We kept guard beside the body of Eleanor while two stolid village policemen tramped round the house, their faces as horrified as our own. I could sense Lyndon's tension as we waited for them to return to us, the deep underlying hurt that this terrible tragedy would bring to his family pride and good name.

The local police could do nothing, but said they would make a full report and the next day no doubt officers from Leeds would arrive at Ackroyd House. Meanwhile, the rooms containing the bodies would be sealed but we ourselves were free to return to Greythorn.

It had stopped raining as we drove back across the fells and a pale crescent moon was shining fitfully between scudding clouds edged with silver. Lyndon drove automatically, his thoughts far removed from the rolling moors and the sleeping villages, and I sat beside him without speaking, aware that anything I might have said would have been an intrusion into his private grief.

The house was in darkness as he let us in through the front door and I guessed that all those inside would be already sleeping, unaware of the tragedy they would have to face in the morning. In the study Lyndon poured out a glass of brandy, commanding me to drink it, informing me that I should occupy the room I had had during my previous stay at Greythorn. I waited at the foot of the stairs while he lit five candles standing in a tall silver candelabra, then with his hand under my elbow we ascended the stairs together. He walked with me to my room, looking round it with a slight frown on his face.

'It feels cold in here Maya, but fortunately the fire has been laid.' Leaning down, he applied one of the flames from the candles to it and soon we heard the cheerful crackle of logs catching fire, filling the dark room with a warm glow and an elusive, fragrant scent. He pulled the curtains and lit the lamp and then after a brief look round the room he said, 'I don't suppose you will get much sleep Maya, but the brandy will help. We shall need to talk some more about the events of today but I think that for the moment we have both probably had enough.'

I nodded wordlessly. I was standing very close to him, only too aware of the powerful feelings he aroused in me. I was staring at him with wide troubled eyes, seeing his mouth edged with pain and the bemused look in his eyes as they stared down into mine, then bending his head he lightly brushed my lips with his. It was over so quickly, that brief fleeting caress, and yet I could feel it still and instinctively my arms reached out to him and as he gathered me close into his embrace I could feel his heart thudding against mine. Our lips clung together with warm passionate intensity and if I never felt it again I knew it then, the hunger, and the anguish and the power of love.

He wanted me as I wanted him, but suddenly he thrust me away from him.

'No, Maya. *No*,' he said firmly. 'This isn't for either of us. I need your help but I have no right to ask for your love.'

'My help?' I echoed stupidly.

'Your very necessary help, my darling – have you forgotten Cora and Jamie?'

Of course I had forgotten them. I had forgotten Eleanor and Roland, I had even forgotten Lyndon's wife, and he was gripping my hands in his until something of his strength brought me slowly to my senses.

'Forget what has happened tonight, Maya. Think if you like that it was only the aftermath of the terrible tragedy we have shared today. Tomorrow it will all start again, the questions, the insinuations and we shall both need to be strong for Cora's sake and Jamie's.'

THIRTEEN

IT SEEMED ONLY a few hours before I was back at Ackroyd House the next morning. There were policemen tramping through the grounds, and holding inquisitions in the darkly curtained rooms. They questioned me about the events leading up to the tragedy and I answered them truthfully, meeting the Inspector's eyes calmly. I had nothing to hide.

Janine wept copiously, her broken English incoherent until in the end Lyndon said testily, 'The girl can tell you nothing more and it is obvious she is distraught! Can't we allow her to leave?'

'We have to establish the facts, Sir,' the Inspector said calmly.

'I'm aware of that, but surely it is obvious that Roger Ackroyd killed his wife and Roland Carnwood and then took his own life.'

Now came the questions about their relationships and I could see that every query was like a knife-wound in Lyndon's proud heart.

The affair filled the newspapers and it was obvious that the North Riding was shaken by the catastrophe that had overtaken one of its noblest families. The villagers from miles around stood outside Greythorn Hall staring dismally through the railings of the closed gates, or peering over the top of the stone walls that edged the grounds. Visitors came and went, the police and old friends, businessmen and magistrates and then too came the clergy. My heart sank when I recognised my uncle's trap in the courtyard one day and I realised he was probably adding his condolences along with the others.

I was surprised when a maidservant came to tell me my uncle wished to see me and I followed her down the stairs and into the study where my uncle sat opposite Sir Lyndon.

'Come in Maya, and sit down,' Sir Lyndon greeted me, while my uncle looked at me over the top of his glasses with ill-disguised curiosity.

'I have come to convey your aunt's and my own condolences Maya,' he began pompously. 'I hope you will make yourself useful to Sir Lyndon whilst you are here.'

'Maya is very necessary to me,' Sir Lyndon said haughtily. 'She is taking care of Jamie. The child needs some sort of stability in his life and there is no one better able to provide it than Maya.'

'Will the child continue to live here, Sir Lyndon?' my uncle asked.

'Well, of course! Where else would the boy live?'

'I only wondered if he would go away to school, in which case Maya would no longer be required here. Not immediately of course, Sir, but when all this tragic business has been sorted out.'

'These are early days yet, Edisford. I cannot say what is going to happen – all I can tell you is that you will be consulted about your niece's future.'

'Yes of course, Sir, I understand perfectly.'

Sir Lyndon rose to his feet and stood beside his desk inviting my uncle to leave. Instead, my uncle queried the funeral arrangements while I squirmed with embarrassment.

'If there is anything I can do in my capacity as vicar of Lexford with regard to the funeral arrangements I shall be only too willing to assist, Sir Lyndon,' he said obsequiously.

'That is very civil of you but arrangements are already in hand for when the police give their permission for the funerals to take place.'

'Might I ask where they will be, Sir Lyndon?'

'My sister will be interred in the family vault at Buckley.

153

Mr Ackroyd will no doubt be buried beside his father and Mr Carnwood's relatives will make their own arrangements, that is all I can tell you at this stage. Now if you will excuse me, Edisford, I have a great deal to do and time is short.'

'Yes, yes, Sir, of course. I must not detain you further but I simply wished to be reassured about Maya here.'

A servant came to show him out but I remained in the study waiting to be dismissed. I sensed Lyndon's exasperation. There was a slight frown on his face as his hands played nervously with the pen lying on his desk and my heart went out to this proud man beleaguered by the effects of scandal and death. As though he sensed my sympathy he smiled sadly, saying, 'Didn't I tell you what it would be like, Maya? All those prying eyes whenever I leave the house, the whisperings of servants round every corner – the lifted curtains whenever I drive through the village street . . . it will go on until they have exhausted every last traumatic detail, every sensual, sadistic titbit of gossip they can assemble. It will touch us all – there is not a single one of us that can escape from it.'

'It could hurt Jamie most of all.'

'Of course. In time he will go away to school and children are naturally cruel. Can you imagine what it will be like for him there when the other boys get to know about his mother and father, and get to know they surely will. This family is too prominent for him to escape.'

'I was afraid for Eleanor. I knew she was meeting Roland, I could see nothing only tragedy in it but I hoped she would realise for herself what might be the outcome.'

'My sister could never see danger, not even when it stared her in the face. She did everything dangerously, thoughtlessly, wildly – but she had great courage and generosity. There was never anything petty about Eleanor.'

'And she was so beautiful. Men would always have loved her.'

'Yes, but beauty is not always a gift to be prized. Sometimes it can be a curse, a thing to be shunned for the sorrow it can bring.'

'May I ask if you have told Cora everything?'

'Yes, everything. There was nothing I could hide for she would have probed and pried to get at the truth if she thought I had tried to keep something back.'

'Oh poor Cora, how terrible for her.'

He stared at me strangely. 'She didn't speak, not one single word. She sat perfectly still until I had told her everything, then she simply rose to her feet and left the room. There were no tears, no screams of anger, nothing at all. Can you understand that, Maya?'

'I think so. I couldn't cry for my parents or for any of the things that were lost to me. It is an agony worse than tears, worse than death. For years after my parents died I longed to weep, I longed to show emotion and scream my agony to the world but I couldn't. It was as though somewhere in my mind there was a gigantic dam and although I pounded with my fists to break it the dam held. There are times when I wonder if it will ever break and my emotions raw and bleeding will be set free.'

There was sympathy in his face, an understanding so rare I longed to run to him and feel again the warmth of his embrace but there was also an invisible line of restraint that I dared not pass.

'Perhaps in a few days you will feel like visiting Cora,' he said. 'In the meantime she is not eating, her tray is being sent back untouched and if this continues I shall have to call the doctor in. She keeps her door locked and I am not sure how long she can sustain this withdrawal.'

'I will go to see her certainly, but I am worried about Jamie. How soon should he be told about his parents?'

'He knows something is wrong, of course?'

'I'm not sure. He seems to have retreated once more into his imaginary world of make-believe figures. I don't seem to be able to reach him.'

'Be patient Maya, as yet it is early days.'

Jamie was sitting on the window seat staring through the window when I arrived back in the nursery. I joined him there and saw again the crowd of villagers sitting on the wall or peering through the gates. Angrily I wondered why the police didn't move them on and I tried to get Jamie to leave the window and return to his books.

'Why are all the people staring at the house?' he asked quietly.

'Villagers are always curious, Jamie. They don't like to miss anything.'

'My mother didn't come, did she?'

'No dear, but you are quite happy living in Uncle Lyndon's house.'

'Oh yes. She won't come now – Nancy says she will never come now.'

'Nancy seems to know a great deal, Jamie. She isn't always right, you know.'

'She's right about my mother. She is dead, isn't she?'

I stared at him anxiously. He was stating it in such a matter of fact voice! I could not believe he could view his mother's death without emotion and I shivered in spite of the warmth of the room. Who were these strange imaginary children who could talk to him about the death of his mother and have him believe it?

'My mother is dead *isn't she Maya?*' he insisted, and sitting down beside him I drew him into my embrace.

'Yes, Jamie she is, your father too, but you must be very brave, Uncle Lyndon will look after you and I am here.'

He nodded his head in a strangely satisfied way then in that same matter of fact voice he said, 'I suppose my father killed her?'

'Why do you say that?' I asked him, startled.

'I heard him say that one day he would kill her. I used to sit on the stairs outside their room and I knew he was beating her. I hated him, I shall always hate him.'

'Oh Jamie no, you mustn't let hatred eat into your heart. One day when you are older you will understand better. Your father was a terribly unhappy man, and how can we tell what feelings drove him to do what he did.'

He was staring at me with his eyes wide open and I realised I was speaking to him as an adult when he was really only a frightened child.

'Why do the police keep coming to the house?' he asked quietly, almost as though he no longer wished to discuss the deaths of his parents.

'They have business with Uncle Lyndon. Jamie – would you like to walk in the park? We could wrap up warmly against the wind and we don't need to go near the edge of the park. Suppose we walk down to the stables?'

He nodded, getting off his seat and walking towards the wardrobe where his coat was kept.

I put a warm woollen scarf around his neck and a similar one round mine. The spring winds were treacherous across the moors and our catching cold was the last thing I wanted. We left the house by the side entrance and set off walking briskly towards the glade.

I could see one or two of the onlookers pointing at us and I knew we were under discussion, but keeping my face resolutely turned in the direction we were going we reached the glade and there the sightseers were hidden from our view.

The leaves were only beginning to uncurl on the beeches and some of the branches still reached up starkly towards the grey sky. The wind moaned dismally along the glade but there were no voices and Jamie held my hand tighter and his small face grew pinched and white. I was wishing we had taken another route when he said, 'Isn't this the glade where the voices come?'

'There aren't any voices, Jamie. It is only the wind in the trees.'

'My mother said there were voices, she'd heard them, and Aunt Cora said she'd heard them many times. Haven't you heard them?'

'No. As I said, it is only the wind in the trees.'

'Who is the lady who walks in the glade? I've seen her many times and sometimes she comes to the house and stands looking up at the windows.'

'Perhaps it's one of the servants Jamie, I can't think of anyone else.'

'She's pretty, very pretty, and she has red hair.'

I stared at him. There was something uncanny about this child and the people of his imagination. He spoke of them as if they were real and I found it difficult to know the difference between real people and the elusive wraiths.

'I don't know anybody like that, Jamie.'

'She's sad, very sad.'

I thought of the girl Cora had told me had drowned on the eve of her wedding and I shivered slightly. If anybody could conjure up her sad wandering ghost it would be Jamie, but catching hold of his hand in a tighter grip I started to run. 'Come on, Jamie! If we run we shall be much warmer – I'll race you to the stables!'

We found Gavin there, with a groom saddling up his horse. He turned round at our entrance and a slow grin spread over his face.

'Well, hello,' he said. 'I knew you were back at the house but I thought Lyndon had hidden you away somewhere.'

'I thought a walk would do us both good. Jamie wants to look at the horses.'

'Why not come for a ride? It's a good afternoon for horse-riding.'

'We're not dressed for it.'

'Oh, Jamie can manage one of the ponies and you can ride side-saddle in that skirt. You'd like that, wouldn't you Jamie?'

Jamie's face lit up with eagerness so reluctantly I allowed Gavin to lead out a pony while I watched them saddle up Cora's horse, a gentle, soft-eyed mare, entirely predictable.

'I don't wish to ride through the gates Gavin. Those people would only stare at us and it isn't fair to the child.'

'I see your point. We'll ride up on the fells behind the house – I don't suppose there'll be many of them up there! They're too frightened of missing anybody going through the front gates.'

I enjoyed the ride, my first since that mad headlong gallop on Roger's black stallion and Jamie too seemed happier as he rode his pony in front of us.

'You have the makings of a fine horsewoman,' Gavin complimented me. 'You sit a horse well and you have style. We must do this more often.'

'I am here to teach Jamie and to spend as much time with him as possible. I'm afraid there won't be much opportunity for riding.'

'Riding is part of his education and Lyndon won't allow him to neglect it. I heard all about your mad dash here on the night of the tragedy.'

My eyes cautioned him to silence but he merely smiled, saying, 'The boy won't hear us, he's too far in front. What do you make of it all?'

'What do you mean?'

'I mean Eleanor and Roland, Roger too if you like.'

'I should have thought it was evident, and really I don't want to discuss it.'

'Are you always the proper unemotional schoolmistress, Maya? Don't you ever feel like tilting your hat at windmills or throwing caution to the winds?'

'No, I can't say that I do.'

'Then you are going to miss an awful lot in life. What do you want out of it anyway – you must have some ideas?'

'Well, of course I have but I don't see why I should tell *you* what they are.'

'Let me guess, then. You want to teach children, other people's children, then perhaps one day if you can find a proper young curate you'll settle down to a life of good works and church three times on Sunday. You'll devote your life to helping him rise to prominence in the church and you'll probably end up by being a good and loyal Bishop's wife. I think that's what you want for yourself Maya, but you'll never ever have had any fun.'

'And you, Gavin, talk a lot of nonsense which is all a very long way from the truth.'

'You haven't told me what you thought about the shootings.'

'Oh surely you must know what I thought – that it was all a terrible, tragic and bitter waste of three lives!'

'But in that moral and praiseworthy little soul of yours didn't you also see it as an inevitable retribution?'

'I saw it as no such thing. I'm going after Jamie. I don't want him to get too far in front.'

I spurred the mare on, hearing his laughter behind me before he too began to gallop, easily catching up with me.

'Do you eat all alone in the nursery night after night?' he enquired, laughing impudently across at me.

'I usually eat with Jamie. I'm not a guest at Greythorn Hall, I'm an employee.'

'You mean Lyndon didn't invite you to dine with us, not even during that mad impulsive drive across the fells? I consider that was very remiss of him. What do you do all evening shut away up there?'

'I mark Jamie's books and read. I enjoy reading.'

'Of course, but books are no compensation for real people, and Cora's shut away in her room playing out her faithless lover, forsaken maiden act.'

'As I said, I don't look to the family for entertainment, and Cora could benefit from your sympathy instead of your derision.'

'It's very difficult to sympathise through a locked door!'

'Perhaps she would open it if she believed you wanted to be kind.'

'She hasn't opened it for Lyndon or for Melinda. Why don't you try? After all, you were living at Ackroyd House, you must have been aware of what was going on!'

'I think we should go back now. Jamie hasn't ridden this far before and it's getting late.'

Obligingly he turned his horse round to ride back with us but I stayed beside Jamie, feeling I had had quite enough of Gavin's taunts for one day. Jamie's cheeks were pink and there was a happier light in his eyes than I had seen of late.

The ride across the fell had tired Jamie and I could see he was sleepy as we ate our evening meal together. The long night stretched ahead of me and although it was snug and warm in the nursery with the curtains drawn and the fire blazing in the hearth I grew impatient with my book, surprised that Gavin's taunts came to interfere with my reading.

I found myself thinking about Cora, shut away behind her locked door. Next morning, plucking up my courage I went out of my room and down to the bedrooms below. I was just in time to see one of the servants coming along the corridor with her tray, so putting myself in front of her I said, 'Is the tray for Miss Cora?'

'Yes, Miss,' the girl replied.

'Then perhaps I might take it. I'll knock on the door and ask if she will let me in.'

The girl looked at me out of wide brown eyes. She was a country lass from one of the nearby villages and I guessed her mind was already eaten up with morbid curiosity and horror at the events of the last few days.

She allowed me to take the tray, but in a gloomy voice she said, 'Eh Miss, she wouldn't open't door fer't master, I can't think she'll open it fer you.'

'Well, I can but try. If she won't let me in I'll return the tray to the kitchens.'

I could see that she wanted to accompany me to Cora's door in order to see what success I had, but after a brief smile I said, 'What is your name?'

'Gertrude, Miss.'

'Well, Gertrude, I suggest you go back to the kitchens and I'll take the tray and see what happens.'

She watched me walk down the corridor and waited, I have no doubt, to hear if I was admitted into Cora's room.

I knocked gently on the door and waited but I could hear nothing from inside the room so I knocked again, this time trying the handle of the door. It was locked of course but I called out to her, 'Cora! It's Maya, please open the door. We have so much to talk about.'

'Go away, Maya,' she called to me. 'I don't want to see anybody and I don't want anything to eat.'

'But you *must* eat Cora. Besides, I can tell you more than anybody else about those last few days at Seaten.'

I knew I could tell her very little that she didn't already know but I was relying on her curiosity being powerful enough to make her open the door for me.

I stood with my ear against the door, listening for any sounds from within. In a few moments I was rewarded by the creak of a chair and the soft fall of a foot on the heavy carpet. Then to my relief I heard the key turn slowly in the lock and the door opened just a fraction.

It was dark in the corridor and I couldn't see her, but using all my strength and carrying the tray before me I pushed the door wider and before she could stop me I was in the room.

Taken by surprise she leaned back against the wall and I stared at her in horrified silence. Her gaunt face surrounded by lank, lacklustre hair seemed to have aged by forty years. There were dark circles round her sunken eyes and a wave of pity swept over me for this girl who had suffered silently and alone. I placed the tray on a small table near the door then I stepped forward to take her into my arms, but she moved quickly to stand behind a chair.

There was anger in her face. 'Don't touch me,' she cried. 'I thought you were my friend but you knew all the time what was happening. You knew but you never told me.'

I stared at her in anguish, and she was quick to follow up her accusation with other words so unfair they left me speechless.

'You *knew* Maya – but you never said a word to me or to Eleanor. You could have stopped it happening. Why, *oh why* didn't you tell me, and now it's too late!'

Weakly I sat down on the edge of the chair and all the time her eyes blazed down at me, hating me, blaming me.

She moved over to the window and stood with her back to me looking out across the park, but I felt her anger like a living thing between us. It seemed like an eternity before I could gather my thoughts into some form of normality, giving me the courage to leave my chair and join her at the window.

'I knew Roland called to see Eleanor, Cora, but I didn't know they planned to go away together, not until that morning. Besides, I was only a governess in Eleanor's house, I had no right to question either her morals or tell

162

her which friends she might have calling upon her.'

'So you decided to say nothing! You watched me preparing for my wedding knowing that he was spending more time with her than with me.'

'But I didn't know for sure. On that morning I asked her to think what she was doing, both to you and to her marriage but she was distraught. Roger had taken a whip to her the night before and all she could say was that she had loved Roland first, while you were still a child. I had no answer to the things she was telling me and my main concern was for Jamie.'

'Jamie!' she repeated dully, as though she had only just thought of him.

'Yes, of course. Jamie too has suffered. He has lost both his mother and his father. If your world has crashed about your ears, so has Jamie's.'

She sank down on the window seat and I watched the varying emotions cross her face. I wished she could cry. Tears would have brought that pent-up release that lay close to the surface and I knew how she hurt and ached inside. I too had longed for tears but they had been denied me, and sitting down beside her I put my arm around her shoulders, silently urging her to tears.

Then I watched them flow down her face, felt her shoulders heave with sobs, but in the end she was calm and some of the strain had left her face.

'You think you will never get over it Cora,' I told her gently, 'but you will. In time the pain will go, believe me. You will never wholy forget or even perhaps forgive, but you are still young and there will be some other man for you, someone who is kind and who loves you and only you. I told Jamie not to nurse his bitterness, or his hatred for his father, I can only beg you to try to do the same, otherwise it could destroy you.'

'I am already destroyed.'

'That isn't true, Cora. You have your family who love you and you are so young. All life is before you.'

'I would like to see Jamie.'

'Then you shall. Come to the nursery as often as you like and in time we can go for long walks together or ride over the moors.

Jamie will respond to your affection, he's a little boy crying out for love. I worry about him when his best friends are those he manufactures.'

'Why did you bring the tray in?'

'I waylaid one of the servants coming along the corridor. Try to eat something Cora, otherwise I must take it back to the kitchens untouched and they will think I have had no more success than they.'

She looked at the tray without enthusiasm, but in the end I encouraged her to eat a little cheese and drink the coffee. Then I waited while she bathed and changed her gown.

'I look terrible,' she said, staring into the mirror.

'Well, of course you do, but in a few days when you've eaten and slept better you'll be fine. My aunt Miranda says the young are very resilient and I'm sure she's right. Would you like me to do your hair?'

She nodded, and after brushing it and tying it back from her face with a watered silk ribbon she began to look more like herself.

'I'll return the tray to the kitchen now Cora, then Jamie and I are going to walk on the fells. Why not come with us?'

'Perhaps I will. I'll wait for you in the nursery.'

I felt decidedly more cheerful as I returned the tray, and particularly so when the housekeeper congratulated me on encouraging her to eat something.

'I thought the poor girl would worry herself into an early grave Miss, that I did,' she said looking at the tray to see what had been eaten. 'She hasn't eaten much that's for sure, but it's a start. We have to be thankful for small mercies.'

Cora was already in the nursery when I returned there. She was sitting at the table with Jamie chatting quite normally while he showed her his painting book, and a little later we set off across the park. There were still plenty of villagers standing around the stone walls surrounding the park and Cora stared at them disdainfully.

'Why don't they go to their homes?' she said. 'What are they expecting to see?'

'I don't suppose they care, they just don't want to miss anything.'

I didn't want to mention the funeral. I thought any word of that should come from Sir Lyndon or another member of her family, and Cora herself didn't speak of it. I knew that they were waiting for the police to say it could take place, and my own personal view was that Cora should not be expected to attend. I was glad when she asked no questions about it but as we approached the glade she said, 'I knew something terrible was going to happen, that night I heard the voices. They were so strong I was frightened by them.'

Jamie was listening to her with great wide eyes and a curious intensity in his stare.

'There aren't any voices Cora! It is only the wind in the trees,' I said stoutly.

'You would never hear them,' she said shortly, 'only the family hears them, and besides, none of the Gaynor women are meant to know real happiness.'

'You mustn't think like that Cora, it's not true.'

'It is true. Look at my mother, she was only thirty when she died and Eleanor's mother was only thirty-two. Look at Melinda and Eleanor and me. None of us have been happy, and we shall all die young, I know it.'

I was wishing I hadn't asked her to come. She was morbidly miserable and Jamie was sensitive enough to be influenced by her mood. I found myself searching for happier things to talk about but I soon realised that Cora and Jamie were walking together in their own private world and I felt shut out and unwanted.

As we reached the stile that led from the park to the fell we saw Sir Lyndon and Gavin riding towards us and I was glad that Lyndon showed no surprise at the sight of Cora, but greeted us as though it was our common practice to walk together across the park. Not so Gavin however, who greeted his sister with the words, 'Well, well! So you've finally decided to enter the world of the living.'

She ignored him and I gave him a look intended to stop him

165

from making further snide remarks while Lyndon changed the subject abruptly by asking if I would dine with the family that evening.

I thanked him quietly and then looked away quickly in order to avoid Gavin's amused smile.

'I shall dine in my room,' Cora said. 'I don't see why I should be expected to put up with Gavin's peculiar sense of humour.'

'You need company Cora,' Lyndon said sharply. 'I believe you are adult enough to ignore your brother's snide remarks and he is surely mature enough not to make them.'

For once Gavin had the grace to remain silent but Cora's face hardened mutinously. 'Perhaps I should dine with Jamie since we are partners in adversity, in any case, it will relieve Maya as she is eating with you.'

Lyndon frowned but decided not to answer and turing their horses they rode off down the hillside. I suddenly found that I didn't want Cora to spend the evening with Jamie. The child was imaginative and in Cora's mood I believed she would be bad for him. However, I was in no position to do much about it and she quite deliberately informed the servant who brought us afternoon tea that she would be dining with Jamie in the nursery later that evening.

I called in to see them on my way downstairs but they barely acknowledged my presence. They were sitting together at the table with a book spread out in front of them but somehow I didn't think they were reading. Normally Jamie would have greeted me with his warm smile but now he merely stared at me with wide, troubled eyes.

'You will see him into bed Cora?' I said. 'No later than eight o'clock. I'll call in later on my way to my room.'

'I'm quite capable of looking after Jamie, Maya, you fuss too much. After all, you are here to teach him, not to act as a nursemaid.'

I felt hurt and strangely rebuked. It seemed as though overnight Cora had changed from someone whom I had regarded as a friend into a grim, uncompromising stranger. I turned away, closing the nursery door quietly behind me. Cora had suffered, was still suffering and I should be forgiving and understanding but still the doubts persisted, making me more troubled than I had ever been at Ackroyd House.

I had not seen Melinda at close quarters since Lyndon brought me back to Greythorn but that evening I noticed a subtle change in her. She seemed more fragile than before but she greeted me warmly.

I had never been blessed with a great many clothes and I was wearing a dress my aunt had had run up for me in the village. For once I had chosen the material myself although my uncle had deplored the colour. It was scarlet, the colour of the Devil he had said, but I knew it suited my colouring and the village seamstress had good fingers so that it fitted me well.

'How pretty you look in that colour!' Melinda said graciously. 'It lights up your face and complements that lovely black hair of yours.'

I thanked her shyly but just then Lyndon and Gavin joined us and the talk became general. I found Gavin's eyes on me and there was admiration in them which brought the rich red blood into my cheeks. Lyndon on the other hand seemed preoccupied and Melinda asked sympathetically, 'I suppose the watchdogs are still at the gates and round the walls?'

'Yes, although what they hope to see now I can't imagine.'

'We could ask them to move,' Gavin said.

'A better plan is to ignore them I think,' Lyndon answered him. 'We shall have to get used to living in a fish bowl until after the funeral which I hope will be soon. I take it Cora is with Jamie?' he said, looking directly at me.

'Yes, Sir Lyndon. She insisted.'

'And you are not too happy about the arrangement?'

'Not entirely. Cora is unhappy, desperately unhappy, and I know how susceptible Jamie is to atmosphere.'

'Then we mustn't let her make a habit of it. I am grateful Maya that you made her leave her room – it is a start at any rate.'

'Perhaps she should go away for a time,' Melinda said. 'A holiday abroad perhaps or a few weeks with Aunt Lettie in Devonshire.'

'Aunt Lettie is too old to cope with Cora's depression and I'm not sure that a holiday abroad alone would help her. Somehow or other Cora has always been a problem.'

'She was always a problem to Eleanor,' Gavin said with a mischievous light in his eyes. 'First with her health, then with her penchant for coveting Eleanor's lovers.'

'Lovers!' Lyndon snapped, raising his eyebrows.

'Admirers then, whatever you like to call them. I always suspected that Eleanor was never particularly chaste.'

'Eleanor is dead,' Lyndon said, and this time he was angry and Melinda too was looking at Gavin with disapproval on her calm lovely face.

'All right – so Eleanor is dead! That surely doesn't turn her into a saint,' Gavin retorted.

'It entitles her to the loyalty of her family. The dead have no facilities for defending themselves,' Lyndon snapped.

I was wishing I was miles away, and as if he read my thoughts Lyndon said, 'I'm sure Maya doesn't wish to sit through our arguments. It would be nice if you remembered that we have a guest, Gavin, and deport yourself accordingly.'

Gavin gave a small mocking bow in my direction, but just then a servant came into the room and whispered something to Lyndon who immediately rose from his chair. 'I must ask you to excuse me,' he said. 'The Inspector is here about the funeral. I am not very hungry, ask them to leave some cheese out for me.'

Gavin was the first to break the silence that followed on Lyndon's departure. 'He's very touchy tonight,' he commented. 'It's a bit of a devil if we can't say what we think any more.'

'Your remarks were in bad taste, Gavin, particularly at this time,' Melinda said, and favouring his sister-in-law with that same mocking bow he said, 'I stand corrected, then. I was merely making conversation but I'll be glad when all this is over and done with and we can act normally again. How do you feel about coming riding in the morning Maya, with or without Jamie?'

'I feel that Jamie should attend to his lessons. There is plenty of time to go riding when those people have moved away from the gates.'

'She rides very well, Melinda. Didn't Lyndon tell you?' he said, smiling across at her.

Melinda sipped her wine, all the time looking at him coolly but I feared his audacity and wondered what he would say next. I was not left long in doubt.

'Did you know Melinda that she rode Roger Ackroyd's stallion all the way from Seaten, in driving rain across the fells with never a thought for her own safety? I'd think twice before I rode Indigo, he's got the temper of the devil, pure vice he is.'

'Then we must congratulate Maya on her spirit and her courage,' Melinda answered him calmly.

'Oh, we must do all of those things, but you didn't ride him back, did you Maya? Had you had enough or was it much cosier in the chaise with Lyndon?'

Stung to anger I retorted, 'You know why I rode him, Gavin, and you know why we returned in the chaise. I'm sure Lady Gaynor is bored by all this talk about my prowess on Mr Ackroyd's horse.'

'But you're not, are you Melinda? Melinda likes to hear about horses, she loves horses, always has done, isn't that so Melinda?'

How I hated him at that moment. Melinda, who had once loved horses and who could never ride again, it was pitiless to hurt her in this way. She seemed not to mind however, and smiling gently she said, 'I am not bored Gavin, indeed I am always delighted to hear about those who ride well. I once did so myself.' She turned to me with a faint half-smile on her lips saying, 'Gavin is like a small spoilt boy who must always be the centre of attraction. If he can't be so naturally and kindly, he resorts to other methods regardless of whom he might injure in the process.'

'Oh – and who am I trying to hurt now, not my dear sister-in-law for whom I have the highest regard, nor our beautiful guest who cares for me not at all. Who *do* you care for Maya? Who has the power to make those beautiful eyes grow dreamy, that

169

stormy mouth grow tender. Is it that young curate over at Lexford or brother Lyndon in that mad dash in the moonlight?'

I felt my face burning with colour but I made myself eat calmly, not caring to look at either of them.

Gavin leaned across the table and poured some more wine into my glass. 'You're not saying anything Maya,' he said provocatively.

'I don't consider that your remarks require an answer. They are infantile and uncalled-for and I agree with Lady Gaynor that you are a spoilt and wilful child who should have been punished long ago. It is possibly now too late.'

He threw back his head and laughed. 'Oh, Maya Wentworth I love you! I wish it had been I who rode with you in the chaise that night.'

'And I am more than relieved that it was not.'

Fortunately we were saved from further sarcasm by the arrival of Lyndon. I thought he looked at Gavin sharply but I could not be sure, and then he was telling us that the police had given permission for the funerals to take place in two days' time.

'I shall be glad when it's all over and behind us,' Lyndon said. 'Now it will start up all over again, the talk and the conjecture, too many tongues wagging and saying nothing they are sure of, too much forced sympathy and too much eagerness to be the first with any titbit of scandal they can get hold of. At least the funeral will be private – surely they will grant us that much?'

For a few moments Melinda's hand rested lightly on his, answered by his look of affection at the sympathy she extended How I wished it was my hand that could rest upon his, and how I longed for his eyes to look into mine with that yearning I had seen in them all too briefly.

Immediately after dinner I excused myself on the grounds of wanting to look in on Jamie. Lyndon and Gavin both rose to their feet to bid me good night and Melinda said, 'One day when all this is over Maya, perhaps you would play for me again. I no longer ride or even walk very far, but listening to music is something I can truly enjoy.'

'I shall be glad to play for you, Lady Gaynor,' I answered and after a brief smile I escaped from the room.

The nursery was in darkness and not bothering to light the lamp standing on the table I moved instinctively towards the window, pulling the curtains wide so that the pale moonlight could illuminate the room. The room was tidy. Jamie's books lay in a neat pile on the table and his painting folder had been put away. I walked across to the door leading into his bedroom but all I could hear were the gentle sounds of his breathing. Quietly I opened the door to find the room in total darkness. Since we had came to Greythorn I had always left a nightlight burning in his room because he had seemed afraid. The night-light was always kept on the table beside his bed but I had to grope my way there in the darkness and long before I reached it a small frightened voice said, 'Who is that? Please go away.'

I found the saucer with the nightlight on it and soon I had its small flickering light shining palely through the gloom. Jamie was sitting up in bed, his face pale and haunted, straining as far back against the wall as it was possible for him to get.

'It's all right, darling, it's me, Maya. Why didn't you ask them to leave the nightlight burning?'

'Aunt Cora said I was far too old for a nightlight. You won't turn it out, will you?'

'No, of course not. What did you do with Cora? Did she read to you?'

'No, we just talked.'

'You talked for a very long time then. What did you talk about?'

'She wanted to know about Nancy and Peter and then she told me about the lady who walks in the glade and the voices she has heard. She told me about the other lady too, the pretty one with the red hair.'

I stared at him, puzzled. Cora had no right to fill his mind with her imaginary people and expect him to talk about his own. I didn't want her to become a feature in Jamie's life, particularly now when she was sad and embittered but I did not know how I was going to prevent it. I waited, sitting on the edge

171

of his bed until I was sure he was fast asleep, then I left him, pulling the door quietly shut behind me.

Jamie was so young. I wondered if Lyndon would expect him to attend his mother's funeral and I could not think that Cora would be there . . .

FOURTEEN

ON THE MORNING of the funeral, Cora stated emphatically that it was her intention to stay away and that she would spend her time with Jamie. Consequently, I was free to attend, if I so wished.

The service was short and without the usual lengthy speeches extolling the qualities of the deceased, and soon we stood beneath the elms in the tiny churchyard at Buckley. The church was nothing like as large as my uncle's but it was prettier, and the churchyard itself not nearly so rambling. There was a feeling of rain in the air and a chill little wind set the daffodil heads swaying and filled the air with a sickly perfume from the profusion of floral tributes that lay all around us. Contrary to Lyndon's hopes, the churchyard and the lanes outside were thronged with people but members of the family were sparse. Only Lyndon, Gavin and a distant cousin stood before the doors of the family vault and I was glad that Lyndon had said that there had already been enough tragedy in Jamie's young life without the additional burden of having to attend his mother's funeral.

I stood with the housekeeper and the butler at the head of a group of servants from both Greythorn Hall and Ackroyd House, while behind us and around us, perched on tombstones and grassy knolls, lining the paths and peering at us from over the walls were the onlookers.

There were many old friends who came to extend their condolences and with them came my aunt and uncle. His face bore its familiar expression of concern, tinged I am sure with disapproval, and my aunt was lumpy and dowdy in faded black which did duty for every funeral it was her lot to attend. They made it their business to approach me and again my uncle expressed his concern that I should have been mixed up in anything so sordid as Miss Eleanor's faithlessness, and demanded to know if it was my intention to remain at Greythorn Hall.

'I must, Uncle. I have a duty to Jamie,' I said quickly.

'Make yourself useful in any way you can to Sir Lyndon,' he adjured, 'and remind him to call upon me if he thinks I can be of service.'

'I will, Uncle,' I promised bravely.

'And don't forget Miss Cora, Maya. That poor unhappy girl will need all the companionship and sympathy she can get.'

'Yes, Uncle,' I said, wishing he would go.

Dutifully I kissed my aunt goodbye and watched them walking down the path towards the gates. They were an odd, ill-assorted couple, she so small and shabby, he tall, strutting down the path like a cockerel, acknowledging the nods and smiles of those who knew him with an air of profound condescension.

At last it was over and in a little group we walked back to Greythorn. I was aware of the strain on Lyndon's face, and the effort it had cost this proud man to brave the stares of the crowd while they talked and whispered in groups about the infidelity and scandal surrounding his sister. Once during the service he looked straight at me and I was joyously though painfully aware of that sudden look of yearning in his eyes. I longed to run into his arms, to hold him close to me while I told him how much I loved him, promising him all of my brave young courage but instead I clenched my hands in the pockets of my coat, looking quickly away in case Gavin should find us staring at each other.

The rain started during our walk back to the Hall and I was glad to run upstairs quickly to change out of my wet clothing. My room felt cold and I was shivering as I struggled out of my coat. I could hear the rain pattering against the window and I was glad of the warm shawl I draped round my shoulders.

Cora sat at the table with Jamie beside her and they both looked up expectantly on my arrival. I was hoping Cora would ask no questions while Jamie was there but I needn't have worried. She seemed entirely devoid of curiosity but I felt that my arrival was an intrusion, that I was not really wanted in the nursery and Jamie too seemed happier to sit with Cora while she read to him from a favourite book.

A servant came to tell us that Lady Gaynor would like Jamie to go downstairs to meet the visiting cousin and when I offered to take him he said, 'I know the way, I can go alone.'

'Very well, Jamie. You'll come back here afterwards, won't you?'

'Of course. Are you coming too, Aunt Cora?'

'Perhaps I will Jamie, after all he is my cousin too.'

That was the start of it and as the weeks and months passed by I began to realise painfully that I was losing Jamie. On the surface Cora seemed to recover from her bitterness. She rode with us across the fells and in the park, she walked with us on the moors and attended church with us at Buckley but I felt I never really knew what she was thinking.

She and Jamie were constantly together. He attended to his lessons but immediately they were over Cora would appear as if from nowhere and would suggest that she and Jamie should go off together, either visiting friends or on some private pursuit of their own.

I became Jamie's teacher, nothing more – but his imaginary friends were back and more real than they had ever been. Left more often to my own devices Melinda told me I could play the piano whenever I pleased and more often than not she came into the drawing room to listen to me. She seemed brighter in the summer months, her arthritis less painful, but when the autumn came round again the old air of fragility was back and I marvelled at her courage when every day seemed filled with pain.

Quite often I rode alone and there were times when Gavin joined me, which made me think he knew that I would be alone.

He was invariably gay and quite often outrageous but I was getting his measure now and he no longer troubled me with his sly innuendos and I gave back as good as I got.

Once Lyndon caught up with me riding across the fell and said, 'Why isn't Jamie with you, Maya? Is he no longer interested in riding?'

'Cora has taken him with her to visit friends.'

'But he isn't neglecting his studies to be with Cora, I hope?'

'No. He is a very good pupil.'

'But you are not entirely happy?'

'Not entirely. I wonder sometimes if Cora is good for him.'

He frowned slightly and I wondered if I had said too much. Cora was his sister and I merely the governess, but I need not have worried. 'I will speak to Cora. She must not be allowed to usurp your position, Maya.'

'Oh please no, I'm sure she is not intending to do that and I don't want her to think I have been complaining.'

He smiled, the smile I loved, warm and personal, and he hastened to reassure me. 'I will be very tactful, Maya, you need not worry on that score. Tell me truthfully, is Jamie better for her company?'

'No, I don't think he is.'

It was out before I could prevent it, and I bit my lip vexedly. I should not really mind Jamie's friendship with Cora – after all, she was his aunt and she had been my friend . . . I was shaken to realise I had put our friendship in the past tense.

Lyndon too had noticed my discomfiture without knowing the true reason for it.

'You must not be unhappy at Greythorn,' he said quietly. 'I feel responsible for your being here and for all the past trauma of your life at Seaten. There are times when I regret involving you at all, Maya, but I felt the need for you to spread your wings, that you were being suffocated by your life at the vicarage.'

'Oh, Sir Lyndon, you were right to involve me and it's true that I was suffocating. I regret nothing and I am sure that Jamie will respond to me again. Besides, one day he will go away to school and then both my influence and Cora's will cease '

'And you will leave Greythorn?'

'Yes.'

'What will you do then Maya – back to the vicarage and those long dreary evenings you were hating?'

'Perhaps, I don't know.'

I felt very close to him at that moment, and believed that he cared about what would become of me. Then, as though he had betrayed too great an interest he said, 'I am glad that you are making use of the piano. Melinda enjoys listening to you and Cora gave it up years ago.'

'How can anybody give up music?' I asked curiously.

'One can learn to give up many things. The dreams of one's youth are pushed aside to make room for sterner things until in the end we learn to recognise those things of value one must hang on to. You are very young Maya, you must not let vague fleeting passions fashion your life.'

He was warning me that I could mean nothing to him, that those warm heady moments of passion were valueless to him, and with despair in my heart I raised my head proudly. I would not let him see that I regarded those moments as anything more permanent than a summer storm.

'As you say Sir Lyndon, I am very young, and the young heal quickly.' With a cool nod of my head I spurred my horse on, leaving him staring after me as I galloped across the fell.

I do not know exactly when he spoke to Cora about her monopolisation of Jamie but I felt that he had done so. She no longer came to the nursery quite as often and when we met she treated me to a cool smile and thinly-veiled hostility. Jamie too seemed more distant and although he continued to pay attention to his lessons he no longer seemed to enjoy our walks or our rides.

One day I stood at the nursery window watching him strolling across the terrace. He was alone but he appeared to be talking to someone and I realised that it must be one of his imaginary friends. He spoke to them as though they were real, at times pausing to listen to replies, at others talking animatedly, and often smiling. When he returned to the nursery later on I made the mistake of asking him who he had been speaking to.

'I don't know what you mean,' he answered sullenly.

'Yes, Jamie you do,' I persisted. 'In the gardens earlier this afternoon. You were talking to somebody but I didn't see anyone there.'

'You never see the people I talk to,' he said sharply. 'Aunt Cora sees them, and she talks to them too, Nancy and Peter and the pretty lady with red hair.'

'You never had a lady with red hair until you came here, Jamie.'

'Of course not, she was never at Seaten.'

'Is she the lady who whispers in the trees?'

'Oh no, she's different.'

'What is her name?'

'I shan't tell you.'

There was a scowl on his face and a hostility he made no attempt to disguise. I thought it was time to speak to Cora who appeared to be encouraging him in his make-believe world. Immediately after tea I went to her room, hoping to find her there.

She greeted me coolly sitting at her dressing table brushing her long flaxen hair with firm brush strokes. Her face had filled out and she seemed more like her old self except for the steely glitter in her blue eyes. They met mine through the mirror, cynically amused, waiting for me to find the right words.

'We never seem to meet these days,' I said, hoping to establish some friendly ground between us. 'I have missed you, Cora.'

'But why should you Maya? We were never close friends and you are here to teach Jamie, are you not?'

So the barrier was already in place. I was the paid employee and she the daughter of the house and I realised immediately the form our conversation must take.

'I am worried about Jamie. He was beginning to forget his imaginary friends but now they are back with him and stronger, oh so much stronger than before. There is also a new one, this lady with the red hair.'

178

She nodded. 'Jamie has learnt that he cannot rely on people, not even those who should be closest to him. Consequently, he relies on his unseen friends who are not likely to let him down.'

'But they are not real Cora, they are figments of his imagination, and yours.'

Her face hardened and the colour rose into her cheeks. Stung by my words she snapped, 'Just because you don't see them doesn't mean that they do not exist! There are people who are sensitive to atmosphere, who have the power to see ghosts or spirits and people of the mist. I could always see them, even as a child. Jamie sees them too.'

'Jamie is open to suggestion. His imagination is very powerful and recently you have spent a great deal of time with him. Are you quite sure, Cora, that you haven't filled his mind with your people of the mist as you call them?'

'You are impertinent, Maya, and you exceed your authority. I love Jamie and he loves me. We have both suffered by the tragedy that destroyed his parents and my fiancé and it is natural that he should turn to me. We have both learnt to rely on those who can do us no harm. Jamie's imaginary friends as you call them cannot hurt him like real people have hurt him. I suppose you will now tell my brother that I am more than bad for Jamie and that it is better if we don't meet at all!'

'I shan't do that Cora, but I am pleading with you to act normally with him. One day he will leave here to go away to school. Children can be inordinately cruel, so what do you think boys of his age will do to Jamie when they realise that he talks to himself?'

'Jamie will learn to talk to them when he is alone, as I did. Nobody knew about my unseen friends, they only came to me when I was alone and I was very often alone when I was a child.'

'I know you were never very well Cora, but Jamie is never ill, his constitution is strong, he is a normal happy child and doesn't need to live in an unnatural dream world.'

'Tonight I shall tell my brother that you are exceeding your authority. I think perhaps that he made the mistake of treating you like a friend, calling you by your Christian name and inviting you to dine with the family. I have no doubt he did so because your uncle is the vicar of Lexford but you are still an employee, Maya, like any other of the servants. You should remember that.'

I stared at her, hardly able to comprehend that this was the Cora whom I had known since childhood, and without saying another word I left her room.

Smarting from her words I went straight to my room. I felt the need to be alone in order to think things over. Perhaps Cora was right. I rode their horses and played their piano and I had dined at their table – perhaps I *had* exceeded my authority and it was only because my uncle was the vicar of Lexford that the Gaynor family had felt I should be treated differently from the rest of their employees. In angry frustration I decided I would not ride again, nor would I play the piano. I would stay within my role as Jamie's governess and behave as they would have expected any servant to behave.

I kept this up for several days until the morning when I was told that Lady Gaynor wished to see me in the drawing room immediately after luncheon. I wore my plain navy-blue dress with its stiffened white collar and cuffs and I tied my hair back from my face to give me more severity, then I presented myself in the drawing room, standing rigidly in front of her.

'Do sit down Maya,' she said smiling. 'There is no need to stand on ceremony.'

I sat down on the edge of a chair, solemn and unsmiling, watching the smile fade from her face and an expression of doubt take its place.

'Are you quite well, Maya?' she greeted me.

'Very well, thank you Lady Gaynor.'

'Then why haven't you ridden Cleo these last few days or played the piano? We do not expect you to spend every hour of every day with Jamie, you are entitled to a life of your own.'

I met her eyes bravely but determined to make my position clear. 'You have all been very kind to me Lady Gaynor and I am grateful, but I do not expect you to treat me like one of the family. I am only employed as Jamie's governess and I would not like the other servants to feel that I am taking advantage of my uncle's position in the area.'

She was staring at me in surprise but she answered me quietly. 'I did not realise you thought on those lines, Maya.'

'I know that village people talk. I would not like them to say I was giving myself airs above my station.'

She nodded and without further argument she said, 'Very well, Maya, I shall respect your feelings but I shall miss your music.'

'May I go now, Lady Gaynor?'

'Of course. I trust Jamie is very well. I cannot climb the stairs to the nursery but perhaps he will come to see me one afternoon.'

'Of course Lady Gaynor, I am sure he will.'

I knew she watched me leave the room but I did not turn round. There was a dull ache in my heart as I ran upstairs to the nursery and once again I felt the need for those tears that always refused to come. For the rest of the afternoon I devoted my time to teaching Jamie the rudiments of algebra and later I walked with him in the park. I tried to interest him in the plants and flowers and the different leaves on the trees, but I felt sure he would have preferred to spend the time with his private friends. Later, I dined off a tray in the nursery and was about to return to my room when a servant appeared to tell me Sir Lyndon wished to see me in his study.

I stood before his desk while he looked at me with a half-smile twitching the corners of his mouth and I tried to look dignified and efficient.

'So,' he said at last, 'you would prefer that we address you as Miss Wentworth and transfer you to the servants' quarters?'

'I said no such thing Sir Lyndon,' I stammered unhappily.

'Perhaps not in so many words, but it is probably what you meant. Now I want you to tell me why you have suddenly adopted this attitude.'

'I felt I was abusing the fact that I came here as a child. Governesses in other large houses do not ride their horses nor do they dine with the family. I felt I was becoming too familiar with the family.'

'With the family Maya – or with me?'

I was conscious of the warm red blood that suffused my cheeks and my trembling hands. 'Oh Sir Lyndon,' I said unhappily, 'surely you could never think that I would trade on that.'

'I never did think so, Maya. A few moments of passion between a man and a beautiful girl who had shared an unhappy experience together . . . a man who had no right to hold you in his arms, a moment of shared passion for which I humbly apologise.'

'It has nothing to do with that, Sir Lyndon, nothing. I know that moment meant nothing to you, I know that men do these things heedlessly and without meaning them.'

'You think I am such a man?'

'I suppose so, since you have just apologised for the incident which you say should never have happened.'

It was now his turn to look confused but not for long. He picked up a paper knife lying on his desk with some irritation and his face became suddenly stern. 'Maya – something has been said in this house to make you say what you did to my wife this afternoon. I can only think it is Cora or Gavin. Most likely Cora, since I have already seen that Gavin derives a great deal of enjoyment from your riding together.'

I looked down at the floor unhappily and he went on, 'Ah, I can see that it *is* Cora, probably because I spoke to her about the time she was spending with Jamie. You must disregard her words Maya. You are employed by me not by Cora and I shall treat you with the same courtesy I would have extended to you as Edisford's niece still living at the vicarage. You are not an ordinary governess. I asked you to help Jamie because the child was wrapped up in a private dream world, and you were succeeding, until this unfortunate tragedy and its aftermath.'

He rose from his chair and came to stand in front of me, then to my surprise he reached out and undid the ribbon tying back my hair, allowing it to fall loose on my shoulders.

'That is better,' he said, smiling down at me. 'Your hair is far too pretty to tie back so severely, and you look nothing like the conventional schoolmarm. Do we agree that your life here shall continue as before?'

'If it is your wish, Sir Lyndon.'

'It is, and we are still good friends you and I?'

'Yes, I would like you to be my friend.'

It was a lie. I didn't want his friendship but because I could never have his love it was something I would have to settle for. At least I felt happier about my position at Greythorn but later when I entered the nursery to see if Jamie was asleep I found Cora sitting on the edge of his bed and the boy still awake, his eyes unnaturally bright.

Not in the least disconcerted by my finding them together she sprang to her feet and with a brief smile bade Jamie goodnight. I walked out of his bedroom with her and after the door was closed she said, 'I am sorry I spoke to you as I did Maya, it was wrong of me but I was hurt and annoyed that you thought I was bad for Jamie, particularly when it was your suggestion that we draw closer together.'

I stared at her, wondering if I had really made that suggestion. Perhaps I had, but not for her to fill Jamie's head with stories of people who didn't exist.

'I suppose my brother has told you how much we value your service here?'

Service! There it was again, that sly insinuation about my status in the household but I chose to ignore it. Instead I smiled politely. 'Sir Lyndon was very kind, Cora. I am clear about my duties and my leisure, and I hope I shall not disappoint him.'

She received this remark with her face set in a mask of polite indifference, then she murmured goodnight.

When I returned to Jamie's bedroom I knew that he was pretending to be asleep. It was obvious he didn't wish to talk to me and unhappily I lit the nightlight before leaving his room.

The following evening I was invited to dine downstairs with the family. The conversation was desultory and mostly we listened as Sir Lyndon and Gavin discussed the affairs of the estate. Cora excused herself immediately after dinner and Melinda asked me to play for her.

A group of farm tenants was being shown into the study as we crossed the hall and I knew that Sir Lyndon would be busy for the rest of the evening. Gavin had left the house and Melinda merely commented on it by saying she wondered which of the various village girls he was flattering at the moment.

Suddenly, I found myself thinking about Emily. Gavin had flattered Emily during that one glorious summer and I wondered if that was why she wouldn't marry Ned. Gavin and Ned were poles apart and I couldn't help but feel that Gavin could have spoiled her for Ned. I wished all over again that I hadn't insisted on her accompanying me to the Hall against her will.

I played for the rest of the evening and Melinda sat quietly, listening. I knew the music she liked best, Chopin and Debussy and I realised with surprise how much my playing had improved with practice.

Melinda herself said gently, 'It would have been a great pity to have cut yourself off from your music, Maya, and from the other things you enjoy. I can no longer ride but I miss it terribly. It was once one of my greatest joys.'

I felt a swift surge of compassion for this lovely woman who was still young and as though she were aware of it she laughed a little. 'I shouldn't allow myself the relief of self-pity and burden others with it, I am so lucky in other ways.'

'You are loved, Lady Gaynor, and love is something to be prized.'

'Yes, I am loved, but it is the love of a brother for a sister, the love of a father for his daughter. Love, passionate love, is a thing of the past, barely remembered and Lyndon should not be asked to live the life of a monk while he is still young and virile.'

'He knows no doubt that if ever he could love a woman like that it would break your heart.'

'Yes he knows, and for that reason he will deny love, believe that it doesn't exist. He would break the heart of the woman he loved before he would break mine.'

I turned my head away and concentrated on the music before

me. She surely couldn't have been warning me not to love her husband – after all, what could she know about those few unguarded moments at the end of a long unhappy day? There was surely nothing in the way we looked at each other and in any case if Lyndon ever loved again it would be a woman from his own walk of life, not some little governess or girl from the village, even if her uncle did boast of being its vicar.

I finished the Nocturne I was playing and turning round, I saw Melinda looking intently into the fire, her face pensive. As I closed the lid on the piano she said with her usual courtesy, 'Thank you Maya, that was charming. I do so enjoy these evenings, that is why I asked Lyndon to speak with you.'

'Yes, thank you Lady Gaynor.'

'Things are better now I hope, between you and Cora?'

'I rarely see her, but she has apologised to me.'

'Cora is a strange, withdrawn girl. I thought so when I came here as a young bride and even before I married Lyndon. She was always resentful of Eleanor, possibly because Eleanor was so full of life while she was delicate. There was a time when I thought she resented me, but after my accident she was kindness itself, often coming to read to me and always willing to run little errands for me until in the end I was sure I had misjudged her.'

'Did she ever tell you about her imaginary friends?'

She stared at me curiously before answering, then she said, 'She told me about the whispering glade and the Gaynor girl who was drowned on the eve of her wedding. Her portrait is in the long gallery – haven't you seen it?'

'Why, no.'

'It is the second portrait on your right. A very lovely girl, not unlike you for colouring, Maya.'

'Then she didn't have red hair?'

'No, she is very dark.'

'Jamie talks about a girl with red hair, but he was only introduced to her after his friendship with Cora began.'

'It's the first time I've heard of her, Maya. I very much fear it is someone Cora has invented.'

'Perhaps Jamie will forget her, forget them all when he is older.'

'Yes, I'm sure he will.'

I watched her struggle painfully to her feet. She did not like people to assist her, preferring to rely on the two sticks she carried. She stood still for a few moments to regain her balance then with the aid of her sticks she walked slowly to the door.

'I think I shall go to bed now, Maya. If you will walk with me across the hall you will be able to go up the stairs and look at the portraits in the long gallery.'

Her bedroom was on the ground floor to save her the effort of climbing the stairs, while Sir Lyndon's rooms were on the first floor overlooking the park. There were other portraits in the hall and she told me who they were, pausing in front of each one not because she was particularly interested but to enable her to rest a little.

'Will you be able to manage from here?' I asked her at the foot of the stairs.

'But of course Maya, it isn't far. Don't forget, the second portrait on your right.'

Bidding her goodnight I mounted the shallow stairs and soon found myself in the long gallery with its portraits of Gaynor men and women from the past on either side. I had no difficulty in finding Caroline. She was so young and it was true she had my colouring, a dark gypsy girl with long black hair streaming in the wind, wearing a dark red dress, standing in the centre of an avenue of trees with one foot poised for flight.

Her slate blue eyes, so like my own stared into mine and she was smiling, a faintly sad smile as though she knew something of the fate that awaited her. I looked closer at the picture. Behind the trees there was a stretch of blue and I realised that she stood within the whispering glade itself, almost as though the glade and Caroline would always have an affinity with each other.

I had not heard Gavin climb the stairs until he stood behind me.

'Caroline Gaynor,' he mused, 'the lady in the glade, the lady who is supposed to haunt the park and bring distress to all the other Gaynor women.'

'Surely you don't believe such things!' I said, staring at him.

'Well, they don't seem to have had much luck, do they?'

'I'm sure none of it had anything to do with Caroline.'

'Perhaps not. She's remarkably like you, Maya.'

'She has my colouring, that is all.'

'She has your eyes, your hair, your colouring and that warm gypsy look that covers a heart as cool as ice.'

'You know nothing about my heart.'

'Perhaps not, but I would like to know more. When will you come riding with me again?'

'I don't know, I expect to be very busy.'

'You can find the time to entertain Melinda, why can't you find the time to come riding with me?'

'Because I am mostly with Jamie in the daytime, and that I presume is when you would want to go riding.'

'Not necessarily. What is wrong with riding in the moonlight? It won't be the first time you've ridden in the moonlight Maya – or would you prefer to drive in the chaise?'

I glared at him angrily, and tossing my head I escaped down the length of the corridor, followed by his laughter.

FIFTEEN

GAVIN VERY PROPERLY asked his brother's permission to take me riding a few days later. Sir Lyndon and Lady Gaynor were driving into the country to see friends in a nearby village and stated their intention of taking Jamie with them. Gavin knew I would be at a loose end so he waited until the family were at luncheon before making his request.

Immediately Melinda said it was a very good idea, and somewhat reluctantly, I thought, Sir Lyndon agreed with her.

'Where do you intend to ride?' he asked Gavin pointedly.

'Oh, somewhere along the fells, and along the proper bridle-paths of course,' Gavin answered.

Lyndon knew his younger brother's reputation in the villages, and I felt sure he wanted none of the villagers talking about me. However his permission was eventually given and soon after lunch we set off on our ride. It was a glorious autumn day with the heather already past its purple best and the bracken golden against the warm Pennine stone. I felt gloriously alive and young as we cantered along the paths, jumping the low stone walls that led onto to the fells.

'You ride as though you've ridden horses all your life,' Gavin laughed.

'If I'd remained in Africa that is probably what I would have done,' I answered him.

'That's the first time I've ever heard you talk about Africa,' he said.

'I know. I don't usually want to talk about it, I want to forget but I did have a pony, I remember. Everybody rode out there.'

'I suppose your entire life would have been very different.'

'Yes, completely different, but it was not to be.'

I spurred my horse on until we were on the fell riding at full gallop. We pulled our horses up breathlessly on top of the crag which fell in a sheer drop to the valley beneath. Below us stretched the landscape with its big sky, green fields and scattered homesteads. There too lay Greythorn Hall in its magnificent remoteness and Gavin jumped from his horse and went to stand at the edge of the crag. With one hand he pointed towards the great house calling out, 'How would you like to be mistress of all that Maya?'

I had dismounted from my horse and was standing beside him. I looked down at Greythorn's turrets and chimneys, its wandering parkland and formal terraced gardens – but I had no difficulty in answering his question.

'I have no thoughts at all about becoming mistress of such a house! It would be pretentious of me and I have had no training for it.'

'But you could do it, Maya. It would be like Caroline Gaynor coming alive again, with your dark beauty. Perhaps then the whispering voices would stop . . . and wouldn't it be something to have the villagers bow to you in the village street? It might even bring that pompous uncle of yours to heel.'

'You talk a lot of nonsense, Gavin!' Greythorn Hall already has a suitable mistress and even if it hadn't, I could never fill the rôle.'

He stood, a hand on either side of me pressed against the summit of the crag and his dark devilish eyes alight with taunting humour.

'Why not think about it, Maya? Melinda's a sick woman who will never have children. Every winter she is worse and one winter she's going to die.'

'How can you speak about her in this way, it's inhuman! Besides what makes you think your brother would ever look at me, even if Melinda died tomorrow?'

'I'm not talking about Lyndon, Maya, I'm talking about *me*.

One day you and I could own Greythorn Hall. Our son would be the next baronet, our son would own the Hall and the land as far as your eyes can see.'

I stared at him stupidly, then I broke free and ran towards my horse.

'You're out of your mind, Gavin. Melinda is not dead, and even if she were Lyndon could marry again and have that son you spoke of. Nothing you are proposing for yourself can ever come true.'

'I know my dear brother, Maya. He'll never marry again, but you and I, we're a perfectly matched pair. Don't you understand, girl, I'm asking you to marry me!'

'You must be mad. I don't believe you.'

'I swear it. Tonight if you like I'll tell them at dinner. After all, I've had a good run for my money, it's time I settled down and you won't regret it Maya. I'll make you a good husband and there'll be a lot for us to look forward to.'

'I want more from marriage than a big house and a lot of servants. I want a man who loves me, a man I can depend on. How could I ever depend on you?'

'Well – you'll never know if you don't give it a try.'

'A try! One doesn't try a marriage. It isn't like a new coat or a pair of shoes. You talk ridiculously – how can I take you seriously when you speak of "trying".'

'I mean it, Maya, and I'm going to ask you again and again until you say yes. Promise you'll think about it, at least.'

I stared at him helplessly. For once his face was serious with the laughter gone from his eyes. He was more adult than I had ever seen him.

I mounted my horse and he came to stand beside me, taking the reins in his hands so that I couldn't move away. 'Maya, I've been watching you these last few weeks, your grace and your beauty. I admire your spirit and the way you sit a horse. I can see you mistress of Greythorn, sweeping down the staircase in that dark dress with the blue glints in your hair and those steely blue eyes of yours.'

'None of those things are enough to base a marriage on.'

'But they're a start, Maya. Greythorn is crying out for you. Years ago when Lyndon married Melinda I never saw her as the real mistress of the Hall, just as my mother never was, but there's something about you that's different and I mean to have it.'

'Do you always get what you want?'

'Almost always, but you I want very badly so will you think about it Maya?'

As I stared at him, a strange, little-boy appeal came into his eyes.

'I can't believe you are serious. I don't believe any of this.'

'Think, Maya, *think*. Never to have to go back to that dreary vicarage and those wearisome tasks you hated so much. Never to have your uncle chastise you and watch every penny you spend, but to live here in luxury and with nothing but good for the future. You'd be a fool to turn your back on it, Maya. I'll get Lyndon on my side, I'll get him to make you think about it.'

'No,' I said sharply. 'Lyndon mustn't interfere. I can think about it without bringing Lyndon into it.'

He raised his eyes and this time there was a strange amused gleam in them.

'He bothers you Maya, that brother of mine. Are you quite sure nothing happened between you after that romantic ride in the moonlight?'

'How can I ever take you seriously when you behave so childishly? Have you forgotten so soon why we took that ride in the moonlight?'

'I haven't forgotten, but tragedy draws people together like nothing else. Why don't you want him to interfere?'

'Because I'm quite capable of making up my own mind without any outside influence. Can we please ride back now, Gavin? I want to be there when Jamie arrives home.'

'I have a pleasant surprise for you when we reach the stables. You will no longer need to ride Cora's horse.'

I stared at him but his face gave nothing away. 'I enjoy riding Cora's horse and she doesn't exercise her nearly enough. I'm

Jamie's governess Gavin, and governesses don't aspire to horses.'

'Just you see what I have waiting for you! Now come on, I'll race you down the hill!'

He won easily. Cora's horse was no tempestuous steed although she responded to my words of encouragement. Nevertheless, Gavin was already waiting for us near the gates so that we could finish our journey together.

The grooms came forward to take our horses and I saw Gavin whispering to one of them. 'Wait here,' he called to me, 'he's gone for your surprise.'

Almost immediately the groom reappeared, leading by the rein a shining black horse and I gasped with dismay as I recognised Indigo, Roger Ackroyd's stallion, the horse I had ridden recklessly through the mist and rain on that fatal night. I stared at Gavin in disbelief.

'You can't mean that you are giving him to me?' I asked incredulously.

'Oh, but I do. He has been well-schooled, and now there is no vice left in him. Roger rode him too hard as he did everything else. He treated the horse like he treated his wife, brutally and inconsiderately. See how gentle he has become.'

I walked across to the horse and fondled his neck, a thing I would not have dared to do at Ackroyd House. He no longer seemed nervous and highly-strung and suddenly I knew that I wanted him, I couldn't bear to think of anybody else having him.

'You're a pair,' Gavin said enthusiastically. 'He's as gypsy dark as you are, Maya. As my wife on that horse you'll be the envy of every high-flung family in the county.'

'Is that what you want from your wife?' I asked, eying him cynically.

'Doesn't every man want his wife to be admired, to see that other men desire her yet know that she is his?'

'Does Sir Lyndon know that you intend to give me this horse?'

'Lyndon, always Lyndon, Maya.'

'He is my employer and the master of this house.'

'I'll tell him tonight at dinner that I've asked you to marry me and that I have given Indigo to you. You'll know soon enough if he objects.'

'I haven't said I would marry you, Gavin. You asked me to think about it and that is all I promised to do.'

The mocking smile was back on his face as I turned and advanced towards the house. He made no effort to accompany me and I was glad to be alone. Gavin had proposed marriage but he had not said he loved me. It was like the craving of a small boy for something he admired and thought superior to the toy his playmate might have. Something to show off with and be envied for, but I knew how quickly a toy could be forgotten and easily discarded. I could not believe that he was serious and I felt a surge of anger against him for amusing himself at my expense.

I was glad that I was not invited to dine with the family and Jamie and I ate our evening meal together in the nursery. He appeared to have enjoyed his outing with Lyndon and Melinda but we had still not entirely recovered our old friendship and immediately after our meal he said he was tired and wished to read in bed.

I felt restless. Gavin's behaviour had unsettled me and I did not want to go down to the drawing room to play the piano. Instead, I retired to my room with a book but I found I could not read either. The fine day had deteriorated into rain. Now a thin mist drifted across the parkland and I felt vaguely sad and uneasy. I decided to prepare Jamie's lessons for the following day so I returned to the nursery in search of some books. From Jamie's bedroom I was surprised to hear him talking to someone and I wondered who it could be. I had thought all the family were downstairs at dinner and there was no reason for any of the servants to enter his room.

I knocked gently on his door and opened it without waiting for a reply. The nightlight was burning and Jamie sat up in bed, pale as he often was these days, his eyes large and shining brilliantly, but there was nobody else in the room. Jamie had been alone.

'I thought I heard you talking to somebody,' I said. 'I came to see who was with you. Who were you talking to, Jamie?'

He set his lips, staring at me in a hostile way as he quite often did these days. 'Jamie,' I said gently, 'I heard you, won't you tell me who you were speaking to?'

'I don't want to tell you.'

'But I already know Nancy and Peter although I can never see them. Are they here now?'

'No.'

'Then who is?'

'You wouldn't know if I told you.'

'No, perhaps not but I like to know all your friends.'

'She's our friend, mine and Aunt Cora's.'

'Well your Aunt Cora is my friend too so why can't we all be friends? It's so much nicer that way. Is her name Caroline by any chance?'

'No, but I know about her.'

'I never told you about Caroline, I suppose that was your aunt Cora too.'

He didn't answer me, but it was there still, that stolid mutinous look on his small perfect face.

'Perhaps you would prefer to tell Uncle Lyndon, Jamie. I don't think he would like you to keep secrets from me and I know he wants us to be good friends.'

Still the child's face was mutinous but now his eyes were troubled and vaguely unsure. Pressing home my advantage I said, 'You enjoy our lessons together don't you Jamie? If not, then you must go away to school. I cannot go on teaching someone who doesn't care enough about me to take me into his confidence.'

'Aunt Cora says my lessons and my friends are different.'

'And she is right, but they needn't be. We were very good friends until we came here, Jamie. Don't you remember how we used to walk through the bluebell wood, you and I, and Nancy and Peter?'

'Perhaps if you didn't tell her I told you?'

'Of course I won't tell her if you don't want me to.'

'No, I don't.' He stared at me solemnly, then as though he had suddenly made up his mind he said, 'I was talking to the pretty lady with the red hair.'

'I see. Do you know her name?'

'Yes, of course. Her name is Emily.'

I stared at him in stunned surprise. 'Emily,' I echoed stupidly.

'Yes. She used to come here.'

'She came with me long ago.'

It was his turn to stare. 'I didn't know you knew Emily.'

'Emily was my friend. I brought her here one summer's day a long time ago and she was very pretty indeed with lovely red hair. I don't know where she is now though, I haven't seen her for some time.'

'I think she's dead.'

I stared at him uncertainly. 'Why do you say that, Jamie?'

'Because nobody sees her except me and Aunt Cora.'

'I think you should go to sleep now, Jamie. Emily's gone and it's long past your bedtime.'

'You won't tell Aunt Cora I've told you,' he persisted.

'No, I promise.'

I kissed him gently and left the room, waiting a few minutes in the nursery in case he started to talk to his unseen guest again.

I felt troubled and unhappy. Did Jamie really see these friends or did he imagine them, and why had Cora invented Emily? She had never been particularly friendly with Emily and why did Jamie think she was dead? I too had often wondered if Emily was dead but had refused to believe it. Not Emily with her enthusiasm for life, her laughing eyes and merry wit. But then I thought about the last time I had seen her, sad and haunted and the way she had left the cottage in the middle of the night, alone and insecure.

I lay awake a long time, my thoughts a confused jumble of Gavin's proposal and Jamie's obsession with Emily, and when I slept my dreams too were troublesome, haunted by sad wandering wraiths so that I awakened unrefreshed, my heart filled with strange forebodings.

Jamie too was pale, his voice so hoarse that I could hardly hear his responses to my questions. He said his throat was sore and immediately after our midmorning break I asked permission from Melinda to summon the doctor. She seemed preoccupied, and I did not think she greeted me with her usual warmth, nevertheless the doctor was summoned and arrived just before lunch. He diagnosed a severe chill and ordered Jamie to bed. One of the servants was instructed to look after him.

Left to my own devices I decided to walk in the park. Anything was better than staying in the house where I was conscious of a strange atmosphere of antagonism. The rain had cleared during the night and the paths had dried so I set out by the conservatory door, walking quickly towards the fells behind the house. I had not gone far when I heard someone calling, and looking round I was surprised to see Cora hurrying towards me. She was breathless as she approached, but by tacit agreement we set off together through the woodland that led to the moor.

Regaining her breath she startled me by saying, 'I'm sorry to intrude upon your thoughts, Maya. No doubt you wished to be alone to think over my brother's proposal.'

I stood stockstill, staring at her incredulously for I had never truly believed Gavin's proposal or that he intended to inform the family.

'You seem surprised,' she said, smiling a little.

'Yes, I am. I did not take him seriously.'

'No, people seldom do, but I believe it is the first time he has ever asked a girl to marry him. Heaven knows he never lacked a pretty girl.'

'No, I'm sure he didn't and that is why I am so reluctant to believe that he has singled me out. You must see that it is madness, Cora. I'm a girl without status, without money, without a real family. We live in different worlds. I *can't* take him seriously.'

'I would advise you to try. He was perfectly serious when he informed Lyndon and Melinda last night over dinner. He thinks you would make a perfect mistress of Greythorn Hall.'

'He said that to Sir Lyndon and his wife!'

'My brother Gavin is not the most tactful of people. I thought I should warn you that Lyndon expects to speak to you tonight after dinner.'

I felt myself trembling nervously, my mouth dry with apprehension. Surely they could not think that I was aspiring to becoming mistress of Greythorn as well as Gavin's wife, oh it was cruel as well as tactless if he had given them that impression.

'Don't look so frightened Maya, my brother Lyndon is not going to eat you. I can assure you he knows Gavin better than he knows you. Gavin he can deal with, he only wants to know if you are interested in this proposal.'

Interested! Was that all marriage meant to these people? A young girl given in marriage to settle a gambling debt, another who was to be asked if she was interested enough. My anger must have shown on my face because she quickly said, 'That was a foolish way to put it, you must forgive me, Maya. What I should really have said was – do you care enough for my brother to marry him?'

'I shall be happy to answer any of Sir Lyndon's questions. I have nothing to hide.'

'I wouldn't be sorry to have you for my sister-in-law, Maya. You are a vast improvement on some of the girls he has been seen around with.'

'I suppose you mean the village girls.'

'And many of the county girls. At least you and I are friends.'

'I thought we were once, but recently I have not been so sure.'

'But we are, Maya. You were right, much of the bitterness is gone and I have started to heal. Soon it will be as though the past never existed for me but I shall remember our friendship.'

I looked at her thoughtfully. Perhaps she meant it. Indeed her face had taken on a new softness, the grim look had gone from it and once more she wore her pale blond hair soft against her cheeks. It could have been the old Cora staring at me, but not quite. The difference was tantalising and I couldn't say what it was until I realised that although her lips smiled her eyes did not.

'How far do you intend to walk?' she asked me.

'I have all afternoon. I could not bear to sit around the house, so I shall be glad of your company if you wish to come.'

'No. I'll go back now. It is quite a climb up there and I have never been fond of walking on the fells. Perhaps we shall meet at dinner.'

'I think I would prefer to eat in my room tonight, but I will see Sir Lyndon in his study later. Perhaps you would tell him that, Cora.'

'Of course.'

She gave me one of her brief smiles before setting off on her way back to the house.

I walked for miles in an effort to be at peace with myself but still the fears persisted. I dreaded meeting Sir Lyndon after dinner. I dreaded the coldness in his eyes where once he had looked at me with friendship and once only with something warmer. I couldn't bear the thought of his voice speaking to me in chill impersonal accents, or the speculation in his eyes if he thought I was a self-seeking fortune hunter. It was all so unfair and unnecessary.

It was half-past nine when I walked down the main staircase to go to Sir Lyndon's study. I heard voices from the direction of the drawing room but there was a light shining under the study door which told me Sir Lyndon was probably inside. I knocked on the door and immediately I heard his voice telling me to enter.

'Please sit down, Maya, I shall be with you in a moment,' he said, signing a letter and placing it inside an envelope. Then he looked at me without smiling and I felt my heart sink miserably.

'You know why I have sent for you, I suppose?' he opened.

'I believe so, Sir Lyndon.'

'I must admit I was surprised. I had no idea you and Gavin had become so close.'

'We have ridden together on the fells, sometimes with Jamie, sometimes alone as we did yesterday, but although he has often flattered me and even flirted with me I have not encouraged him. I was very surprised by his proposal of marriage.'

'You mean that you had no idea of his intention?'

'I mean exactly that.'

'Then what did you say when he made it?'

'Well, I did not believe him. I told him it was impossible, that I could not take it seriously.'

'But he asked you to think it over. I presume you are doing that now.'

His face was haughty and uncompromising. Stung by the thought that he believed his brother could just propose marriage to me and that I might actually consider it, I replied, 'Since he asked me a great many times to give it serious thought Sir Lyndon, yes I am thinking it over.'

'And he offered incentives I have no doubt, like money and position, perhaps even this house and all it contains.'

'How could he do that, Sir Lyndon, when you are the master of Greythorn Hall and Lady Gaynor is its mistress?'

'Gavin would find a way, I am sure. Most girls would be tempted if the prize he offered proved rich enough.'

'Most girls would be tempted to marry a member of the Gaynor family. Most girls would not wish to think it over.'

'I agree, but then a clever girl would not wish to appear too eager and often the pursuit is more pleasurable than the kill.'

I had never thought that one day he would look at me with such acute dislike and that I too might wish to rake my fingers down that stiff handsome face. At that moment I was hating him with every fibre in my body and I jumped to my feet, my face pale with anger.

'I have told Gavin I will think it over, Sir Lyndon, and I shall do that! I am not a fortune hunter or any other kind of adventuress. If I do decide to marry him I shall be a good wife wherever he chooses to take me. I will never give any one of you cause to say he has made a mistake.'

I stared at him forcefully for several seconds, then I left the room. I was bitterly angry, but I was hurt, too. I loved him, even when he stared at me with such bitter disapproval and when his tongue lashed me with its sarcasm. How could I marry Gavin when I loved his brother, and yet how could I not marry him when it was all out in the open and things between us could never be the same . . .

I paced my room, obsessed with the idea of marriage to Gavin when I didn't love him, and angry at the rest of them for thinking I had aspired to such heights. I couldn't think what my position would be in this household if I accepted Gavin's proposal, on the other hand what would it be like if I didn't? No more long, charming evenings playing to Melinda, or exhilarating rides over the fells with Jamie, and Lyndon's kind teasing voice would be cold when he spoke to me. My mind was in a turmoil when I went into the nursery to see if Jamie was sleeping.

He was coughing restlessly so I gave him a dose of his cough mixture and saw him settled before I returned to the nursery, surprised to find Gavin there, sitting at the table with a book in his hands.

'Don't tell me you really enjoy cramming this sort of stuff into Jamie's head day after day,' he said, scowling down at the book.

I didn't answer him but went to sit across from him at the table. He looked up suddenly and smiled.

'I suppose Lyndon's had his little say. Does he approve or not of our engagement?'

'Not,' I answered him firmly. 'Gavin – how could you tell him I would make a good mistress for Greythorn Hall, particularly in front of Melinda?'

'Who told you I made that remark?'

'Is it true?'

'I may have made it in passing. They both know what I'm like, surely Lyndon doesn't hold it against you.'

'I'm very much afraid that he does. You've spoiled everything for me here, I suppose you know that?'

'Surely you can't be serious. What have I spoiled, your lessons with Jamie, your position as governess, that halfway feeling of being neither a member of the family nor a paid servant? You'll be my fiancée, soon to be a member of the family, Jamie'll go away to school where he should have been months ago and for the first time in your life you'll have status in the community. Think straight, girl.'

'We don't love each other,' I blurted out, painfully conscious of the cynicsm that came immediately into his eyes.

'Why must you women be so obsessed with love? I love you enough to offer you my name and everything else I possess – and I want you Maya, I want you as I have never wanted anybody else. I know that the only way I'll get you is to marry you, more's the pity.'

'I expect better things from the man I marry. I expect fidelity, and I want him to love me to the exclusion of all others. I don't just want to be a possession, a thing, something he wants and can't get any other way.'

'So you've already decided against it. My brother Lyndon was so sure you would accept. He thought your idea of thinking it over particularly contrived. He will be surprised when I tell him you have decided to turn me down.'

Stung to anger by Lyndon's forecast I said, 'On the contrary Gavin – I have decided to accept your proposal. Your brother will be able to say that he was absolutely right in what he thought about me.'

SIXTEEN

LIKE EVERY GIRL before me I had dreamed of what it would be like when I found the man who wanted to marry me. I would be desperately in love with him of course, and he would be tall and handsome, generous and kind. Gavin was tall and handsome and he was generous with gifts of flowers and jewellery but he was not particularly kind. He was undeniably cynical and although his love-making was passionate and demanding it did not make me happy. I was not in love with him and as the weeks passed by I become sure that he was not in love with me. Somehow I did not feel that he had the capacity for love as I saw it, but I had no cause to complain about his attention.

Sir Lyndon was invariably polite. As soon as our engagement was announced he suggested that I should no longer be expected to teach Jamie and that he would advertise for a governess immediately. I begged him to allow me to continue to teach the child, saying that the wedding was some time off and I had nothing better to do. Gavin on the other hand complained that I put Jamie before him and that now that we were engaged I should be thinking of him and only him.

Cora received the news with obvious pleasure and she surprised me by wanting to make plans with me for the future, and even offering her advice regarding bridesmaids and my wedding dress.

'I suppose Emily would have been one of your bridesmaids if she'd still been living in Lexford,' she said one afternoon when we walked with Jamie in the park.

I hadn't got as far as thinking about bridesmaids, and in answer to my doubtful surprise she added, 'She was your favourite friend, wasn't she Maya? Perhaps she would have refused – after all, she could have felt out of her depth in county society.'

I felt irritated by her words but I recognised the truth in them. I would be marrying into a prominent family with a legendary history. Without Cora telling me I knew that Emily would have stuck out like a sore thumb amongst the spoilt county belles, even though her beauty would in many cases have been superior to theirs. Faced with the half-smile on Cora's lips I couldn't help but think that I too might feel out of my depth.

Naturally my uncle and aunt were overwhelmed by the news of our engagement and seemed unaware that Gavin had not asked their permission. I was informed that they would delve into their pockets in order to provide me with an adequate trousseau and I was quick to assure them that I now had a little money of my own which I intended to use for this purpose.

Lexford and the villages for miles around received the romantic news with avid interest, and now when I drove along the main street I was greeted with smiles and bobbed curtseys. I believed that many of the younger girls looked at me enviously, and once Gavin remarked after he had driven me through the village that it wasn't nearly as much fun now that he was spoken for.

'I suppose you've flirted with most of them at one time or another?' I said, entirely without jealousy.

'All the pretty ones, Maya. It saved me from boredom and no doubt brightened their dull lives.'

'You haven't lost any of your conceit by becoming engaged to me,' I retorted waspishly.

'On the contrary I have acquired much more. Did I tell you that I've asked Lyndon to give a ball for us at the end of October? We don't want it to interfere with Christmas and the weather usually isn't bad enough to keep people away at that time.'

'What did your brother say?'

'He agreed. Wear your most glamorous gown Maya and show all those people who'll be dying to know what you look like that I've chosen a beauty.'

'I haven't a glamorous dress.'

'Well, there's plenty of time for you to acquire one before then,' he said smiling. 'Why don't you wear one of Eleanor's dresses, she always had plenty and they were brought here from Seaten. I do get a little tired of seeing you in those governess clothes.'

As the date of the ball grew nearer I was consulted about whom I would like to invite and only my aunt and uncle sprang to mind. I had no close friends, but then as an afterthought I mentioned the name of Miss Lawford, my old headmistress. I knew Aunt Miranda would not come. She had sent me her blessing but the tone of her letter had been doubtful, as doubtful as my own thoughts.

Oh, those lovely golden October days when I should have been ecstatically happy instead of plagued by problems about the future. I had only to see Lyndon to know that I was fooling myself if I thought I could be happy with Gavin and although he was invariably polite to me the kindness he had shown me as Jamie's governess was no longer evident. He did not want me as Gavin's wife and I smarted angrily, believing it was because he thought I was a self-seeker and only interested in the prestige such a marriage would bring me.

One evening over dinner Cora pointedly asked what I intended to wear for the ball, and I decided to be honest with my answer.

'I don't know, Cora. I have never owned a ballgown. There was never an occasion to wear one.'

'But you'll be the belle of this ball, Maya, so you must have something quite lovely.'

Sir Lyndon looked up sharply. 'If you care to go into York or Harrogate Maya, I'm sure you will find something there. Have the gown charged up to me.'

I knew that my face was flaming with embarrassment but I

made myself meet his gaze bravely. 'Thank you Sir Lyndon, but that won't be necessary. I have a little money put by, and I shall ask the village dressmaker to run something up for me. She is very capable.'

'You can't appear at the ball in something made by the village dressmaker,' Gavin said sharply. 'Don't be so proud Maya! Why not accept Lyndon's offer to treat you to a gown, and isn't it time you dropped the Sir and started to call him Lyndon?'

I burned with shame. I had never felt so inadequate, not even during the holidays from Miss Lawford's school when the other girls who had invited me to their homes possessed wardrobes filled with dresses and I had only the bare minimum. I wanted to run from the room but I knew that was not the answer. Once more meeting Lyndon's eyes, I was aware of a strange compassion in them. At that moment we were close, I felt it. However much he wanted to be angry with me, just then he felt only sympathy. Then lifting my head proudly, I shattered that moment which was all too fragile.

It was Melinda who came to my rescue, echoing Gavin's first suggestion to me. 'There are a great many of Eleanor's gowns in her old room, Maya. You are about the same height, so one of them will fit you beautifully.'

'Yes, of course!' Cora said. 'Why not wear one of Eleanor's gowns? They were always expensive and because she was flamboyant, often daring.'

Nobody contradicted her. They were all aware that her bitterness towards Eleanor was a permanent thing, but Gavin laughed saying, 'Don't be too daring darling, I don't want our guests to think I have chosen a hussy.'

'In the morning we will look at those gowns together Maya,' Melinda said smoothly. 'Eleanor had good taste and there will be something for you I am sure.'

'Thank you Lady Gaynor, I shall be very grateful,' I murmured.

' "Melinda" please Maya, now that you are to become part of the family.'

I had never been in Eleanor's room before but as soon as I entered it I could see her sitting at her dressing table brushing her long dark red hair, or lying with it spread out across the pillow in the large, four-poster bed. The room was elegantly beautiful as Eleanor herself had been and I exclaimed with appreciation at the soft green carpet and heavy damask drapes and bed hangings.

'Eleanor always had taste,' Melinda said. 'Cora tried to emulate her in many ways but it was never possible. She did not have Eleanor's flair, nor her personality.'

The wardrobes were still filled with her clothes, and surprised I asked, 'Did she leave some of her clothes here after she was married?'

'She left most of her ballgowns. Roger was not a ball-going man, he was a sporting man so she left them here for when she came without him. Look at them all Maya, I'm sure you will find one to suit you.'

I picked out three or four of them and laid them on the bed for Melinda's inspection. I deliberately did not choose white or ivory, not wishing to appear too bridal, and of course crimson and black were out of the question. Instead I chose pale blue and turquoise, a gown in a soft shade of coral and one in gold. One after the other I held them up against me so that Melinda could criticise and in the end we decided together on the coral. It lit up my face and set off my blue-black hair and unusual eyes, but more than that it gave a willowy grace to my figure with its long sweeping skirt and the tiny bodice that fell away from my shoulders. The gown was plain except for a trail of coral chiffon roses which fell from the waist to the hem-line. Looking at me critically Melinda said, 'You have great beauty, Maya. You will make Gavin very proud of you.'

On the night of my engagement ball, I stood beside Lyndon and Gavin at the entrance to the ballroom receiving our guests, while Melinda sat next to her husband acknowledging their greetings charmingly. She would be unable to dance and I felt sorry for this woman who had once danced so joyfully in her husband's arms. The two brothers looked remarkably handsome in their dark evening dress and as Gavin and I started to dance I was acutely aware of the gleam of admiration in his eyes. 'You're beautiful Maya,' he murmured against my hair, 'I saw it, even in those dull governess clothes, I know it now. All the fellows here are envying me, all the girls are madly jealous.'

I didn't answer him. Standing beside Melinda's chair Lyndon was watching us and then he turned away abruptly as though he couldn't bear to watch us together. A few minutes later I saw that he was dancing with Cora while Melinda sat chatting to a group of elderly ladies settled beside her.

I danced often with Gavin, but then I danced with other men, men who talked to me about hunting and horses and there were some who tried to flirt with me and others who tried to interest me in various committees and charities.

My aunt and uncle appeared to be enjoying themselves and my aunt was wearing a new gown which I felt sure she must have had specially made for the occasion. It was a dark, serviceable blue but she wore her prized cameo as well as a long gold chain and as she had once said to me, 'Nobody expects a vicar's wife to be too fashionable.'

I felt that Gavin was showing me off to the county as he might have exhibited a prize horse and my smile became forced, and my conversation flagged. I was hurt that Lyndon hadn't asked me to dance with him. He had danced with one or two of the ladies present and as the evening wore on I longed for it to be over so that I could get out of my borrowed gown and retire to my room to lick my wounds. I was standing in a small group listening to their talk about people I did not know, with a set smile on my face, when Lyndon joined us and immediately invited me to dance.

I felt nervous, angry with myself that I stumbled during our first steps on the floor, then as his arm tightened in order to steady me I gave myself up to the joy of dancing with him. He was slightly taller than Gavin and to my surprise his dancing was smoother and more effortless. We danced in silence, and once I caught Melinda's and Cora's eyes on us from the edge of the floor. I wanted that waltz to go on forever. I felt so right in his arms, but slowly the music came to a stop and he was escorting me across the floor.

'Thank you Maya, that was charming.'

His smile was brief, impersonal, and I longed for him to stay and talk to me if only to show that we were still friends. Forlornly I watched him return to Melinda's side, leaving me miserably and strangely alone.

I know that the ball went on and on until the early hours of the morning and I danced dutifully with my fiancé and those others who asked me, and then I stood in the hall watching our guests depart, more weary than I can ever remember feeling. It was not the dancing that had tired me. I loved to dance and I was young enough to dance my feet off but my weariness came from something inside, some strange feeling of dread that I had done a terrible thing in promising to marry Gavin Gaynor.

If I went through with this wedding I would spend the rest of my life living a lie, day after day having to pretend something I didn't feel, and all the time so terribly aware of how much I loved his brother. I knew now that what I should have done was to have had the courage to leave Greythorn, but I could neither have faced my old life in Lexford nor had the strength to cut myself off from Lyndon.

Melinda had retired to her room earlier and at last I was free to go to mine. Gavin appeared well pleased with the evening, saying 'We must do this again after our wedding, darling! Can't you rustle up some more relatives or friends – tonight they were conspicuous by their absence.'

Miss Lawford had declined to attend, saying that her health had not been good recently but she wished me well and hoped that I would take my fiancé to see her. Otherwise, only my aunt and uncle had been present at the ball and again I experienced that sharp pang of inadequacy.

'Perhaps Maya does not wish to have a grand wedding but would prefer something quieter,' his brother said calmly, and throwing him a look of gratitude I said, 'I would much prefer it.

I haven't any friends living close by and few relatives, you must know that Gavin.'

He frowned, the frown of a small boy who hated to be thwarted.

Quickly, Lyndon added, 'Perhaps a quiet wedding would be best in view of the recent tragedy. In fact, it would be more suitable.'

Gavin gave a short laugh. 'I wonder if we shall spend the rest of our lives keeping a low profile because of Eleanor?'

'This is hardly the rest of your life and that particular tragedy is still very recent.'

'Oh well – Maya must make up her own mind. I would like to be consulted from time to time.'

I was trembling when I reached my room. What had I done? Was I really going to marry a petulant child whom I did not love? Had I really burned my bridges behind me until there was no escape?

Gavin decided that the wedding should take place in the early spring and as I rode across the fell with him I asked where he intended us to live when we were married.

'Why, here at Greythorn of course!' he answered, surprised.

'But this is your brother's house. You surely don't want us to live here always?'

'Why ever not? I help Lyndon to run the estate, and I certainly don't intend to saddle myself with the expense of buying a house when there's this enormous place hardly occupied. I couldn't simply buy any old house, it would have to be a large one and then there would be the servant problem with all the attendant worries.'

'So you expect to live at Greythorn just as you have always done – Cora too, I suppose?'

'Oh, Cora'll marry one day. After all, she's quite a catch. She got some of my grandfather's money as well as some that our mother left her. Besides – she's not bad-looking. Some days she's even pretty when she remembers not to look so solemn.'

'I don't think I want to live at Greythorn for the rest of my life.'

He looked at me impatiently. 'Don't you be difficult, Maya. Think instead that one day the Hall is going to be ours. If we haven't moved out we shan't have to move back in shall we? Think about it that way.'

He didn't begin to understand how I felt. He was a man accustomed to having his own way and marriage wasn't going to stop it. He would expect me to be a possession without a thought in my head unless it was prompted by himself. More and more I began to think of how I could get away. I felt ashamed and appalled by my stupidity in ever thinking our engagement could work, and all the time I listened to him making plans for the wedding my mind was absorbed with the need to stop it.

Cora remarked that I had made no plans of my own, either regarding my wedding dress or my bridesmaids. 'Time's going on Maya,' she remarked, 'shouldn't you be thinking about these things?'

'Everything seems to be happening so quickly, Cora. I had thought that perhaps you would like to be my bridesmaid.' In truth, I had just thought of it that second, but Cora was not to know. All the same, I was surprised by her answer.

'Oh, I don't think so, Maya. After all, only last spring I was thinking about my own wedding. There'll be enough gossip as it is and you know what people will say.'

'No, what can they possibly say?'

' "Poor girl, she's had to settle for being a bridesmaid again." I couldn't bear that, Maya.'

'Surely they wouldn't be so cruel!'

'They would delight in being so cruel. Isn't there anybody else you would like to ask?'

'I suppose I could ask one or two of my schoolfriends. We haven't kept in touch but I could write to them.'

'Well, why don't you, but if I can help in any other way I will.'

'I would like Jamie to come to the wedding.'

'Oh, he's old enough to go to weddings, Lyndon only draws the line at funerals. Do you want him for a page?'

'No, he'd hate dressing up. Have you spent much time with Jamie recently, Cora?'

'No. You didn't seem particularly keen on the idea.'

'Only when you were so unhappy yourself and he was so fanciful. Did you ever mention Emily to him?'

'Emily.'

'Yes. He talked about a pretty lady called Emily, a lady with red hair and he said she was probably dead.'

She stared at me, then almost flippantly she replied, 'He could well be right about that. They never *did* find her, did they Maya?'

'Was it you who spoke to Jamie, Cora?'

'Well – why should I speak to him about Emily when I hardly knew her? Oh look, there's Melinda driving the chaise – shall we catch up with her?'

I delved into my small savings in order to purchase things for my trousseau and was touched to receive a parcel from Aunt Miranda containing several lengths of lace and crêpe de chine which she had been hoarding for that special purpose for years. My aunt and uncle viewed her gifts with some relief and I was encouraged to take them to the dressmaker in the village.

Suitably flattered, the good woman's clever fingers made me beautiful underwear from the crêpe de chine but I told her to hang on to the lace as I had not yet made my mind up what I wanted from it.

'It would make a beautiful wedding dress,' she said, 'and there is so much of it.'

'You may be right,' I told her. 'Are you sure there is enough for a wedding dress?'

'Enough and to spare. Besides Miss Maya, the shops charge so much and I can copy anything you see.'

'I'll make up my mind soon and let you know.'

I did not like going into Harrogate or York with Cora. She had far more money than I and invariably encouraged me to spend money that I did not have. Usually our trips ended with me watching Cora try on gown after gown which she invariably bought while I left the shop empty-handed.

'Don't you mind?' she asked me one day.

'No, of course not. I know I can't afford them.'

'Why don't you take over all of Eleanor's things? She'll not need them again and it's such a waste for them to be hanging in her room.'

'They haven't been offered to me Cora, besides there's no reason why they should be.'

'I'll speak to Lyndon. I'm sure he's merely overlooked them.'

'I'd rather you didn't, Cora. If Lyndon had wanted me to have them he would surely have offered them.'

'As I said, he's probably overlooked them.'

To Gavin's frustration I still devoted much of my life to Jamie. We worked at his lessons, and in our leisure time we walked or rode together. Lyndon was still paying my salary and I felt the need to earn it: when I tried to explain this to Gavin he seemed impatient and uncomprehending, but as I was rapidly finding out, he deliberately refused to understand those things he disagreed with.

Surely, I thought, he can't expect Lyndon to keep us at Greythorn when we are married, but more and more as the weeks passed I came to the conclusion that this was exactly what he did expect.

Out of sheer exasperation I mentioned the matter to Cora but to my surprise she simply laughed. 'Gavin's money is tied up like mine so that neither of us can touch it without Lyndon's permission. He is generous fortunately and I was to have control of mine when I married. I don't know about Gavin, he's always been a spendthrift, and a bit too fond of the good life. I suppose he buys you expensive presents. Half the village girls must be wearing some bauble he's handed out at one time or another.'

Stung to retort I said, 'Perhaps he's making sure I'm marrying him for himself and not the things he can give me.'

'You may be right.'

'He gave Indigo to me and spent some time schooling him.'

'Lyndon schooled Indigo, but I'm not sure he meant to give him to you.'

I stared at her in astonishment. 'Then why didn't Gavin tell me? Oh, this is quite terrible. I can't take him under these circumstances.'

She shrugged her shoulders unconcerned. 'No doubt he knows that Gavin has given the horse to you. I shouldn't worry about it if I were you, Indigo's a beautiful horse and whether Lyndon likes it or not you are going to be a member of the family.'

Whether he liked it or not! That just about summed it up. Cora was amused by my feelings of disquiet. Somehow I no longer thought of her as my friend and there were many occasions when she could not resist introducing barbed sarcasm into her conversation.

'I should thank Lyndon for his work with Indigo, or he will think me very ungracious,' I murmured.

'I don't suppose Lyndon's noticed – after all, he's very busy.'

I went to him that night in his study after dinner, and when I had blurted out my thanks and apologised for not thanking him before, he waved a careless hand, saying, 'It doesn't matter, Maya. Are you quite happy with the horse now?'

'Very happy. He's quite gentle now but I was afraid of him before.'

'You should have been, you did a very brave thing in riding him that night.'

I blushed at his unusual praise and smiling a little he asked, 'Who told you that it was I who had the horse schooled?'

'Cora told me.'

'I see. Well, all I ask is that you enjoy him. He needs a lot of exercise. I have given instructions that when you are not riding him yourself one of the grooms must ride him.'

'Thank you Lyndon, you are very kind.'

He rose from his chair and came round his desk to open the door for me. I raised my eyes to his as I drew level and I wondered if he saw in them all I had tried to hide. He smiled at me gently, but his smile was warmer than it had been recently.

Gavin saw me leaving the study and grinning at me he said, 'Have you and Lyndon been burying the hatchet then?'

'I was thanking him for having Indigo schooled for me.'

He raised his eyebrows maddeningly. 'Who told you about that?'

'I shan't tell you, but apparently it was true.'

'Well, it can only have been Melinda or Cora, and I suspect Cora. That girl's getting altogether too malicious, why the devil doesn't she mind her own business!'

'Why didn't you tell me?'

'I didn't see that it mattered who gave you the horse, he's yours anyway.'

'I thought it only polite to thank your brother for his share in the gift.'

'Oh well, I suppose you're right. There's a race meeting tomorrow – are you interested?

'Not tomorrow, Gavin. I have to go into Lexford for some fittings and there's Jamie to think of.'

'Oh Jamie, always Jamie. You're not thinking of keeping this up once we're married I hope.'

'Lyndon is paying my salary and I must earn it. I've told you before that I intend to teach Jamie until your brother says it is no longer my concern. Try to understand, Gavin.'

The sulky little boy look was on his face again and I realised with some dismay that it had ceased to trouble me. It troubled me even less the following morning when Lyndon told him with some asperity that he could not leave the estate to attend the race meeting. There was a dispute between two separate homesteads which needed sorting out and one of the workmen had had an accident the previous day and labour had to be transferred.

Gavin left the house with poor grace but Lyndon seemed more preoccupied than usual while I doubted if I could ever make a mature adult out of Gavin after we were married.

I attended to my fittings in the morning but in the afternoon Cora invited me to ride with her across the fells. Jamie had gone on a visit to some neighbouring friends with Melinda and because the day was so fresh and bright I began to look forward to the outing.

We rode towards Lexford but instead of going through the village Cora suggested that we climb the fell to Ash Meadow. I wondered if Ned was still working the farm with his father and if he missed Emily. It was singularly quiet round the farmhouse as we passed the gate. A farm dog slept in the cobbled yard and sheep grazed on the fells, but no smoke rose from the chimneys and I surmised they were all out on the land.

Cora rode behind me as we climbed higher and suddenly I was aware of the figure of a man sitting at the top of the hill, his back resting against the stones. He was staring down into the valley beneath him, deep in thought, and not wanting to ride too close to him I turned Indigo in the direction of the lower slope.

Cora drew my attention to him. 'Isn't that the boy your friend was seeing?' she asked from behind me.

I pulled up the horse and looked towards the crag. She was right, it was Ned Rakesby sitting so pensively on the hillside staring down at his father's farm.

'Will you wait for me Cora, I'd like to talk to Ned,' I said already guiding Indigo up the slope.

'I'll ride on, you can catch me up eventually,' she called.

I was almost on top of Ned when he awoke from his trance, jumped clumsily to his feet, and stood fidgeting with his cap while I approached.

'Hello Ned,' I said, smiling at him. 'I didn't know it was you at first but Cora recognised you. How are you?'

'Well enough, Miss Maya, I didn't expect to see you round 'ere.'

'Well, I'm not really very far away. There didn't seem any signs of life round the farm – are your parents not at home?'

'Mi mother died last November so there's only me an' mi father now, miss.'

'Oh, I'm sorry Ned. Had she been ill long?'

'No, it were very quick towards th'end.'

215

He seemed ill at ease. His eyes wavered when they met mine but something I could not control made me persist in my conversation with him.

'Are those your sheep up on the fells, Ned?'

'They are fer now, but mi father's sellin' t'farm so they'll soon belong to somebody else.'

'Selling the farm, Ned! But what about you, this is your livelihood.'

'We don't get on, mi father'n me. 'E says it's me that's sent mi mother to an early grave. They've niver forgiven me for Emily.'

'But that's cruel, Ned. You loved Emily, you wanted to marry her, how can he do this to you?'

'Well, ye see Miss Maya, she went away an' she's never come back. You know what it's like in t'village, every time mi mother went to t'shops, an' when we went to t'church, all of 'em starin' at us an' whisperin'.'

'Oh Ned, don't I know it, but it's so unfair – you can't let a lot of old busybodies ruin your life! I'm surprised at your father. What are you going to do?'

'Well, mi father's got a little cottage in Lawton, and I suppose I could go wi' 'im but 'e's niver mentioned it. I knows what I'm goin' to do.'

'What's that Ned?'

'I'm goin' to join up. They're wantin lads in th' Army an' I know nowt but farmin'.'

I stared at him in dismay. 'Oh Ned, why didn't you and Emily think about the future more, why were you so foolish?'

He stared at me hopelessly, then surprised me by saying, 'I 'ear you've got engaged to Gavin Gaynor, Miss?'

'Yes Ned, and please don't call me Miss, you always called me Maya before.'

'That was afore ye got caught up wi' th' gentry.'

'I haven't changed. I'm still the same girl you helped to climb back into her bedroom up the trunk of that old elm tree.'

'I wish we had those days back wi' us, Maya.'

'So do I Ned, oh so do I.'

'Aren't ye 'appy then, bein' engaged to 'im?'

'I don't know, Ned. Sometimes I wonder if I care enough.'

'I cared enough, Maya, I worshipped 'er, I'd 'a followed 'er to the ends o' the earth an' I'd a' tried all mi life to make 'er 'appy. She knew that an' still she wouldn't marry me.'

'But *why* Ned? I could never understand why. She cared for you enough to let you make love to her, so why wouldn't she marry you?'

'I never made love to 'er, Maya, I never laid a finger on 'er.'

I stared at him in disbelief, and in some impatience he cried, 'It's true, I never touched 'er. I loved 'er, I wanted to marry 'er, respectable, like our folks wanted it.'

'Then who Ned, *who*?'

'It's not fer me to say, Maya. She's gone, it's best left alone.'

'No Ned, it isn't. You knew who was responsible – why didn't you defend yourself, why didn't you say?'

'I couldn't let 'er down. If I'd defended misself where would Emily a' bin? I knew 'e wouldn't marry 'er, 'e'd niver any intentions o' marryin' 'er.'

'Did he know?'

'Oh, 'e knew all right. I told Emily I'd kill 'im if I ever saw 'im an' she begged me to keep out of it. That were when she first said she'd marry me – if I'd keep out of it – but then she changed 'er mind. I didn't amount to much at side of 'im.'

'*Who was it, Ned?*'

'I can't tell ye that Maya, an' I'd rather ye didn't ask me. I must be gettin' back now, there's milkin' to do an' mi father gets peevish if I'm not there i' time to do it. I 'opes you'll be very 'appy Maya. 'E doesn't deserve anybody as nice as you are.'

I stared down at him. I already knew who was responsible for Emily's baby. I didn't need Ned to tell me, and again I saw her warm blushing face whenever the name of Gavin Gaynor was mentioned. And I had been the one to insist that they meet! I felt suddenly sick with anger at the hopeless wasted years and some of my despair must have shown in my face because Ned took the reins of my horse firmly in his grasp, crying, 'No Maya, no, you must think, don't do anythin' reckless. You love 'im, you must forgive 'im!'

'I can't forgive him Ned – and I don't love him. I think I hate him!'

Snatching the reins away I urged Indigo down the hillside, jumping the stone wall recklessly and without a thought for our safety. I had forgotten Cora who had ridden on ahead of me, forgotten Ned standing on the hillside staring after me. All I wanted now was to get back to Greythorn, and using my whip I urged Indigo on faster still until the gates of the Hall lay before us, with the long drive up to the house.

SEVENTEEN

TWICE I HAD ridden Indigo as though the devil himself pursued me – the first time with my heart filled with dread, the second with such a deep hatred consuming me I was unaware of the speed or the flying hoofs beneath me. Now I pulled him up sharply in the stableyard and he reared on his haunches, whinnying shrilly. The grooms ran towards us, their faces frightened and one of them said, 'I thowt 'e were runnin' away wi' ye, Miss.'

I did not respond, but dismounted, leaving Indigo in their care. Outside the stableyard I took to my heels and ran, arriving breathless in the hall minutes later. The house felt quiet. I remembered then that Jamie was out with Melinda and Cora was probably waiting for me still on the fell. Then I heard men's voices coming from Lyndon's study. I could not hear Gavin's amongst them, so I wandered through the house, looking in every room that I came to.

On being informed by a servant that he had not been seen since luncheon, I bit my lip with frustration and went into the library to wait. I could hear Lyndon's visitors leaving, then shortly afterwards I heard Gavin speaking at the study door. I could not hear what was being said but I wished Lyndon would go away out of the house. I wanted to speak to Gavin alone.

He came into the library whistling cheerfully, and on seeing me smiled and came towards me.

'I knew you'd gone riding with Cora, Maya. I have just seen Indigo in the stables, and he looked as though you'd ridden him hard – and unwisely, I might add!'

'I've been talking to Ned Rakesby on the fells near Ash Meadow.'

'Have you indeed, and who, might I ask, is Ned Rakesby?'

'You know very well, Gavin.'

'You surely don't think I know every village swain around these parts. Girls yes, the men no. Who is this Ned Rakesby?'

'Somebody who once said he'd kill you if Emily hadn't prevented it.'

I saw the wary look in his eyes even if the nonchalant manner persisted. Turning his back on me he walked over to the table, his hands hunting through the periodicals that were always kept there.

'One can never find anything in this place,' he muttered. 'I suppose Lyndon's got it.'

I walked round the table to stand near him.

'Look at me Gavin, and listen when I'm speaking to you.'

'My, but my beautiful fiancée is very demanding this afternoon,' he said, but close to him I was aware of the dark flush on his face and that he was ill at ease despite his sarcasm.

'You knew about Emily's baby – didn't you Gavin! You knew that she was desperate!'

'Emily? What Emily?'

'You know very well who I'm talking about so don't prevaricate. She came here to tell you about the baby, didn't she? You knew it was yours.'

The petulant sulky look was back on his face. 'Oh, don't go on about it, Maya. She could have married that chap Rakesby and they'd have been right for each other. Why the hell didn't she?'

'What did you say to her when you knew?'

'I told her there was no proof that it was mine, nor was there. She was no angel, your little Emily. When it came to raw passion she could have taught you a lot! Be reasonable, girl – you surely didn't expect me to marry her! You are not too confident about how you fit in here, so Emily would have been a disaster.'

'She knew you wouldn't help her. What effect did that have on her?'

'Gracious – how can I remember now? I told her to marry Rakesby and I said I'd give her money. They'd have had a good start together, what with his father's farm and my money.'

'You think money's the answer to everything, don't you Gavin, that it can buy everything!'

'Well – most girls, a good many girls, would have been glad of it.'

He was walking towards me with that maddening half-smile on his lips, a smile that was meant to placate me as no doubt it had placated many other women. Suddenly, terrifyingly I was back in that other room years before, sheltering in Anya's arms while that big negro with a half-smile on his face came towards us with the butt of his rifle raised on high. Without a second's thought I rushed towards Gavin raining blows on his face with my whip while the pent-up sobs of all the years racked my body with agony and the scalding tears rolled down my face. I heard his cries of pain but I could not stop. I went on hitting him until I felt the whip wrenched from my hands and strong arms gripping my struggling body. Through a red haze I dimly heard Lyndon's voice saying over and over again, 'Maya for God's sake stop!'

Through the curtain of my tears the room began to take shape. Not a room filled with the scent of oleander blossoms and my mother's body lying still across the doorway, the dark blue sky ablaze with stars – but another room, lined with books and above me Lyndon's face shocked and angry. Dazed, I looked towards the door where Miranda and Cora stood white-faced and afraid, then I turned to stare at Gavin. Blood was pouring from a deep red cut along the side of his face and there was blood on his hands where he had covered his head and face to defend himself.

I stared at him in horror then sank trembling into a chair with my head in my hands. I have no memory of the following hours after Lyndon snatched the whip from my hands. I only recall dimly that he gave instructions for the doctor to be sent

221

for and then I found myself sitting alone in his study waiting for him to come to me. I felt no sense of regret or shame, no compassion tempting me to minister to Gavin's hurt, no anguish that something between us was irrevocably over. It had never been love. Gavin did not have the capacity for loving and I was only capable of loving unwisely and hopelessly.

I sat before the fire while outside the study I was aware of voices and hurrying footsteps and gradually the events of the afternoon took shape. I knew now that Cora had intended me to see Ned Rakesby sitting on the hillside where his sheep were grazing. She must often have seen him there and she had been insistent that we rode that way. What I could not believe was that she had done it out of friendship. Her motives were far more sinister. In spite of the fire I felt cold and I dreaded the contempt I would see in Lyndon's eyes when he eventually came to me. I was shivering with the effects of shock, holding on to the arms of my chair with my teeth chattering uncontrollably. I heard the door close but I dared not look up. Instead I continued to stare straight ahead of me as though to memorise every leaf and twig outside the window. Lyndon came to sit opposite me at his desk, but one look at my stricken face and shaking hands made him reach for the brandy bottle, pouring out a generous measure in a glass. I could not take it from him, nor could I hold it without spilling the contents, and he held it to my lips so that the strong sharp liquid could trickle down my throat.

I coughed as it burnt my throat but in just a few minutes I felt calmer and the shuddering had stopped. Lyndon had gone back to sit in his chair and although I stared at him helplessly there was no contempt in his eyes, only anxiety. Bit by bit I poured out my story, keeping nothing back. I told him about Africa and that last dreadful night and I told him about Emily and how much I had loved her. I told him why I had suddenly hated Gavin with all my being and the need I felt to make him suffer and that was the first time he spoke.

'Why did you promise to marry him, Maya? Love doesn't suddenly turn into hatred. It is true it can be killed by ill-use and suffering, but not immediately. Usually it dies slowly, painfully and with many doubtful misgivings.'

I had told him so much I might as well tell him everything.

'I should never have said I would marry Gavin. I didn't love him, but I thought you believed I was an adventuress, a girl who had wormed her way into your household and intended to take advantage of it. A girl who had nothing – but intended to have everything.'

'And did my opinion matter so much that you were prepared to marry my brother out of pique, or because your pride had been hurt?'

'It wasn't just my pride, it was everything. I loved you so much Lyndon, it was so easy for you to hurt me.'

I put my head into my hands and sobbed for the second time that afternoon. Once I had thought that tears would make the hurt go away, now I was realising that they were only a temporary release for pent-up emotion. Time alone would take the deeper hurt away.

He left his chair for a second time and pulled me to my feet to stand within the circle of his arms. 'Oh my dear,' he murmured unhappily, 'I had no idea. I did not think that you would read so much into those few unguarded moments. I had no right to make love to you, it should never have happened.'

'I wanted you to make love to me. I think I loved you from the first moment I saw you years ago but I didn't know it then. You were so sensitive to my loneliness, and later you were so kind to me and I hurt for you when I knew Melinda would never be well.'

'And I got you out of your uncle's house into something more adventurous and all in all you came to look upon me as some sort of deliverer, your white knight perhaps?'

'It may have been like that, I don't know, I have never loved anybody before. I never want to love anybody again.'

'Oh, but you *will* Maya, believe me. You are very young and very lovely. One day the right sort of young man is going to come into your life and you'll smile about this confession and wonder how you could ever have been foolish enough to make it.'

223

'I know you don't love me Lyndon, I know you love Melinda and I'm glad. I love her too, she's good and kind and sweet, but I haven't been foolish, I have been very wise to love you. One's first love should always be for a good man, an honourable man. If I never love again I shall not regret loving you, even when I know it can never be returned.'

He was looking down at me helplessly but I could not read the expression on his face. With a small smothered cry he murmured my name, 'Maya, Maya,' and crushed me for a brief moment in his arms. Letting me go so abruptly I stumbled and would have fallen if he had not caught my arm to prevent it.

He stood away from me and this time his voice was practical, impersonal. 'You realise Maya that you will not be able to remain here after the events of today?'

'I know.'

'When will you be prepared to leave?'

'Tonight, please. It will not take me long to pack my things.'

'And you will return to your uncle's house or is there anywhere else you can go?'

'I could go to Aunt Miranda's but not tonight. I shall have to return to Lexford and tell them my engagement is broken. They will not make me very welcome after *that* news.'

'I will speak to your uncle, Maya. It will not be left to you. Now go upstairs and pack your things and I will have a tray sent up to your room. I will drive you to Lexford as soon as you are ready to go.'

It did not take me long to pack and although the tray arrived I was not hungry. I looked round the charming room where I had been so happy and I longed to go into the nursery to see Jamie but I thought the kindest thing was for me to stay away. The gowns that had been Eleanor's I left hanging in the wardrobe taking only my own things with me, and in less than half an hour I was walking down the stairs. I stood hesitantly in the hall, looking round at the graceful pillars and sweeping staircase that I would never see again. I moved slowly towards the study, memorising every picture, every ornament and piece of furniture on the way, but before I had reached it the drawing room door opened and Melinda stood looking at me.

'Please come in here for a moment, Maya. Were you really going without saying goodbye?'

Unhappily I followed her into the room. She was alone, looking at me sadly and with regret.

'I am so sorry it has ended this way,' she began gently. 'Lyndon has told me what prompted your assault on Gavin and I can understand your anger with him. Of course you would no longer wish to marry him after that.'

'No, Lady Gaynor, how could I? I would always remember Emily.'

'Gavin has always been wild, too good-looking, too sure of himself and in many ways the girls welcomed his advances. I'm not saying your friend was of this calibre but on the whole everything came too easily to Gavin, and afterwards he invariably lost interest in his toy of the moment.'

'Is he very badly hurt?'

'He will be scarred, probably for life. His face needed stitching.

'Oh my God,' I murmured, sinking down into a chair where I sat trembling.

'Lyndon tells me you met a man this afternoon who told you he was not the father of your friend's child. Did you go specially to meet him?'

'No. It was Cora's suggestion that we ride up there. I think she meant me to talk to Ned, I think she knew about Emily and Gavin.'

'I see.' She stared at me without speaking for several seconds, then she said something which troubled me whenever I thought about it, long after I left Greythorn Hall.

'You see this house as a beautiful thing, Maya, standing serene and peaceful in the midst of its parkland, but over the years terrible things have happened to the people who lived here. I have never heard the voices in the whispering glade but Eleanor heard them and she is dead. So did Roland and Roger. There were others too, and now I wonder who will be the next.'

'I can't think that Emily ever heard them.'

'Perhaps not, but who is the lady with red hair that Jamie talks about? Does the child really think he sees her or is he open to suggestion? Very soon, Maya, I am going to ask my husband to have them drag the mere.'

I stared at her with horror. 'You think Emily is in the mere?'

'I think it is more than likely.'

We were still staring at each other when Lyndon came for me, then without another word I walked with him from the room.

At the vicarage we were received with some surprise, and immediately Lyndon asked my uncle if he could speak to him alone in his study. My aunt and I sat in uncomfortable silence in the kitchen. She explained that a fire had not been lit in the drawing room and invariably she now retired to bed early while my uncle stayed up to prepare his sermons.

She listened as I explained the bare essentials of my broken engagement and the necessity for my leaving Greythorn.

'Does that mean that you will be living here, Maya, that I must dispense with Miss Peabody's services?' she asked anxiously.

'Not at all, Aunt Edith. I shall go into Lancashire to stay with Aunt Miranda for a time and Sir Lyndon has always been most generous. I have been able to save a little money and of course I will no longer need to provide for my trousseau.'

'You paid the dressmaker, I hope, for the things she made for you?'

'Yes of course, and I shall ask her to return the lace. I shall not be needing it now.'

Sir Lyndon was leaving and summoned by my uncle we both went to the door to see him depart.

He took my hand, looking down at me gravely. 'If there is anything I can do for you Maya you must not hesitate to ask. A reference, a letter of introduction and I will see that a sum of money is placed in the bank for you.'

'Oh no, Sir Lyndon, that won't be necessary, I have enough for my needs.'

'Well, we shall see. Goodbye, Maya. Thank you for what you have been able to do for Jamie.' I felt the clasp of his hand long after he had gone.

We stood and watched him walking down the path towards the carriage then we turned to go inside. I don't know what Lyndon had said to my uncle but although he was clearly ruffled, he kept silent. My aunt was obviously curious but he said curtly, 'If you will come into the study Edith, I will inform you of what Sir Lyndon has said to me. Perhaps you will make some tea, Maya.'

I made the tea and afterwards we drank it in silence. Excusing myself, I said I would like to retire as I felt very tired. They offered no objection and wearily I dragged myself up the stairs to the room I had had as a child.

I lay fully clothed on the bed unable to sleep, going over and over in my mind the events of the day. I heard my aunt come up to bed and later my uncle, then as I had done through all the days of my childhood I lay listening to the branches of the elms tapping against my window and the sound of the wind echoing mournfully around the house.

I was determined to leave Lexford as early as possible before the news of my broken engagement became the main topic of conversation in the village. My aunt said she would retrieve the lace from the dressmaker so that I need not say anything to her, so taking just the bare essentials I left the vicarage in the late morning, intending to call and see Mrs Roper on the way. There were few people about because it was Sunday and church had already started. Mrs Roper rarely attended now in the morning although she invariably went to Evensong – and I felt pretty sure I would find her at home.

She greeted me with surprise and went immediately to make tea. I sat at the table in the old familiar parlour and looking at me closely she said, 'Somethin's wrong Maya. Do ye want to tell me?'

I started at the beginning and told her the whole events of the day before, leaving out only my conversation with Lyndon. I even told her Melinda's suggestion about dragging the mere.

'I allus knew there were somethin' goin' on wi' Master Gavin. She were allus out when he rode down t'street. She'd come in at night wi' 'er eyes shinin' like stars an' I never saw 'er like that wi' Ned. I don't suppose 'e ever loved 'er.'

'No, Mrs Roper, nor me. Gavin loves only Gavin.'

'She must a' bin mad ever to suppose 'e'd marry 'er.'

'Being in love gives us many strange ideas.'

'Ey lass but it's wrong that you should suffer fer 'er mistakes. Can't you forgive 'im, can't you go back to 'im an' leave all this in the past?'

'No, Mrs Roper. I can't forgive him and he'll never forgive me. I've spoilt his pretty face and Gavin is very vain, besides, I don't love him. That fact will hurt him as nothing else has hurt him. He won't be able to forgive me for not loving him.'

She shook her head dolefully, nor did I think she fully understood. She came to the door with me and I ran down the street before the rest of them emerged from the church. There was only one train into the city on Sundays and I had to wait at the station for over an hour before it came.

I was grateful for Aunt Miranda's loving commonsense and for the first few days she asked no questions but allowed me to tell her everything in my own good time. She listened quietly, occasionally shaking her head and when the sorry tale was told she said, 'I was worried about that engagement of yours, Maya. Your letters should have been full of it, full of *him* but they weren't. It was always the other one you wrote about and I have ever been a one for reading between the lines.'

'I have to forget about him now, Aunt Miranda. I must find work, rebuild my life so that I'm too busy to dwell on the past – but I don't know how to start!'

'You can stay here as long as you like, Maya. You like it here, don't you?'

'Oh yes I do,' I answered truthfully. I loved her warm cottage and the wild hills, even though my heart told me often that the man I adored lived on the other side of them. I relished the quaint country lanes and warm bustling villages but there was no work for me and I was too young to spend my life living on Aunt Miranda – whether she welcomed it or not.

I wrote a long letter to Miss Lawford telling her that my wedding plans were off and asking her if she knew of anything I could do. I told her that I had been working as a governess and could provide her with excellent references, and if there was nothing at the school perhaps she knew of some child or elderly person who could offer me employment.

She wrote back immediately, inviting me to go to see her and my heart lifted somewhat. Surely she would not have invited me if she didn't have something in view.

I packed a small valise in case I had to stay overnight and told my aunt I would return as soon as possible with any news I might have. She watched me go with an uncertain smile on her face but my hopes were high as my pony and trap clattered along the narrow lane towards the town in the valley.

I was surprised at how little Miss Lawford had changed in the years since we had last met and she greeted me warmly. Sitting in her study with the sound of girls' voices outside in the gardens, it seemed like another world, a calm charming world in which I had been happy, with no thought of the turmoil to come.

I told her all that had happened to me since leaving her care and shaking her head sadly she said, 'If only your uncle had allowed you to stay here Maya, none of these things would ever have involved you.'

I nodded regretfully. 'I suppose I would have still been here, happy in my own little world, doing the thing I loved best and untroubled by other people's tragedies.'

'I wonder if that life was ever intended for you, Maya? I thought about you a great deal after you left the school and I reached the conclusion that you were a girl who needed to spread her wings, find life, perhaps even suffer a little. I watched Mary Reardon doing the work I had offered to you and became convinced that she was right and you would have been wrong.'

I stared at her anxiously, shaken by her words.

'Oh – you could have done the job with more flair, Maya, you would have filled their hearts and minds with a vision that Mary has never heard of and they would have adored you, while plain, plodding Mary works so hard but with so little imagination.'

'Mary is still here, then?'

'Yes. She is happy here and I have no complaints about her work.'

'I thought perhaps that there was a place for me here, that Mary had left.'

'No the place isn't here Maya – although I do know of someone who is looking for a secretary. Would you be interested in such a position?'

'I'm not sure. I don't know very much about being a secretary.'

'There is a lady living in the village who is writing her memoirs. Her husband was quite a famous explorer and she travelled with him widely. You may have heard of him – Sir Edward Gillespie.'

'Oh yes, of course I have heard of him, but I didn't know he was dead!'

'He died last year and his widow came to live here. She is elderly, well into her seventies, but she is a very alert and capable lady.'

'What would my duties entail, Miss Lawford?'

'Some research perhaps, taking notes, I'm not very sure. She has said she needs help and I have already spoken to her about you.'

'What did she say?'

'She wants you to call and see her, today if possible Maya, directly after tea perhaps. You must stay here tonight. There won't be time for you to get back to Lancashire.'

I wasn't sure about my ability to act as a secretary. It was a far cry from teaching a small boy but it was work. I needed to work, not only for the money but to fill my mind and my heart and leave little time for brooding.

I would never have guessed that Mrs Gillespie was seventy-four years old. She was small and spry with thick silver hair and china blue eyes in a pink and white face. She looked more like a delicate doll than a woman who had accompanied her husband on dangerous expeditions, and as if she read my thoughts she said with twinkling eyes, 'You are thinking this surely cannot be the woman who has tramped the Amazon jungles and slept out on ice floes.'

I blushed, apologising shyly for any such thoughts I had harboured.

'Don't apologise my dear, I am frequently misunderstood, and I am not nearly as fragile as I look. I suppose Miss Lawford explained what I am looking for.'

'Yes, but I'm not very sure if I shall fit in.'

'I'm sure you will. She spoke very highly of you and I have great faith in her judgment. She said something about a broken engagement, I'm sorry my dear.'

I smiled uncertainly, and she said briskly, 'I don't suppose there's any chance that in a few weeks it will all be on again?'

'No chance at all, Mrs Gillespie.'

'Your reference from Sir Lyndon Gaynor is very good. He speaks highly of your talents, Miss Wentworth.'

'That is kind of him.'

'I met Sir Lyndon once in London, at a dinner where my husband was the guest speaker. I found him very charming and very handsome, but his wife was not with him. I believe she is an invalid?'

'Yes, that is so.'

'And you were engaged to his younger brother?'

'Yes.'

She was looking at me very intently and I felt sure she understood more than my words had conveyed.

'Ah well,' she said briskly, 'work is the best remedy for a broken heart. How soon will you be able to start, Miss Wentworth?'

I stared at her in surprise. She had asked me very few questions but seemed more than willing to take me on Miss

Lawford's recommendation endorsed by Sir Lyndon's reference.

'I need to collect my clothes and other things from my aunt's house in Lancashire, but I can return here before the weekend.'

'That will do splendidly, and of course you will live here and I shall call you Maya. We must not be too formal. Come with me and I will show you your room.'

I followed her through the house and up the stairs. It was a charming room she showed me into and my eyes lit up with pleasure.

'I can see that you are pleased with it, Maya. The wardrobes and the drawers are all empty, and there are pretty views from the windows. Those dark Pennine hills terrify me,' and to suit her word she shuddered realistically.

I laughed. 'I can't believe that, Mrs Gillespie. I have read about your travels with your husband.'

'You and I are going to get along splendidly my dear, and when my memoirs are completed I know of several people who would be glad of your services. Always provided you don't find another young man in the meantime! You are a very lovely girl.'

I was happy with Mrs Gillespie, and true to her words after my job finished with her I was employed by a retired general for the purpose of writing memoirs of a very different kind. The next four years passed quickly enough. I enjoyed my work, met interesting people and even travelled a little but inwardly I felt permanently scarred by the past, just as Gavin's face would be permanently scarred by my riding crop.

I was always careful to keep my aunt and uncle informed about my movements, determined to give them no cause to say I had disappeared into the blue without a thought for their existence. And yet, news of my aunt's death was the only correspondence I ever received from them in all of those four years. There had been no cards at Christmas or for my birthday, and it was almost as though Lexford had never existed for me. I had been a great disappointment to them always, and perhaps they felt they could never forgive me.

When my uncle's letter came I knew at once that it could not contain good news. Nothing was mentioned about the funeral arrangements but when I asked my employer's permission to travel north he immediately gave it.

Secretly I wondered how I was going to bear seeing the village again and those dark brooding hills that could suddenly become wildly beautiful. I expected to be stared at curiously by the villagers and to rekindle by my presence the old scandals which were best forgotten. I made up my mind that I would not linger in Lexford or visit remembered places – for this would only cause me pain.

EIGHTEEN

I HAD NOT expected to sleep, consequently I rather welcomed the first grey shafts of morning light that fell across the floor. It was only just after half-past six when I stood at the window after washing in the ice cold water from the jug in my bedroom.

The villagers would no doubt be sleeping late as it was Saturday yet by mid-morning the high street would be thronged because Saturday was market day in these parts. I was already dreading that journey along the main street and I dawdled with my packing. Actually I could have done it in less than five minutes but to kill time I purposely made myself take out some things from my valise, folding and refolding them before replacing them. I wondered what time Mrs Roper appeared and then realised with something like shock that my uncle had not mentioned her and I had only assumed she would still be working at the vicarage.

It was almost eight o'clock when I heard footsteps coming up the path from the gate, then I heard a door close somewhere in the house and the sounds of crockery from the kitchens. I wanted to talk to Mrs Roper before my uncle left his room so I hurried out of the door and down the stairs.

A woman was humming to herself in the kitchen and I opened the door with a smile of greeting on my lips which died instantly at the sight of a complete stranger setting out cups and saucers on the table. She was a remarkably fashionable stranger, who favoured me with a look of surprised appraisal.

'Good morning,' I said. 'I expected to find Mrs Roper here.'

'Mrs Roper hasn't been here for some considerable time. I am Mrs Gilmore. I live at Higher Edge.'

I knew Higher Edge. It was a large, prosperous house at the other end of the village. Seeing my surprise she explained, 'The poor vicar has been quite distraught and I have been coming in to help him with his work and to get him the odd meal. We must all help one another at such a time.'

'Yes, of course. My name is Maya Wentworth. I am the vicar's niece.'

'Yes. Your name has been mentioned from time to time. I'm afraid you are too late for your aunt's funeral.'

'Yes, I know. My uncle neglected to tell me when it would take place.'

'I'm really not surprised. Everything at sixes and sevens, that poor man has far too much to do and your aunt was little or no help to him recently. Will you be taking breakfast, Miss Wentworth?'

'No thank you, just a cup of tea, but please don't trouble. I can get that for myself.'

'It's no trouble. While I'm making for two I can make for three. Are you here indefinitely, Miss Wentworth?'

'No. I am leaving today. There is nothing for me to do here.'

She sniffed. 'Well, I don't know about that . . .'

'I mean, not with you to help him, Mrs Gilmore. I am sure my uncle is very grateful to you.'

Mollified she eyed me up and down before saying, 'Now let me see – aren't you the young lady who was engaged to Mr Gavin Gaynor from Greythorn at one time?'

'Yes, for a short while.'

'You knew he was married, of course.'

'No, I didn't know.'

'They were married in the summer. She's years older than he is but a very wealthy woman. I hear her father has vast estates in the North Riding and as she is his only child she will bring Mr Gaynor a sizeable fortune.'

'I hope they will be very happy together.'

'I'm a stranger in these parts myself. I came here with my

husband who had interests in wool but we were only here a few months when he died. I liked the house and decided to stay on here. I keep myself busy with church matters and I like country life. Will you be visiting them at Greythorn?'

'I'm afraid not, there won't be time.'

'Well, no. And I suppose there's always liable to be an atmosphere after a broken engagement.'

'Perhaps.'

'Well, as I said, the young man has done very well for himself. She's no great beauty but then they tell me he's not nearly so dashing since that scar appeared on his face. Happened on the hunting field, I believe.'

I was on dangerous ground so I changed the subject rapidly by asking about Mrs Roper.

'Oh, she's not worked here for three years or more. Left the vicarage without giving her notice she did, right in the middle of the day, just after lunch. She doesn't even attend the church here now but prefers to go elsewhere.'

'Did she quarrel with my aunt and uncle?'

'The woman was quite ridiculous. Of course your uncle was right not to bury that girl in consecrated ground with her having drowned herself in the mere. He was absolutely right but Mrs Roper took the huff and walked out on them. Like the vicar said – why should he make an exception for Mrs Roper's daughter, then the families of any other suicides would expect him to do the same for them.'

My legs were shaking as I sat down at the table but I don't think she noticed. She was busy at the stove and I kept quiet knowing that my voice would have betrayed me if I had spoken.

'I suppose you knew Mrs Roper's daughter?'

'Yes. We were friends when we were young.'

'Flighty I believe, and headstrong. All the village was agog with it but I refrained from asking too many questions. After all, my husband and I had been here such a short while and I didn't want to appear too curious. Pretty, was she?'

'Very pretty.'

'Flighty too?'

'Warm and generous, and she loved life.'

She turned round to stare at me. 'You sound quite fond of her, Miss Wentworth.'

'I was, very fond. Would you mind if I took my tea up to my room Mrs Gilmore, I still have some packing to do and I want to get away early.'

She passed me the tea cup and hearing my uncle's footsteps on the stairs I was glad to escape. I wished him good morning and he seemed vaguely embarrassed.

'I suppose you have met Mrs Gilmore. She's a charming woman, been like a rock to me in my sorrow, insisting on getting my meals and helping me in the evenings. I don't know what I would have done without her.'

'I'm glad Uncle, I think your breakfast is almost ready.'

I hurried upstairs and drank the tea sitting on the edge of my bed while my mind digested all she had been able to tell me. They had found Emily's body in the mere and Gavin had married an heiress. It made me even more determined to call upon Mrs Roper and before half-past nine I had said my farewells at the vicarage and was hurrying down the village street towards her cottage.

There was a new spruceness about it. A new door with a polished brass knocker stood slightly ajar and there were new curtains at the window and new paint on the window frames. Assuming the cottage still belonged to her I knocked briskly on the door.

Mrs Roper herself opened it and her eyebrows shot up with delighted surprise when she saw me standing there.

'Maya!' she exclaimed. 'Bless ye a' never thowt to see you again! Come in, 'ave you 'ad breakfast?'

'I wasn't very hungry, Mrs Roper and there was a strange woman in the kitchen.'

'Oh, 'er. Mrs Gilmore. She's aimin' to move in there, that's fer sure an' the vicar's that flattered 'e doesn't know whether 'e's comin' or goin'.'

'She surely hasn't got designs on my uncle?'

'It wouldn't surprise me. 'Er 'usband left 'er a nice little pile

237

an' ye know 'ow tight-fisted t'vicar allus was. 'Er money'd be just what 'e's needin'.'

Despite my avowal that I was not hungry, toast and marmalade appeared on the table as well as fragrant hot coffee, and my appetite reawakened.

'Did ye come up for yer aunt's funeral, Maya? I niver saw you there.' Mrs Roper asked.

'I did, but it had already taken place.'

'Yes, last Thursday. I went to the church to pay me respects but I never go to the services now.'

'No, I believe not.'

'I suppose the vicar was within 'is rights not to bury Emily, but it was 'urtin' to me, her mother.'

'Where is she buried, Mrs Roper?'

'Up at Greythorn.'

I raised my eyebrows in astonishment.

'Sir Lyndon came to see me. 'E could see 'ow distressed I was, she 'ad no call to be buried in a pauper's grave an' that's what they were proposin' to do with 'er. She's put away in the private cemetery there. I'll allus be grateful to 'im for that an' 'e's bin kind in other ways.'

'How?'

'Well, we sat an' chatted long into the night an' I told 'im about my 'usband an' 'is long illness and 'ow perhaps I 'adn't bin able to care for Emily like a' should've done. 'E gave our Rosie an' 'er 'usband a nice little cottage on the estate an' they both work for 'im, Joe on the land an' Rosie at the 'All. It's made a difference a' can tell ye. They gives me enough to make me comfortable an' I looks after their children when they're not at school.'

'I'm glad the funeral was private, Mrs Roper. There would be no prying eyes at Greythorn.'

'Well, a few of 'em turned out to stand round the gates. Sir Lyndon came to the funeral, but the rest of us was family.'

'And Gavin?'

'No signs of 'im. Ye knew 'e was married, Maya?'

'Mrs Gilmore told me.'

'My, but that Mrs Gilmore made good use of 'er time.'

I smiled. 'Yes, I suppose she did.'

'They do say she's no ravin' beauty and she's older than 'im, but there's money there an' she's an only child.'

'I wonder if he ever comes to Greythorn?'

'Rosie says not. It's rumoured that 'e an' 'is brother 'ad words afore 'e went. I shouldn't be surprised, nothin' like Sir Lyndon he is, now 'e's a real gentleman.'

'And easy to love,' I thought silently. Perhaps if I never came back to Lexford in time I would be able to put his memory behind me, but not yet. In this place surrounded by the scenes of my childhood, every lonely hill was a constant reminder of his charm and the low timbre of his voice, every twist in the road an ache to see him riding towards me on his big chestnut horse, with that sweet smile softening the sternness of his face . . .

Deliberately I made myself ask about Melinda.

'Poor lady, she doesn't improve any. Rose says she just gets weaker every day.'

'And Jamie, I suppose he's gone away to school?'

'No. The poor lad 'ad a nervous breakdown, as though Sir Lyndon 'adn't enough to worry about. 'E's still not completely 'imself an' spends too much time wi' Miss Cora. She's no good fer 'im. She's eaten up wi' bitterness, they do say. It's almost as if she's payin' Master Jamie back fer what 'er sister did to 'er.'

'Oh no, Mrs Roper, that would be terrible!'

'Well, it were terrible Maya. It's morbid it is, the two of 'em allus walkin' in the glade or round the road along the mere. Sir Lyndon 'as 'is estate to attend to, 'e can't allus be expectin' to keep 'em apart, although they do say 'e's warned Cora to leave the boy alone.'

'Perhaps Jamie would be better off at school.'

''E's not well enough to go there yet. 'E 'as a tutor goin' out fro' Seaten every day, a nice young feller who teaches privately. 'E can't leave the area cause 'e's got an invalid wife too.'

'I would like to see Jamie again but it isn't possible.'

'Ye don't feel you could visit the 'All?'

'No, I couldn't do that.'

'Then why don't you take a walk on the fell, if there's time

239

that is. Like as not you'll see Master Jamie an' Miss Cora settin' out on their walk later on.'

I was hesitant. One part of me wanted to get away quickly, the other wanted to linger among old haunts and scenes that held memories, both sad and happy.

'I don't want to see too many of the villagers, Mrs Roper. I ought to get away quickly so that they don't have too much to talk about.'

'You can go out at the back o' the cottage. You'll be on the fell i' no time an' they'll all be busy round the stalls on market day.'

I pretended reluctance. Inside I knew I would climb the fell to take one more look at Greythorn, and as if she read my thoughts Mrs Roper settled down to tell me more of the village gossip, talking of my aunt's illness and Mrs Gilmore's pre-occupation with church matters and the care of my uncle. Her resentment of my uncle showed through it all and a little later I bade her farewell and was glad to get back out into the fresh air. It was a cold grey day which did nothing to beautify the rolling moors and stark hills, but I was aware of a strange excitement as I climbed the fell above the Hall. Even against its background of Pennine grandeur the house stood proudly, its grey stone unmellowed by sunshine, the parkland shrouded in a faint floating mist. Beyond the whispering glade the mere looked dark and brooding, its waves whipped up by the chill breeze that was blowing across the fells.

I stood looking down, my back resting against a crag and because the weather was dismal I wondered if Jamie and Cora would take their customary walk. I had almost decided to turn back when I saw them emerge from the conservatory at the side of the house. Jamie was so tall and grown-up! I was surprised to see that Cora wore only a dress which she had not bothered to cover with a warm coat. There seemed an urgency about their walk as she led Jamie towards the glade and he allowed her to pull him along, almost like a sleep-walker.

I watched them curiously as I walked down the fell towards the path, then from out of the front door I saw Melinda toiling painfully on her two sticks in the direction they had taken. A manservant followed her and even from where I stood I could tell he was remonstrating with her to return. She waved him aside impatiently and continued with her painful journey.

Without thinking I found myself running now down the hillside as fast as my legs would carry me, acting recklessly in answer to my fears, jumping the low stone walls until I came at last to the wall surrounding the park. I prayed desperately that the door in the wall would be open. It was seldom used but before I reached it I found a spot where the wall had crumbled and I managed to climb over this without too much difficulty. At last I was in the parkland, running through the shrubbery where the branches of the brambles tore at my clothing as well as my face and hair. When I reached the lawns the going was easier and I ran down the slope towards the glade. Melinda was there, leaning against a tree gasping painfully and hearing my footsteps the servant turned and regarded me helplessly.

Through a haze of pain she stared at me and then recognition suddenly dawned. 'Maya – go after them! I think she's gone mad, she's taken Jamie to the mere!'

'You must go back to the house, Melinda. Let me help you.'

'Don't you understand, Maya, *she's taken Jamie to the mere*. Go after them and the servant will bring help.'

I could not ignore the urgency in her voice nor her wide-eyed terror. Once more I took to my heels and ran. I could see the mere shining dully at the end of the glade but there was no sign of Cora or Jamie. I ran on to where I could stand on the shingle at the edge of the lake with the waves tumbling towards me. Then I saw them.

They stood where the water swirled around them, already up to Jamie's waist while Cora walked backwards, encouraging him at every step. Her pale hair streamed in the wind, her skirts eddying around her while overhead the thunder rolled in the fells. I called to them but my voice was lost on the wind, and oblivious to my clothes, without a second's thought I plunged into the water and felt myself carried foward by its current. It was bitterly cold but the compulsion to reach those two doomed figures was stronger than my fear.

'No, Cora no!' I called. 'Hold on, Jamie, I'm coming.'

She never looked my way, but the sound of my voice penetrated through to Jamie's senses and as though he had suddenly been aroused from his stupor he looked towards me and instant terror filled his eyes. He started to struggle. Reaching them, I added my strength to his struggles as I desperately strove to remove his hands from Cora's grasp. The boy was sobbing with fright but still she hung on and then from somewhere behind us I heard a man's voice and she let go of the boy and turned her attention on me.

She was so strong. In spite of my peril I remembered the strength of those slender white hands and suddenly I was fighting for my life as she drew me further and further away from the shore. Now my feet could not even find the bottom of the lake and as she dragged me underneath the surface I could feel the reeds clinging to my skirts. Gasping, we surfaced again and all I could see above me was the blur of her face distorted by hatred and a determination to take me with her.

I was tiring and she knew it. My arms ached with the efforts I had made to defend myself and all I wanted was to float on into the middle of the lake and let the water take me peacefully so that I didn't have to fight any more. Dimly I heard again the sound of a man's voice, then there were other voices and I was struggling again as I felt strong arms encompass me and the voice told me to lie still and not struggle. I remember the sensation of floating then other hands reached out to take me and I was lying on something hard and firm while blankets were laid over me and underneath my head. I was safe – that at least I remembered, then I knew nothing more.

I have no idea how long I slept but the swish of curtains roused me and I turned my head on the pillow to see a maid shutting out the dusk. Weakly I struggled to sit up and the girl spun round saying, 'Oh Lord Miss, I didn't mean to wake you.'

'What time is it?' I murmured sleepily.

'It's nigh on five o'clock an' pourin' with rain. I'll tell the 'ousekeeper you're awake, Miss.'

There were so many questions I wanted to ask but they

refused to take a logical form and while I was still struggling with my memory the door opened and the housekeeper came into the room. I stared at her blankly for several moments then recognition dawned.

'Am I at Greythorn?' I asked in surprise.

'Yes, Miss Wentworth. Sir Lyndon gave instructions that you were not to be disturbed but now that you are awake I'm sure you will be wanting something to eat.'

'Oh no, I'm not hungry. Is Jamie safe, and Miss Cora?'

'You mustn't talk too much. I'll have some soup sent up to you. You have had a terrible experience, you need to sleep some more.'

I struggled to sit up against the pillows. 'Oh, please tell me if Jamie and Cora are safe. I don't care about food.'

Very firmly she pushed me back against the pillows, straightening the bedclothes with a set face, ignoring my questions and I watched her bustle out of the room in a wave of despair.

The maid brought the soup on a tray and from the way she hurried in I knew she had been warned not to answer my queries. Filled with frustration I made myself eat. The soup was delicious and surprisingly I enjoyed it. I felt warm and lethargic. The escapade in the lake now seemed remote until it could have been a dream and again I slept. The next time I awoke the curtains were drawn back and a thin watery sun fell across the bed and I realised it was daylight.

The house was quiet and my watch had stopped so I had no means of knowing what time it was. I looked round the room curiously, relieved to see that a dressing gown had been placed over the arm of a chair close to the bed. I felt no worse for my experience in the lake and I was determined to leave my room now to find some answers to the questions that were tormenting me. The robe and the night-gown I was wearing must once have belonged to Eleanor since they fitted me perfectly and no doubt I would have found them becoming if my hair hadn't looked such a sight. It hung lankly onto my shoulders and I was pale and hollow-eyed, even though I felt perfectly well.

Thrusting my feet into Eleanor's slippers I let myself quietly out of the room, standing for a moment or two outside the door, straining my ears for any sounds from downstairs. Now I remembered the layout of the house. Without meeting anybody I made my way to the nursery, listening at the door before entering it, but everything was silent.

I stood in the doorway looking round at the familiar room. It was strangely tidy. No books lay on the table, not even the old familiar painting books. Then of course I realized that Jamie was no longer a small boy and he must have developed new hobbies.

Quietly, I moved over to the door leading into his bedroom and stood listening, hardly daring to breathe in case I missed some movement inside the room. It was as silent as the grave, and disquietened by the metaphor I made myself open the door.

The room was empty, the single bed covered by a bedspread as though it has just been freshly made or had not been slept in. The entire room had an unoccupied air and a feeling of dread entered my heart so that I stood shivering, my fears taking shape. A sound behind me made me spin round with a little cry only to find Sir Lyndon standing in the nursery doorway. In answer to the panic in my eyes he said quickly, 'Jamie is quite safe, Maya. He hasn't occupied this room for some time.'

The relief of knowing the boy was safe made me feel suddenly faint and he came forward quickly to take my arm.

'You shouldn't be up Maya,' he scolded gently. 'Come, I'll take you back to your room.'

'Oh please, not before you've told me that everything is well. Nobody would answer my questions. Don't you see – I've got to know!'

We stared at each other, and eventually I saw his face relax into a little smile and he said, 'Of course Maya, but it's cold in this room. Come down to the study where there's a fire. It is still very early you know.'

'No, I didn't know. My watch has stopped and there was no clock in my bedroom. What time is it?'

'Just after seven-thirty.'

I knew now why the house was so quiet, and it felt cold as I followed him along the corridor to the head of the stairs. He took my arm as we descended and I was glad. My legs were trembling and I realised I was not nearly so well as I had thought.

A blazing fire burnt in the grate and the study felt blissfully warm as Lyndon drew up a chair and gently pushed me into it. He stood looking down into the flames, his face unusually pensive although his first words surprised me.

'You did a very brave thing, Maya. You could quite easily have lost your life.'

'I didn't stop to think. I had to get to Jamie, but why did Cora try to push me under the water? Why does she hate me so much?'

'Did she hate you Maya, I wonder? Poor, mixed-up Cora who at times hated everybody, even Jamie.'

'Why did she try to kill him?'

'Perhaps we should ask that question last of all. Perhaps we should go back to the beginning when Cora was a child. She was always delicate, a pretty, spoilt, ailing child who missed out on all the enjoyment the rest of us took for granted. All those parties and balls when I would see her sitting on the landing upstairs looking through the balustrade watching the dancing before she was hustled back to her room.

'All those long golden summers when we filled the house with our friends while she could only look on, having no friends of her own. When I remember those days, I see that even then she lived in Eleanor's shadow and Eleanor was beautiful and gay and full of life. Gavin too, teased her about her inability to play games, ride a fast horse or dance until dawn. I always made myself be especially kind to Cora, but then Melinda came here and once more she felt neglected and shut out.

'Perhaps it was inevitable that she should fall in love with one of Eleanor's young men. There were so many of them, but unhappily she picked on the one Eleanor herself loved. It was always accepted that one day Eleanor would marry Roger Ackroyd just as one day I would marry Melinda Graves. Don't ask me why Maya, but I hope it is a custom that will one day die out and our families will be content to let the next generation choose for themselves.'

'I hadn't been in this village long before somebody told me that money married money.'

245

He smiled a little. 'Perhaps it's true. On the other hand it may be because these are the people we grow up with. We live in the same environment like peas in a pod. We are brought up to look upon the people in the villages as men and women who either work on the land or come to us as servants, whilst those who live in similar houses are the sort of people we should marry.'

'Where does that place me, I wonder?'

'In this class-ridden society you belong to the professional class by virtue of your uncle's profession, and you would be expected to marry within that class, to someone like that young curate who once stayed at the vicarage with your uncle and aunt.

'Eleanor did not love Roger Ackroyd, of course. I thought I had never seen a more unhappy bride but Cora on the other hand believed she had lost a rival. She set herself out to comfort Roland Carnwood and he, poor man, was beside himself with jealousy and despair. He turned to Cora torn by these two emotions, but as the weeks and months passed he realised the mistake he had made.

'Eleanor was desperately unhappy and he was still in love with her. You know the rest, Maya. What you don't know is how things have developed here after you left Greythorn. On the surface, Cora seemed to have recovered from the effects of the tragedy. As you may remember, she started to take an interest in things again, riding and visiting neighbours, buying clothes and books, but then we had trouble with Jamie.

'More and more the child withdrew into himself and those imaginary friends of his grew in number until Melinda and I ceased to exist for him. Only Cora satisfied his need for companionship and I began to wonder if her air of wellbeing was merely a facade, while secretly her anger and despair were affecting the child.

'When I remonstrated with her, her eyes grew sullen and sly and I felt sure I had been right in my assumptions. On the surface she appeared to obey my instructions, but I discovered her twice leaving his room in the early hours of the morning and I had him removed to a room on the main landing close to my own apartments.

246

'Melinda, too, warned me about Cora and disturbed me also when she said that perhaps it was Cora who had deliberately pushed her down the stairs during that New Year's Eve party.'

I stared at Lyndon, appalled by the suggestion, but then I remembered Melinda's conversation with me when she herself had said she was sure she had been pushed on that fatal night. I could not believe that Cora could have been so cruel, but Lyndon went on, 'Think, Maya. A sad, lonely ailing girl surrounded by other people's happiness, other people's love and laughter, and that one split-second of envy that enabled her to destroy something of that air of wellbeing. Perhaps she didn't even mean it to destroy Melinda's health forever, but just momentarily to hurt and punish her.'

I tried to think about Cora as I had first known her but unhappily I could only remember her face filled with hatred as she tried to push me down through the dark green water and the choking weeds. In a small stunned voice I said, 'She tried to kill me. Why does she hate me? I have nothing she could envy me for!'

'She hated you because she believed I was in love with you.'

I stared at him with the warm blood flaming in my face, an instant denial on my lips. 'Oh no, Lyndon. How could she ever have thought that? You gave her no cause.'

'She saw us together the day Eleanor died. She saw me leaving your room and that last mad embrace. When I threatened to send her away if she continued to influence Jamie she said she would tell Melinda that she had seen us together. Poor Melinda has enough to hurt her without the additional worries of a faithless husband.'

'Oh Lyndon, that was cruel! Surely she understood that it had been just that once, that foolish unguarded moment born out of sadness and a shared traumatic experience. You gave her no cause to think that I ever meant anything to you. I was simply an interlude, like Gavin's interlude with Emily.'

I saw him wince almost as though I had struck him, and a degree of sternness entered his voice that had not been there before.

'If Cora had seen Gavin with his arms around you in the

middle of the night she would have thought little of it. She knew that I did not go in for such meaningless adventures.'

In spite of all I had listened to that morning suddenly I felt a wild surge of happiness as the meaning of his words became clear. Lyndon did care for me. Now, whatever happened to me in the future, however lonely and dismal my path through life might prove, I would remember this and be comforted.

He made no effort to touch me but his eyes said all that his words might deny and I felt strangely at peace.

He smiled gently. 'You see Maya, how easy it has always been to forget about Cora in the face of other emotions.'

I stared at him doubtfully, then my eyes opened wide with apprehension. 'But you saved her Lyndon, surely you saved her?'

He shook his head sadly. 'I went back for her and the men got the boat out. Time and again we dived into the lake but nobody knows its depth out there in the centre and we couldn't find her.'

'She deliberately took her own life?'

'Yes. I think that yesterday something irrevocably snapped in Cora's brain. She told Melinda she was taking Jamie to the lake, a thing she often did on a fine day, but when Jamie told Melinda they were going into the mere to look for his mother she became desperately afraid. She saw them setting out along the path and despite her infirmity she tried to go after them. It was some sort of miracle that found you watching the house from the fell, and another miracle that I was in the house when the servant came back for help.'

'I saw Melinda struggling on her sticks. It was that that sent me flying down the hillside. I knew something was terribly wrong. I hope Melinda is no worse for the episode.'

He smiled a little at my concern. 'Melinda is no worse than usual Maya, but she becomes increasingly frail. She, too, did a very brave thing that afternoon.'

I nodded wordlessly. Melinda had qualities of bravery and sweetness that made her very dear to him. However much I loved him, however much I meant to him I at least was young and strong and able to stand alone. At that moment I resolved that this time when I left Lexford I would never return.

NINETEEN

I WORKED HARD on completing the general's memoirs with him, so hard that I had little time for self-analysis or brooding on memories that were best forgotten.

A new employer was already waiting for me when it was time to leave the general, this time a lady who wrote children's novels, to be followed four months later by another lady who wrote and illustrated books on wild flowers and fauna.

Between the two of them I was kept busy and happily I found myself a little cottage which, although sparsely furnished, I enjoyed turning into a home.

The two ladies helped me with odd pieces of furniture and ornaments they did not need, and Miss Lawford too came forward with a bookcase and several small tables. The bedroom furniture I bought at one of the sales in the area and I took pleasure in decorating the cottage myself and running up curtains for the tiny windows. I planted wallflowers and nasturtiums in the plots outside the front window and I was happy with my apple and plum trees in the garden at the back of the cottage.

It surprised me how quickly the weeks ran into months and the months into years and as I walked home through the dusk on my birthday I realised with something approaching surprise that I was twenty-eight years old!

Twenty-eight and unmarried! I had one or two male companions, young men I had met in the homes of friends, and one of them was my employer's nephew. They took me to concerts and beauty spots in the summer and there were times when they flirted with me, but I had no desire for a deeper involvement and they respected my wishes. In the main, they could not understand why I was contented with my unmarried state and I also think they assumed an unhappy love affair in the past had made me afraid. They asked few questions and I in turn was happy to drift along in these untroubled waters.

There were plenty of letters waiting for me behind the door as I let myself into my cottage that evening and I picked them up deciding to read them over my solitary meal. Most of them were birthday cards from friends I had made in the area, but there was also an envelope bearing Miss Lawford's familiar handwriting and this I opened first. She stated in her letter that it was now some time since she had seen me and she hoped I was well and happy. She needed to see me on my next day's holiday and would I please let her know if I could call on her, stating the date and time.

I smiled to myself. Her letters were always precise and businesslike, but she had been responsible for putting me in touch with every one of my employers and I now believed she had another one lined up for me.

Apart from Mrs Roper, she was the only person I had ever told about my experiences at Greythorn and although I hadn't confessed my feelings for Lyndon, she had guessed them.

'My dear,' she had said. 'You are too young to spend the rest of your life in vague regrets. This man is married and although I am sure he is worthy of your love and that you are important to him you must put it all behind you. There is no future in loving a man who already has a wife, and a man moreover who lives in a different walk of life.'

I agreed with her, but until I found somebody to take his place I was content to go on from day to day, living my life peacefully and untroubled by thoughts of love.

I wrote to her by return saying that I would call upon her at the school the following Saturday afternoon. I was glad that the day turned out to be fine. It was April and a watery sun struggled to shine through the gold-tipped rainclouds.

Miss Lawford greeted me warmly and listened to my tales of what I had been doing and where and with whom I had spent my leisure hours. Shortly before four o'clock we heard the patter of running feet in the corridors outside and the high sound of girls' voices as they laughed and chattered on their way out of the classrooms. Excusing herself Miss Lawford said, 'I must talk to one or two of the mistresses before they disperse,' and hurried away on her errand.

I went to stand at the window, watching groups of girls walk arm in arm along the paths leading through the gardens and nostalgically I thought of those careless happy years when I too had been a schoolgirl at this same school.

I turned round when the door opened, expecting to see Miss Lawford there. My eyes opened wide however when I saw Lyndon standing there, looking at me with that slow sweet smile which I remembered so well and which still had the power to make my heart tremble in my breast.

'How well you look, Maya,' was his greeting, and then he closed the door and came over to the window to stand looking down at me.

I continued to stare at him incredulously and his smile widened. 'I wasn't sure how I could find you but then I remembered Miss Lawford and I hoped she would be able to help me.'

'You wanted to find me,' I stammered.

'I wanted very much to find you.'

'But Lyndon, why?'

'Because I want you to come back with me. Because I can't live without you – put it any way you please.'

'But Melinda?'

'Melinda died eighteen months ago. I could have come for you much sooner, and Heaven knows I wanted to come but it was too soon, too soon to erase Melinda's memory and I was afraid that you might never want to see or hear of Greythorn again. There had been too much unhappiness, too many tragedies.'

'Oh Lyndon, I shall never forget Greythorn, and I would never have forgotten you. Heaven knows I've tried.'

'Are you going to marry me, Maya?'

'Oh yes, my darling.'

'We'll be married by special licence somewhere in London. I don't want to make you face all those prying eyes around the villages at home. In time, their tongues will stop wagging and you will be simply accepted as the second Lady Gaynor. You can appreciate that, can't you Maya?'

'Oh yes, I can. I know how those tongues will wag. Most of them no doubt saying hurtful, untrue things they know nothing about. I don't really care what they say, they can speculate all they like. I love you Lyndon, I've always loved you and I want to make you happy. I shall spend the rest of my life trying to do that.'

I didn't hear Miss Lawford come back into the room. With Lyndon's arms around me and his lips on mine the world and its occupants all seemed very far away.